WE MET
LIKE THIS

WE MET LIKE THIS

A Novel

....

Kasie West

S

**SATURDAY
BOOKS
NEW YORK**

First published in the United States by Saturday Books,
an imprint of St. Martin's Publishing Group

EU Representative: Macmillan Publishers Ireland Ltd, 1st Floor, The Liffey Trust Centre, 117–126 Sheriff Street Upper, Dublin 1, DO1 YC43

www.saturdaybooks.com

Title page art: lemons © Nadezhda Zubova/Getty Images

Library of Congress Cataloging-in-Publication Data

Names: West, Kasie, author.
Title: We met like this : a novel / Kasie West.
Description: First edition. | New York : Saturday Books, 2025.
Identifiers: LCCN 2025000262 | ISBN 9781250349149 (trade paperback) |
ISBN 9781250349156 (ebook)
Subjects: LCGFT: Romance fiction. | Novels.
Classification: LCC PS3623.E84478 W4 2025 | DDC 813/.6—dc23/eng/20250108
LC record available at https://lccn.loc.gov/2025000262

Our books may be purchased in bulk for specialty retail/wholesale, literacy, corporate/premium, educational, and subscription box use. Please contact MacmillanSpecialMarkets@macmillan.com.

First Edition: 2025

10 9 8 7 6 5 4 3 2 1

To Christine, my fun and supportive mother. I promise that only the good parts of the mothers in my books are based on you.

WE MET LIKE THIS

PROLOGUE

"There?" he breathed into my ear, his finger pressing on just the right spot, as if he'd studied my body for years and knew exactly how to make it hum with pleasure.

"Yes," I said, unable to keep my knees from falling open as he worked me to near release. How could he know the exact spot when this was the first time we'd ever met in person? He hardly knew me at all. We'd literally matched the day before on a dating app and set up a date for tonight. Dinner conversation was subpar and the food was less than subpar. What was I doing? My rule was three dates, at least! And never in a car. I wasn't some horny teenager. I was a romantic. I liked fun banter and late-night talks and effort!

"Don't stop," I said when his finger slid out of me and his hand moved up my side to cup my breast.

"Let's slow down," he said, "take our time . . . go inside?"

"Yes, back inside," I said with a moan.

He let out a breathy chuckle.

We sat in the driveway of what I assumed was his house. Was it his parents' house? He was twenty-seven, but that meant nothing these days. Who could afford housing? Even if he was . . .

"Ah, ah, yes," I said on a sigh. He had unbuttoned three buttons of my top and moved aside my bra. My nipple was in his mouth that was applying slight suction while his tongue swept back and forth along my peak. My ribs knocked into the gear shift and he adjusted my position.

After the less-than-impressive dinner, he'd driven me back here to my car. I meant to get out of his, walk the thirty feet to where mine was parked on the curb, and drive home. Instead, we'd met each other's eyes. His were a warm brown. He had thick, wavy hair and a wide smile. He was handsome despite the terrible conversation. And then, without knowing who initiated it, we were kissing. Not some sloppy kisses that left my mouth wet and the rest of me dry. This man knew how to kiss. Long, languid drawn-out kisses, his mouth soft, his breath hot, his tongue sure.

"You said you were a software engineer, right?" I asked now. Did software engineers study human anatomy? How was he so good at this?

"Yes," he said, releasing my nipple. I shouldn't have asked him a question. "You're a literary agent?"

At twenty-four, I was well on my way to becoming a literary agent. But right now, I could only claim, "Assistant to a literary agent."

"What's an assistant to a literary agent do?" he asked, his eyes intense on mine, like he was trying hard to focus on anything but the exposed breast just under his chin.

"We read lots of emails and lots of books. What about you?"

"Mostly coding. Sometimes rewriting other people's codes. Troubleshooting projects. Compliance." My hands were on the buttons of his shirt now, undoing them one by one. Why had I turned this night back to conversation? We'd already proven we were horrible at that. At least with each other. But this—I snaked my hand inside his shirt and along his bare chest; he drew a shuddering breath—this we were proving to be exceptionally good at.

I put his hand back on my breast and he chuckled, but his calloused thumb traced a slow circle and my eyes fluttered closed with the sensation.

"Um . . ." he started.

"Margot," I filled in for him, opening my eyes.

"I know your name," he said. Then his brows shot down. "Do you remember mine?"

Shit. I honestly didn't think this date was going to last more than an hour after his first words to me were "The problem with dating apps is that not even the best programmer can replicate a fraction of real human interaction."

"Right," I had said. "Hi, nice to meet you."

The next few minutes had been him studying the menu in complete silence. I'd tried to ask him what he was ordering several times, polite small talk, but his eyes never left the page, like anything outside of whatever he was thinking wasn't important. Instead of responding to me, he started talking about how fonts were created, and how whoever designed the menu had used the wrong one. He ignored the waitress when she came over as well. I had to hold up my finger, silently asking her for more time because he was still talking. Not even I, a total book nerd, could talk for ten minutes about fonts. Especially not in a way that made it sound like I should be put in charge of all the world's lettering choices. He was arrogant. That was obvious.

I could normally carry a conversation, but I found myself at a loss for words. He was right, this was the problem with dating apps. Not even the best programmer could replicate real human interaction. So you didn't know, until you were sitting in front of a person, whether you were actually compatible or not.

"Uh . . . something with an A?" I said now.

He gave a single laugh. "You *really* don't remember my name?"

"Aaron?"

"Oliver," he said.

"I was close!"

"You call that close?"

"I do." I leaned forward to kiss him.

He inched backward.

"They have the same feel," I insisted.

"Margot . . ."

"Seriously?" I asked, my panties still around my ankles.

"Let's get to know each other a little better."

"I think the getting to know each other is what's ruining it," I said with a smile.

He shook his head, a smile on his lips too. At least he had a sense of humor. But he didn't resume our makeout.

I pulled my black lace underwear the remainder of the way off, over my heels. "Oliver, you said?"

"Oliver," he said.

"I think we both know we're not a match." I had known from the minute he ignored the waitress. I should've left then. I took his hand and placed my panties in his palm. "But it was fun." I climbed out of the car, adjusted my skirt, and walked away.

CHAPTER 1

Three years later

"Wait wait wait wait . . ." Sloane, my roommate, started. She was in her pajamas, bonnet on her head protecting her curls, and sipping a glass of white wine. She'd come out of her room when I got home and perched herself on the couch, ready for me to summarize the date. For as long as we'd been roommates (more than two years now) this had been our ritual. "You're telling me you *gave* him your leftovers?"

"Yes," I groaned, pouring myself a glass of wine from the bottle on the counter.

"The guy who cuts his meat into tiny pieces?"

"My dad nearly choked on a piece of steak once," I said, carrying my wine to the couch. "Had to get the Heimlich from a fellow restaurantgoer and everything. Maybe Lance has too."

Sloane curled her lip. "Did he still hold his fork in his entire fist while he ate?"

"It's unique," I insisted.

She rolled her eyes. "A free meal is a free meal no matter who you have to eat it with, I guess."

I cringed. "I paid."

"You paid last time!"

"I know. I panicked. He started talking about flat-earth theory. And he was on the wrong side of that argument! I practically threw my credit card at the waiter." I don't know why. I didn't have extra funds just lying around to pay for all dates. At twenty-seven, my job was still the same one I'd had for the last four years—assistant to a literary agent. And even though in the last couple years I'd gotten to take on a few of my own small clients, in every other way it was the same: same responsibilities, same office, same boss, same barely livable salary. We should've split the check. I usually split the bill on dates, but Lance was into the *I pay this time, you pay next time* idea. As if there were going to be an infinite string of *next time*s.

"Thank god he brought up his thoughts on the Earth's shape," she said. "Or you would've been in love with him by next week."

"I would not have," I said, but only half-heartedly. We'd met in a yoga class three weeks earlier when I'd stumbled and knocked him over while attempting the Warrior 2 pose. We'd exchanged numbers before the class was even over through whispers and giggles under the annoyed glare of the instructor. Lance was cute and asked me questions about myself, a low bar, yet one many men couldn't make it over. He'd made it to date three. I thought we were on our way. Then he brought up his conspiracy theories and the perfect future I had envisioned came crashing down.

"I'm just saying . . ." she sang.

"You have no room to talk," I said to Sloane. "You're happily

WE MET LIKE THIS 7

in a relationship now. You've forgotten about the discovery phase. The discovery phase is the absolute worst part of a relationship. I hate having to start from zero with someone, to answer the same questions over and over again and ask the same questions over and *over* again. Decide if we're compatible over and over again."

"So you were willing to live with fist fork for the rest of your life so you could avoid having to explain what a slush pile is again?" Sloane twisted her smartwatch on her wrist.

"Among other things," I said. We both knew I wasn't going to marry Lance, despite how much I tried to convince myself his habits were charming.

"You know what this means?" Sloane said.

I took a sip of wine. "No, it doesn't."

"It does."

"I don't want to. I don't need them. I'm meeting people the real way."

"In yoga class? That's the real way?"

"Yes! It was romantic." I was a romantic at heart. It was why I wanted to be a literary agent. I wanted to put love stories in the hands of the hopeless romantics of the world. Plus, I was really good at seeing what did and didn't work in a story. At seeing how to shape a book into the perfect combination of conflict and romance. And through years and years of reading love stories, I wanted my own. Not one that involved swiping right. I'd seen it happen not just in stories but in real life, time and again. Why couldn't it happen for me?

"It really wasn't," she insisted. "Your meet-cute obsession is narrowing your field of potentials. How many new people can possibly cross your path when you go to the same four places every day?"

"Rude."

"True."

"Dating apps are no better. They are all a big, unromantic scam, wasting our time and money. A software engineer once told me that they can't re-create real interaction anyway, so they're a pointless way to meet—"

"I don't need another rant about how you wish you lived before social media and apps and how true romance only happens organically through shared experiences, history, and in-person chemistry. This attitude is why you're still screwing Rob."

I gasped and heat crawled its way up my neck and clung to my cheeks.

She pointed, her wine sloshing over the edge of the glass in her opposite hand. "I knew it! Dammit, Margot, you should have to put five bucks in the Bad Decisions jar for that." She gestured toward the jar on the bookcase that had started as a joke and was now an even bigger joke because it was half-full of money.

"I am not screwing Rob!" Which was true. I just still occasionally, against my better judgment, *wanted* to screw Rob, which was why my cheeks were cherry red at the moment. Rob was my boss and the last real relationship I'd had. *Real* being a relative word. Our timing had been off from the very beginning. He was going through a divorce, he was emotionally unavailable, he was . . . my boss. It had been a relationship full of shared looks, bathroom makeouts, and weekend rendezvous. It was filled with high highs and really low lows. It was wrong. *God*, I knew it was wrong. But in the midst of all the boring dates I'd been going on for the last several years, sometimes it felt like the only exciting thing in my life. Sloane was the only person in my life who even knew about that so-called relationship.

She stood. "Sit down. I'm going to make you your special slushie and you are going to download the dating apps again."

"Nooooo!" I whined.

She headed for the kitchen. "You prematurely deleted them."

"I didn't. I was on the edge of something with Lance."

"The edge of the Earth?"

"Ha, ha." I reached for the book I'd left on the coffee table earlier and sank deeper into the couch. I opened it to where a piece of dental floss was acting as a bookmark. "Maybe I'll just stick to my book men from now on," I said. "Celebrate a Me Era where I read more and work on a promotion and, you know, be more consistent than once every six months with yoga. I don't need a man."

"Is it possible to read more than you do?"

"It is," I assured her.

"You're right, you don't need a man. And I agree with that promotion thing, make that happen, it's long overdue. But"—she pushed a button on the blender and the sound of ice being pulverized filled the room for sixty seconds—"everyone needs a little fun."

I knew why she really wanted me back on the apps. She thought without them I'd become preoccupied with Rob. It was hard not to when I saw him day in and day out.

My book was plucked from my hands and she held out my drink.

"Don't lose my spot!" I called as she shut it and deposited it on the table.

"Spot is safe," she said as I accepted the drink.

Then my cell phone was placed in my free hand.

I sighed, resigned, took a sip of slushie for courage, and cringed. She'd made it strong tonight. I scrolled to the app store and pushed the get button on my go-to dating apps. I watched the little cloud and arrow symbols as the icons were brought to life on my screen. The more colorful they became, the more my heart sank. This should've felt like I was taking charge of my life. So why did it always feel like I was giving up?

CHAPTER 2

I knocked on the frame outside the open door to Rob's office and then leaned my upper body just over the threshold. "Hi, good morning, I finished reading Janet's rom-com yesterday and I had a few suggestions. Do you want me to email them to you or do you want to discuss them face-to-face?"

Sloane would make me put five dollars in the Bad Decisions jar if she saw me right now, too many buttons undone on my shirt, my dark hair curled into beachy waves, my plum-colored lipstick on, leaning into my boss's office at just the right angle for a cleavage view.

After my terrible date last night and the walk of shame back into the dating apps, I needed some excitement, but Rob was too preoccupied with his computer to give me much of anything. "An email is fine. I'm doing lunch today with Kathy Green, so—"

"The editor?" I asked, taking a step forward and straightening my shoulders. Los Angeles was not New York. It was rare that he met face-to-face with editors here. Like me, he usually pitched over emails or phone calls or, unlike me, on his quarterly New York trips.

"Yes, I'm pitching her Sarah's book. She'd be a good fit, yes?"

"She'd be a great fit." I'd worked hard on Sarah's book. I was the one who'd found it in the slush pile of emails that came into Rob's inbox from authors hoping he'd represent them. It was my job to comb through those emails, pick out the promising ones, and sometimes . . . most of the time . . . pass them on to Rob. But not before giving him my notes for story improvements.

Occasionally, Rob let me junior-agent on authors I personally found. Share most of the responsibilities in exchange for a small cut of the commissions. But Sarah was not one of those cases. He thought she was going to be big. He handled clients he saw the most potential in.

For the last three years, Rob had promised me that *soon, very soon*, I could be a full-fledged agent. It was beyond frustrating that I hadn't been promoted yet, because my clients did decently well, they earned royalties, they made best-of lists.

"What time is the meeting?" I asked. My eyes went to the clock on the wall in his office. It was ten. "Should we walk over together?" He had promised me the last time he had a local meeting that I could come *next* time so I could meet more editors in person. Face-to-face was so important to build rapport.

He finally looked over at me from where he'd been typing who-knows-what on his keyboard. His eyes lingered on my blouse, then jumped to my lips. "Just me this time. I'll take you along next time. It would be good for you to see the master at work." With those words he gave me a flirty wink.

He was handsome, really handsome, with dark hair, piercing

blue eyes, and a strong nose. Plus, he was charming, always saying just the right things at just the right time. That was how I'd gotten into trouble before. But today I wasn't going to let him charm his way out of a promise. I crossed my arms over my chest, suddenly wishing I'd buttoned my shirt all the way up to my chin. "That's what you said last time." I sounded like a petulant child. I kind of felt like one.

"Did I?" he asked. "Well, this meeting is more just old friends catching up with a pitch thrown in the mix. I wouldn't want you to feel like a third wheel."

I mentally pulled up the list my sister, Audrey, had given me years ago about the art of negotiation. She was the most successful person I knew in real life, so she often became my internal compass.

Common interests. That was one of the C's. "I'd be a great second opinion on Sarah's book. Two people excited about a project is better than one."

"I have this one." He picked up a stack of papers from his desk and held them out. "Will you file these with the rest of the contracts?"

Rob wasn't about compromise (one of the other C's) because he had all the power. He was dismissing me now. Redirecting me. And I was letting him—walking forward, taking those papers, and leaving his office. I pulled his office door shut behind me even though it had been open when I arrived. It was my passive-aggressive form of rebellion. I quickly filed his contract in the agency file room and went back to my desk in the lobby, where I'd been stationed for the last six months. Ever since the office's receptionist had taken a better job across town. Rob had promised they were still looking for a replacement. That it would happen *soon, very soon.*

I seethed while answering phones, responding to emails and receiving packages, because it was better to be angry than hurt. I hated that Rob still had the power to hurt me.

As he was leaving the office at eleven forty-five, Rob said, "While I'm gone, will you reach out to Kari and see if you can schedule a phone appointment for later this week?" as if he hadn't rejected me that morning.

I clenched my jaw and nodded. Kari was his top client and I enjoyed talking to her, hearing about her latest projects or ideas or her struggles and blocks. But not even the thought of talking to Kari could loosen my jaw.

"Great," he said. On his way out the door he turned back. "Oh, and I probably won't be back in today. Why don't you treat yourself and leave at four instead of five." He took two steps backward and the door swung shut between us. He stood for a moment, staring at me through the glass like I should mouth a *thank you* or blow a kiss. He was obviously expecting *something*. When I did nothing, he looked down at his phone and walked away.

I let out a frustrated grunt, sent an email to Kari, then did what I often did when I was dissatisfied with my job: typed in the address for my dream agency in New York—Mesner & Lloyd Lit. Getting a job there as an agent was a pipe dream without more stats on my résumé and as long as the word *junior* was still in my title.

I took my phone out of my purse that was tucked under my desk and shot off a text to Sloane: I thought sleeping with your boss was supposed to get you ahead in your career.

I stared at my phone, waiting for her to chime in with some empathetic frustration that would make me feel better, but she was obviously actually working today.

She was a film agent. It was how we met four years ago. One of Rob's clients was working with her to sell their film rights. Sloane and I were on the phone weekly trying to iron out the details. She had thought *I* was the lit agent, because of how little she had talked to Rob. Eventually, she and I were having weekly lunches. Then, when we found out our leases were ending at the same time, we decided to become roommates. One of the best decisions I'd made in the last several years. The *only* good decision? No. I shook my head. There were others, even though I couldn't think of any at the moment.

I was starting to put my phone away when I saw a little red notification next to one of my dating apps. Ugh. I'd matched with a couple guys the night before, under Sloane's watchful direction. But I'd avoided looking at the apps ever since.

The message waiting now read: Should we just start by exchanging full body pics, save ourselves some time.

I rolled my eyes.

Phase one of dating-app swiping consisted of collecting a wide array of potentials. I tried to match with as many people as possible to give myself a fighting chance. This was my least favorite phase because I'd end up chatting with a handful of guys, most of whom didn't want to have conversations at all. Even the conversations that had promise still felt forced, and I loathed that with all my romance-loving soul.

It was the opposite of a meet-cute. The opposite of a chance encounter or eyes meeting across a crowded room or hands accidentally touching on a handrail. I wanted a mixed-up coffee order or a fighting over the same taxi or reserving the same book at the library and both getting called to come pick it up and then both realizing we had the exact same taste in books. I wanted a knocking someone over in

Warrior 2 pose and him not turning out to be a conspiracy theorist . . . Stupid Lance.

As I unmatched Mr. Picture Swap and swiped through a few more possibilities, my finger paused on the next screen and I chuckled. The photo was a familiar face.

Oliver.

Ever since our terrible date three years earlier he and I had bumped into each other across multiple platforms over and over again. He must've deleted the apps as much as I did. Every time I'd downloaded them again, like a reset, his face was there waiting. Sometimes I swiped left on him, rolling my eyes as I remembered how he'd ignored the waitress and me, gave a boring monologue on font usage, and then proceeded to get me all worked up only to leave me to fend for myself that night. And sometimes I'd laugh and swipe right, and we'd exchange a few funny remarks and move on until our next reset. Today, I swiped right.

Immediately the word *Matched* filled the screen. He must've thought it was a funny tradition at this point too.

He was still very cute—big brown eyes with long lashes, light brown wavy hair, a full smile. So many men didn't smile with their teeth in photos, but he did.

So we match again, I typed in the chat. I like your new profile pic.

His response was fast: Norah! Hello.

Funny.

They're the same feel, right?

I laughed out loud, then clamped my mouth shut and looked around. I was alone. I mean, they kind of are, I responded. I wasn't going to let him win on the name-forgetting front by admitting I'd been wrong. It had been three years, but I still had my pride.

His next message read: You have a new profile pic too. You got a dog?

No, it's my friend's dog. I need people to know that animals love me.

But do you love animals is the question.

I smiled, then typed: It depends on the animal. That specific dog in that specific picture . . . no.

Ha! Well, being adored is much better than adoring. And that dog adores you.

Truth. The potted plant on the corner of my desk looked sad, drooping leaves with brown edges. I picked up my water bottle and drizzled some water into the parched dirt.

How are you? was his next message.

You know . . . still here trying my luck with these impersonal torture devices.

He responded: Same. I thought you worked during the day. Did you change jobs?

No. I'm at work right this second, I replied. Working away. You still coding?

My phone buzzed with his response: I started my own business, actually, so I work from home now. But yes, lots of coding involved.

Do you make fonts?

Please don't remind me of my oration on fonts. It's a low point in my life.

But I can't look at a menu without thinking about it. You need to know the consequences of your actions. This was actually a true statement. There'd been many times I had unwillingly remembered our first date. It had been such an odd juxtaposition of incredibly boring followed by incredibly sensual that left me more irritated than anything.

A message appeared on my screen: Sleeping with your boss kept you doting and horny.

The message made me physically recoil before I realized it was Sloane responding to my *getting ahead* text. I spun my chair away from the front door so I was facing the back wall.

I thought that was from this guy I was messaging, I texted back.

She replied: And I take it he wouldn't use doting and horny in the same sentence?

That is the main problem.

A message from Oliver buzzed through at the top of my screen: Which font would you like me to draft an apology letter in?

I laughed, then pressed the phone icon next to Sloane's name before I confused message threads and responded to the wrong person.

She picked up after three rings. "Your fingers too tired to text?"

"I wanted to hear your beautiful voice," I said.

"Valid," she responded.

"Do you remember me mentioning an Oliver? I went out with him once three years ago and have matched with him off and on ever since."

"Best-car-makeout-you've-ever-had guy?"

"Yes!" Best makeout period.

"But he was otherwise painfully boring and inconsiderate."

I cringed. I had probably said that too. "Not *painfully*. Okay, painfully. And yes, was rude to the waitress and didn't ask me any questions about myself, but instead talked about something completely irrelevant. We had absolutely nothing in common." I liked artists and filmmakers and writers. They were easier for me to relate to because we had shared interests and oftentimes shared goals. Plus, people outside the creative field didn't understand the sometimes all-consuming nature of the job.

"We are not meant for talking," I said. "Only making out, apparently." That combination hadn't happened to me before or since.

"I wonder if he still has your underwear."

Speaking of something I hadn't done before or since. "I'd be offended if he didn't." I thought about the shocked look on his face when I'd done that. He'd probably thrown them away immediately.

"It *was* pretty badass. Anyway . . . what about him?"

"He's the one I was chatting with when you sent me that text."

"You're going for a round two? He could probably use a matching bra. Make it a set."

I snorted. "No. And considering how many times we've matched over the years, this would be a round ten."

"Round ten's the charm?"

"Not happening."

"Probably a good call. I have to go. The office phone is ringing. Wait, are you at work?"

"Yes, I'm working."

She laughed and hung up.

I really did need to work. I sighed, spun back toward my computer, and started reading through emails sent by writers hoping Rob would represent their books. An hour or so into reading, my eyes starting to sting from staring at the computer screen for so long, I got curious and reached for my phone again.

A couple messages were waiting from Oliver. The first read: I didn't mean to shame you into going back to work. You should definitely message on company time.

The second one read: If we're going to ghost each other again, let's give a warning this time.

Ghost was a strong word, reserved for someone you were interested in. Oliver and I were not that. We had established on day two of knowing each other that we would never be that. I typed: Is it considered ghosting if a warning is involved?

We'll call it a haunting, he responded.

Did you have that word ready to go? That was fast.

No, I'm just really clever.

I narrowed my eyes. You had that word. You're reusing banter on me? Recycled banter is unacceptable.

For the record, this is the first time I've used it, but I guarantee fifty percent or more of my banter will be unoriginal. If that is a deal-breaker, haunt me now.

That wasn't on my dealbreaker list before but I'm going to add it now.

What else is on this list?

Oh you know, the usual: doesn't know the difference between their, there, and they're, hits the snooze button fewer than three times, has never seen Dirty Dancing, thinks the earth is flat.

Right . . . the usual.

As I was about to respond, asking him what his were, the front door to the office opened and Rob came in holding a Styrofoam box and some sort of iced coffee.

"You look . . ." He paused just inside the door.

"What?" I asked when he didn't finish. I looked down at my shirt to make sure another button hadn't come undone or anything.

"Happy," he finally said.

I could feel the leftover smile on my face from the chat I'd been having with Oliver. I slipped my phone back into my purse by my feet and cleared my throat, trying to channel some seriousness. "I'm good. Fine. I thought you were out for the rest of the day."

"You seemed so angry when I left, I thought I'd bring you some lunch and a chai." He set the offerings on the desk in front of me.

My eyes shot between the food and him. Did he really think a bribe would work? It did mean he was thinking about me in his meeting. I felt my resolve melting. Maybe it *would* work. I managed to keep my face neutral. "Thank you."

"You're welcome," he said, not feeling the need to keep a smile off his face. He sat on the edge of my desk, one of his strong hands picking up the rake in my desktop garden and dragging a pattern in the sand.

"How did the meeting go?" I asked.

"It went well. She wants me to send over Sarah's full manuscript. Can you do that before you leave today?"

"That's great. And yes, of course."

He stood.

"But Rob?"

He stopped before he'd even taken a step. "Yes?" He gave me the smoldering stare that had gotten me into trouble more than once.

It was not going to work on me today. Especially if I

stopped looking at his eyes. I focused on a dark freckle on his cheekbone. "I've been here four years. It's time for me to make the jump to full-time agent."

"You're right," he said with a nod. "We'll talk about what the path to agent looks like soon."

"Right," I said, somewhat shocked he didn't push back. I could feel the surprised look on my face and I smoothed it to confident (another C). "Right. Thank you."

As he walked out the door for the second time that day, my chest expanded with excited anticipation. Things were happening. Maybe I was finally going to take some steps forward in my life.

I opened the Styrofoam box, ready to dig into whatever lunch he had brought me. It was a few bites of soggy salad and a quarter of a chicken breast smothered in barbecue sauce.

His leftovers.

CHAPTER 3

"Hey, Mom," I said, answering my phone while changing lanes.

Her voice rang out over my car's speakers. "Hey, honey. How are you?"

"I'm good. Just on my way home from work. How are you and Dad? Any food roulette this week?" My parents were pretty technologically savvy, but they were helping to "work out the glitches" of a food-ordering app one of their friends had developed. Once the week before they'd ended up with a feast to feed twenty, and the second time they'd ordered a cake instead of the burgers they had been trying for. The app had a lot of glitches.

She laughed. "No surprises this week."

"Because you haven't used it?"

"Possibly . . . What about you?" she asked. "Still dating your yoga studio guy? I loved your meet-cute story."

So maybe I talked about meet-cutes too much if my mom knew the term and everything. "No, actually. He turned out to be a flat-earther."

She laughed. When I didn't join her, she said, "Wait, are you serious?"

"Unfortunately, very."

"I'm sorry, I know how much you want to find love. Fingers crossed that your guy is waiting for you at the nearest train station or chicken farm. Have you checked the chicken farms?"

I chuckled. "Maybe I should. But in the meantime, I'm back on the apps."

"You're swiping for dates?"

"Unfortunately," I said.

"Is that Maggie!" my older sister called out. She was the only person who called me Maggie. Had since I was little. "I was just going to call her." The sound of the phone changing hands was followed by my sister's voice. "Hi."

Audrey had the perfect life. The perfect real estate investor husband, the perfect five-year-old twin boys, the perfect house, the perfect wardrobe. I (along with approximately five hundred thousand viewers a week) knew this because she had a popular YouTube channel all about her life called Success from the Inside Out.

She had always been a go-getter. Where I spent my elementary years on the playground, she ran for and was nominated student body president. Where I spent my high school years writing movie scripts starring my latest crush, she spent hers organizing food drives and heading a remodeling committee for the cafeteria. In college, I was more social than studious, while she double-majored in interior design and business. If she was running up a mountain, I was telling her I'd take the long, scenic way around it. She was good at standing out. I was good at blending in. We didn't spend a lot of time walking the same path, but she was always giving me advice, always pushing me, always telling me how to walk my path better. Without her personality to go along with it, however, her plan wasn't working.

"Hi," I said with a smile. I hadn't seen her in a couple weeks, but we talked all the time. Despite our differences, we were very close. "Are you stocking Mom's fridge?" My sister only lived a couple miles from our parents and she often swung by after a grocery run with fresh fruits and veggies.

"Yes, without me, these two would be dead already."

"I'm fifty-seven, not a hundred and seven," Mom said from the background.

"I'm helping you make it to a hundred and seven," Audrey returned. Back to me she said, "The twins have a T-ball game this Saturday. Nine o'clock. Can you come?"

"Isn't that a bit late for them?" I asked.

"Funny. Nine in the morning."

"I know, I know. I have a brunch with friends but maybe I can come for the first part." It wasn't that I didn't want to watch my nephews chase around a ball for an hour on a Saturday morning. I loved seeing them. It was just that they lived about an hour away, depending on traffic. I would not make it back by eleven. The last game I went to, between traffic and parking and the game itself, had taken five hours out of my day. Five!

"I'll text you the address," she said.

"The boys were more interested in the orange slices after the last game than me, Audrey. Do they even care if I'm there?"

"Of course they do! And I want to see you too."

"Me too!" Mom called.

"I'll try." What I meant by that was I'd seen which argument would win that morning—the guilty side or the *screw it* side.

"I have to run," she said. "Samuel just spilled some juice on Mom's carpet. See you Saturday!"

I pictured the phone being shoved back to Mom as my sister rushed off to save the carpet.

My mom laughed as she came back on the line.

"Is your carpet going to live?" I asked.

"It was a tiny drop. But you know your sister."

"I do."

"How is work?" Mom asked.

A car to my right lay on their horn and made me jump. It shouldn't have. I'd been driving in Los Angeles traffic for years now; horns were like white noise.

"You're hands-free?" She'd obviously heard the horn as well.

"Yes," I said. "And things are good. I talked to Rob today about dropping the *junior* from my title." *Talked* was a strong word, but I'd mentioned it and he hadn't shut me down.

"That's great, honey. See, you don't need to move to New York. You can find success right here in the publishing industry."

I hadn't found success at all yet, but this was one of the other main reasons I hadn't started my career in New York in the first place—my family, my friends, everything was here, thousands of miles away. I knew I could be a literary agent anywhere, but the heart of publishing was still in New York and that's where I knew I'd eventually need to go if I wanted to build a strong foundation. "Maybe," I said.

"Do you really call your boss Rob?"

"What?" I started to say, but then realized what she was asking. "What else would I call him?" My heart picked up speed as if this was the final clue she needed to discover that I was more familiar with my boss than I should've been. She would be so disappointed in me, and I wasn't sure I could handle Mom Disappointment right now. I was already on a roll of disappointing myself.

"Mr. Bishop," she said.

"We work in a small office. There are just three agents and two assistants right now and we're familiar with each other. It would be weird to be so formal."

"When your dad and I got married, I called his mom Mrs. Hart for years." Yes, my last name was Hart. Another reason, Sloane assured me, that I was so enamored with romance.

"Well, yeah," I said. "She made me call her Grandmother. That should say everything."

Mom laughed. "True."

"You can call my boss Mr. Bishop anytime you want, Mom," I said.

"I'm older than him. I would call him Robert."

I gave a barking laugh.

"When would I ever talk to your boss to call him anything?"

Never. The answer was never, and I would keep it that way.

"Oh! Dad is organizing things in your old room," she said. I was grateful for the subject change. "He's thinking about turning it into an office." My old room had gone through several iterations since I'd left. It had been a workout room with a stationary bike, a craft room, with rolls of ribbons and stacks of material. Now they would add a desk and a computer to the room, it seemed, but my twin bed would still exist, along with the bike that never left the craft room and the ribbons that would never leave the office.

"You can get rid of all of it, Mom. I don't mind. It's your house. What things of mine do you still have, anyway?"

"I don't know. Probably some old handwritten scripts. Remember when you wrote those?"

I let out a breathy laugh as a memory of me sitting on the floor beneath my desk so my mom wouldn't catch me, headlamp on so I could see, writing late into the night. Another memory, just as vivid, quickly followed: Audrey, in the light of day, flipping through the handwritten pages and telling me she'd researched the odds of getting a script made into a movie and they were devastatingly low. "And that's for the very best scripts," she had said. Even as a child, my sister always had a mind for business.

"Nope, don't remember that at all," I told my mom now.

"Well, it was a long time ago."

"It really does feel like ages ago." I took my exit off the freeway toward my apartment.

"You were so creative back then."

"Thanks, Mom."

"No, no, I'm sorry. You're still very creative," she said, as only a mom could.

"I'm just teasing you, Mom. I was creative." On the total wrong path, but creative.

"Are you okay?" she asked after a couple beats of silence.

"I'm fine. Why?"

"It's just lately you seem so . . ."

She could've filled in the end of her sentence with any number of words—unmotivated, preoccupied, adrift—and been right.

"Unhappy," was how she actually finished the sentence. A word that hadn't even come into my mind.

I pressed my brakes as I took the turn into my neighborhood. "I'm not."

"Maybe you need some goals. When I'm feeling down, I challenge myself to a new twenty-one-day habit."

"I'm not feeling down, but I'll keep that in mind. And like I said, I am sort of embarking on a new twenty-one-day habit in the dating world." That's probably about how long it would take before the apps provided me either bliss or misery. Either outcome would prompt me to delete them.

"How so?" she asked.

"I call the apps finding a needle in a haystack. The hay is the people I have to work through to find the needle which will probably end up stabbing me in the eye once I grab hold of it."

"Sounds like you need to get off the apps," Mom said.

I laughed. "You're telling me. But I haven't given up. You know everything takes me twice as long to accomplish than the average person. And, Mom, I'm fine, very fulfilled." Sure, not at work and not at all with my love life or my health goals . . . but I had really great friends and family. And that was something.

"If you don't come to the T-ball game, at least come see us this weekend. We'll order some food and watch a movie."

"As long as we don't use *your* glitch-filled app." Great, my life sounded so pathetic that my mom felt like it needed to be filled with rom-coms and sugar in order for me to find joy again. How could I show her that I wasn't someone to pity when I felt so pitiful?

CHAPTER 4

Good morning, beautiful

That was the message waiting for me when I woke up, from not one but two people I had matched with the day before. With all my heart, I wanted it to be a sweet, genuine sentiment, but when every other guy sent the same message after a few short exchanges, it no longer felt genuine.

I unmatched both of them and sat up with a stretch.

My room was cold. It was late April, which brought us perfect weather outside, but Sloane had once read that the optimum temperature for sleeping was sixty-eight degrees and she took her sleep very seriously. I pulled on my robe and stepped into a pair of slippers I kept at the foot of my bed, then exited my room.

Our kitchen was a good size for an apartment. Probably bigger than we needed, considering neither of us liked to cook. It had a small island and two long countertops. It had a large oven that we never used; instead we'd bought a Crock-Pot, then an Instant Pot, and finally an air fryer, all of which we also never used. The one appliance we religiously used was our coffee maker.

I poured myself a mug now. Sloane joined me, sliding her mug next to mine. I obliged, filling her cup.

"How many *good morning beautiful*s today?" she asked.

"Two," I said.

"Should we write a book for men titled *'How's ur day going' and other things you shouldn't type into a chat box because every dude bro across all platforms does?*"

I took a sip of my coffee and hummed in agreement.

"I mean, I know a literary agent. I bet we could get that published," she said.

"We might need to work on the title. It's a bit long."

She poured some vanilla creamer into her mug, then added a dash to mine. "I think it's perfect."

"Speaking of agents, I asked Rob about a promotion."

Sloane's eyes went wide and she slapped the counter with her hand. "It's about time! Good job. What did he say?"

I took my coffee to the table and sat down. A vase full of dying flowers dropping their petals occupied the middle of the table. They weren't mine to throw away or they would've been in the garbage at least three days ago. Maybe that was just my jealousy speaking. I couldn't remember the last time I'd gotten flowers. "He said we'd talk about what that entails soon. Or something like that." I didn't remember exactly what he said but that was the gist of it.

Her happy expression faded as she slid into the chair next to mine. "That sounds like classic Rob. Always later."

"It felt different this time."

She patted my arm. "I hope you're right."

"I am."

"Good. That's great. I'm proud of you. Make sure you bring it up again sooner rather than later."

She was right. I needed to make sure it happened this time.

My phone gave a chime.

"Ooh," Sloane teased. "More *good morning beautiful*s await."

I groaned and took another sip of coffee to fortify myself, then opened the app that had the little red number one in the corner indicating an awaiting message. Only it wasn't a message. It was a blurry picture with the warning from the app: click to view

"What?" Sloane asked.

I must've made some sort of noise. "A picture from Oliver."

"Of what?"

"I don't know." I held my breath and clicked on the pic. It cleared to an adorable photo of him crouching down by a golden retriever, a bright red leash in someone else's hand. The dog's mouth was open in a smile and its tongue flopped out to the side. Oliver was wearing running shorts and a T-shirt, a sweat ring around the collar. His hair was damp, which made his waves more pronounced. His brown eyes sparkled with happiness and gave me a wave of butterflies that hadn't been activated by an online exchange in a while.

"Not a dick pic, then?" Sloane asked, raising her eyebrows at my smile.

"Unless this dog's name is Richard." I turned the phone so she could see.

"Ah, cute," Sloane said, then she squinted a little. "And the dog's cute too."

I typed: You have an adoring dog?

"He's actually better-looking than I remember," Sloane said, inspecting the end of one of her long braids.

"I know, right?"

She flung her braid over her shoulder. "But you're not going to go out with him?"

"Attraction is not our problem."

"So if he asks you out you'll say no?"

"He will not. I promise you. We swiped as a joke and are now talking to pass the time in between real matches. He doesn't even have my number. We chat in the apps."

"You have some real matches, then?"

"I'm working on it," I insisted.

"He's too cute to be a time passer."

"Looks aren't everything. Believe me." I shuddered, remembering our date.

The chime sounded again and Oliver's message read: My neighbor's dog. I wanted you to see that animals are in love with me as well.

And your feelings for animals? I asked him, because he had asked me that same question.

This particular dog is my favorite, he replied, not really answering my question, but I'd given him a snarky reply to that question when he'd asked it, so I deserved it.

"I need to get ready," Sloane said with a big yawn. "Tell your boyfriend that all future Richard pics need to go through me."

"Not my boyfriend."

"Considering your years of matching and chatting history, he is probably the most consistent, healthy relationship you've had in a long time." She laughed as she walked down the hall.

"Ouch," I called after her. "Not cool!"

Back in my phone I typed: Is this a recycled pic or did you take it just for me?

I told you I wouldn't use recycled material on you. All original.

I actually think you told me at least fifty percent of your material would be recycled.

Oh, right. I knew I said one or the other.

Hey, that's not a bad idea, though. We could help each other out. There's obviously something wrong with our banter on these apps if we both continually end up back on them. Maybe you should run all your pickup lines by me before you use them on women from now on. If he was still single, he was obviously still making the same mistakes he had made with me.

And you'll run yours by me?

Well, duh. This isn't a one-sided service, I typed.

First advice: strike duh from your vocabulary.

I huffed. Completely? Or just when responding to men?

More the second.

Ha! Will attempt. Does that mean all sarcasm must go or just the bits that make men feel stupid?

You can say duh to me all day long, but other men . . .

Oh, sure. You have feelings of steel but those other men, they need to be handled delicately.

Exactly. I like it rough.

A smile took over my face, but before I even responded, another message came through: In the most innocent of contexts, of course. Where did your mind go?

My first advice to you: Wait until at least after a first date for dirty talk.

Good thing we already had one of those then.

I blinked at his message. Was this the same Oliver who had ignored me and the waitress, crowned himself the king of font choices, only read nonfiction, and told programming jokes that I didn't understand? Maybe this was the Oliver that had known exactly what to do with his tongue.

Maybe he really would be a fun way to pass the time between real matches.

CHAPTER 5

The front door to the office opened with its cheery little chime and Rob's teenage daughter, Danielle, walked in. Yes, Rob had a sixteen-year-old daughter. He was forty-two. Another reason the stars weren't aligned for us.

Dani had a backpack slung over one shoulder and she was staring at her phone as she approached my desk.

"Hi," I said. "I haven't seen you in a while."

She squinted at me like she didn't remember who I was. I'd literally met her at least a dozen times. Not to mention all the stories I'd heard about her on car trips to Palm Springs or San Diego or the handful of other weekend getaways Rob and I had taken over the last two years. Stories about her soccer matches and her school dances and her purple hair dye. All told while he ran a slow finger along the underside of my arm or placed my hand on his thigh. Weekend trips were some of the few times I felt like we were actually a couple and not some shameful secret.

"I like your shirt," I said to her now. "I'm a huge Arctic Monkeys fan." *Huge* might not have been the right descriptor, *moderate* would've been a better one, but I felt myself trying to impress the girl standing in front of me, who was clearly unimpressed.

She looked down at her shirt. "I don't know them. I thrifted this."

"You should know them!" Why did I sound so overly enthused about this suggestion? "I'll make a list of their top five songs for you. An introduction to the band, if you will."

"Right . . ."

"Margot," I said.

"No, I'm Dani."

"Oh, I know. *My* name is Margot."

She gave me a once-over. "Okay," she said, her eyes saying *I didn't ask.* "Where is Gloria?"

Gloria was the old receptionist. "She got a new job . . . six months ago."

"Oh. Is my dad here?"

"He stepped out a little while ago. You can wait here. He should be right back." I pointed to the chairs. Behind those chairs were bookcases filled with books. Mostly clients' advance reader's editions and hardcovers and foreign versions, but there were other books as well. It was my favorite part about the lobby. Sometimes, when things were slow, I'd sit in one of the wingback chairs and read. "I'll call and let him know you're here."

She held up her phone. "I'll just text him and wait in his office."

"Oh, yeah, right."

She walked down the hall and I buried my face in my hands. Why did that feel like a failed interview? Why did I care what Rob's daughter thought of me?

"You know why," I muttered.

Angry at myself for constantly blurring the lines between boss and potential boyfriend, I pulled out my phone to check for messages from actual potential boyfriends.

How's your day going? A message from a guy named Peter.

Not good. I messaged back.

Several minutes passed before he replied: Would sitting on my face make it better?

Wrong answer, buddy. I hit the unmatch button.

I checked all the other apps, but that was the only message.

My finger clicked on Oliver's profile, and without thinking about it, I sent him a message: "Would sitting on my face make it better" is the wrong response to "My day is not going well." Your PSA for the day to help you with the ladies.

Five minutes later he responded. Huh. Seems like a perfectly normal response to me. Romantic, even. Second date talk?

I smiled. Talk for if, and only if, I have in fact already performed said act.

Noted. This is invaluable information. I'm sure to succeed on the apps now.

I gave a curt nod as if he were in front of me to see it, then typed: You're welcome.

Is this hypothetical or did this actually happen?

I answered: Actually happened.

Tell me you unmatched him.

Immediately.

My favorite message of the week: If I promise you a carrot can I go for a ride?

Did she mean a literal carrot or is that code for something?

I'm not sure.

Was this her first message to you?

Yes.

Well, I don't blame her, you do look rideable. I hit send before I thought twice about it. What had gotten into me? I wasn't exactly the talk-dirty-over-texts type. But with Oliver, it was different. We weren't trying to date each other, and that gave me a freedom I didn't usually feel when chatting with guys.

Rein it in, Margot, Oliver texted back.

I responded: You couldn't pass up the pun. I hope you used that on her.

I didn't think of it until now. For her, I said nothing.

But the carrot, Oliver! The carrot!

If only I knew what it was code for . . .

I laughed. I might be more motivated by a literal carrot. I'm hungry.

So . . . why are you having a bad day?

You know how other people's dogs love me . . . other people's children? Not so much.

I assume you have some evidence to back up this claim.

I glanced down the hall Dani had walked minutes before. It was empty. The look my boss's teenage daughter just leveled me with after my attempt at trying to relate.

I don't accept this evidence. Children and teenagers are not the same thing.

Are you speaking from experience? You've also made a teenager hate you?

I WAS a teenager, he responded. And I was cold to most adults.

But I'm twenty-seven! She's not supposed to think I'm old yet. I'm practically her peer.

Bless your wannabe young heart.

Twenty. Seven!

The same as forty-seven to a teen.

What would that make you, Mr. Thirty-year-old? Fifty?

At least.

I looked up at the sound of shuffling feet that preceded Dani heading for the door. "Leaving?" I asked.

"My dad said he's going to be forty-five more minutes." She rolled her eyes.

"Sorry about that," I said, as if I were solely responsible for her dad's schedule.

She shrugged and pushed open the door.

"Hey, Dani! How old do you think I am?" I called, because I lacked self-control.

The confusion that overtook her face was understandable, but that didn't stop her from saying, "I don't know . . . thirty-something?"

I shouldn't have asked and I definitely shouldn't have gasped at her response. I cleared my throat and tried to save it with a "Good guess."

"Bye," she said, not even caring enough to ask if she was right.

I grumbled and turned my attention back to my phone. You're right. Who needs teenagers to like us anyway? I'll always have books.

I snapped a pic of the bookcase in the lobby and sent it off to him.

Your collection?

My collection is much bigger. This is the office. What about you? Big bookcase?

Is bookcase code for something else?

I smothered another laugh as Cole, the assistant to Rebecca and Dusty, the other agents in the office, passed through the lobby on his way to the cubicles, where I also used to sit, at the end of the hall. He gave me a short wave. When he was out of sight, I texted: No, not this time.

If I told you my book collection was all digital, would you hold it against me?

Yes.

Understandably.

Do you still only read nonfiction or have you gained some culture in the last three years?

That was the first strike against me, wasn't it? he asked.

It was the first five, I assured him.

Rob walked into the office fifteen, not forty-five, minutes later. And as if to prove how much a guy holding a book really did bring to the table, he was turning a page with one hand while opening the door with the other. An act that took considerable skill.

"You just missed your daughter," I said.

"She didn't wait?" he asked, lowering the book and pausing at my desk. He smelled good, familiar, like pine and mint. He was wearing fitted slacks and a blue button-down shirt that matched his eyes.

I realized that *my* eyes were traveling up his body, so I quickly shuffled some papers on my desk, averting my gaze. "She thought you were going to take longer."

"I thought I might. Better to underpromise than overpromise in these types of situations."

I stopped mid-paper-shuffle, hoping he meant what he said. If he was underpromising me so I wouldn't get my hopes up, maybe our talk about my future here would go even better than I anticipated. "Is now a good time to discuss things?" I said. His afternoon schedule seemed pretty open.

He rested his hand on my desk, leaned down, then said in a low voice, "You look beautiful today, by the way. And yesterday . . ." His eyes went to my blouse as if he was reminding me that yesterday I had undone one too many buttons.

I shifted in my seat as a shiver went down my spine and settled between my legs. No. We were keeping this professional. I was focusing on my goals. "Thank you, but that's not what I meant."

"I'll be in my office," he said, and left.

I knew why he said that. It's what he always used to say when he wanted me to follow him.

Marjorie, you will stay in your chair until you have yourself under control. Margot was not short for Marjorie, but every time I was contemplating something stupid, I used that name on myself. My dad sometimes called me Marjorie. As if my name didn't have enough syllables, didn't hold enough weight. Maybe that was the problem. I was one syllable short of being taken seriously in life. Thinking of my dad was supposed to snap me out of my terrible thoughts.

I took a deep breath. It did.

I was good. The flutter in my stomach was all but gone. I could do this. Other people didn't decide my fate, my sister used to tell me often. I did.

I stood and faced the hall. I would talk to him about *my* future, not *our* future.

The office phone rang, stopping me short.

Maybe other people did control my fate.

CHAPTER 6

"Bishop, Maxwell, and Shore Literary Agency, this is Margot, how can I help you?" I chirped in my cheery phone persona.

"Margot, just the woman I want to talk to," came the familiar voice of Kari, Rob's long-standing and best client.

"Hi, Kari. How are you?"

"I'm okay. Well, no, I'm not. Rob rejected one of my proposals this morning. Told me to rework it."

"He did?" That was a surprise. What Kari touched was gold. She wrote commercial, feel-good romance that sold exceptionally well. Most of the time she didn't even run ideas by Rob; she would just turn in another beautiful family-centered, tug-at-your-heartstrings book that needed very little work before being sent along to her editor.

"Yes. He did. I thought of an idea that has taken over all my creative energy and I want to write it."

"Why doesn't he want you to?" I was used to phone calls where I had to talk clients down or help them figure out what

Rob really said or meant. And I fully expected to play Rob Translator in this instance as well.

But then she said, "The book is a thriller-slash-romance with a horror-style ending."

My eyes went wide. "Oh. Well, um . . . your readers won't be expecting that. They're used to happily ever afters."

"That's what Rob said. He said I couldn't screw with my brand."

"He said *screw*?"

"I speak Rob. That's what he meant."

"Right." Of course she did. She'd known him longer than I had.

"You know the market," she said. "You talk to editors. How do you think something like this would be received?"

"It might be a hard sell," I said.

"But not impossible?"

"Definitely not impossible." I needed to shut my mouth. She was not my client. I was overstepping here.

"Can you work on him?" she asked. "I don't even know if Rob has read *any* of my last five books. But you have, right?"

"What?" Unless I was the junior agent on a project (and I definitely wasn't for Kari Cross), clients usually didn't realize I was the one giving the feedback on their books. Rob would sometimes use the royal *we* when relaying notes, but mostly he just forwarded them as if they were his own. I assumed he read through my comments and agreed with them. I also assumed he read the books himself. But maybe with clients like Kari, who consistently put out good books and had for years, he didn't feel the need to. After all, at the end of the day, her editor was the one whose opinion about content mattered most.

"You're the one reading and making notes on my books?"

"Um . . ." What was the point in denying it? She obviously knew. "Yes. I love your books."

"Your feedback is always spot-on. But I'm ready to try something new. I'm not saying I'm going to completely give up traditional romance. I love writing romance. But this idea has grabbed me by the tits and it won't let them go."

"Sounds . . . painful."

"It is! So you'll talk to him? Rob?"

"I'll try. I'm sure you said everything that needed to be said. Not sure my opinion will matter."

"I can be kind of brash, and sometimes alpha males like Rob dig their heels in and need, I don't know, a softer ask. I hate that I have to play this game, but can you do that?"

"I can certainly try," I said.

"Great! Because this book is getting written and I need him on board." With those words, she hung up.

Speaking of a thriller/romance with a horror-type ending, how would me getting up and walking into his office right now, after his obvious invitation to join him, play out? Hopefully with both mine and Kari's needs being met. The need that involved all my clothes firmly in place.

I walked down the hall and stopped in front of Rob's closed office door. I took a deep breath and turned the handle with a knock.

He was in front of his desk, sitting on the edge, as if he thought his pull was too strong for me to resist. In the past, he would've been right. "I wasn't sure you'd come," he said, even though his position in the room contradicted his statement.

I left the door wide open, a sign of *my* intent, and stepped inside. "I actually have a few things I want to discuss," I said, crossing my arms and staying outside the area rug that anchored his desk. "I just got off the phone with Kari."

"I miss you," he said, like he hadn't heard me. He pushed himself off his desk and took three slow steps forward.

Shit. My body liked that statement. I needed to flee. Come back tomorrow after I'd given myself a million lectures about why this couldn't happen again. About how wrong this was. About my future. About how it shouldn't . . . *couldn't* include him. Even if a relationship with him were appropriate, he'd broken my heart several times over. I didn't need to hand it back to him for another attempt.

I stayed where I was. "I'm here every day."

"You know what I mean."

"Yes, I mean, no, Rob. I'm here to talk to you about Kari."

He stepped past me and looked out the door and down the hall both ways before he shut it and turned to face me. "Did you know that when you look at me, sometimes you bite the inside of your cheek, which causes these adorable little dimples to form on your chin?" He was in front of me now, and with those words, he brushed a light finger over my chin.

"Rob . . ." I started, staring at the wood floor by my feet.

"It drives me crazy."

"No, I didn't realize I did that." I lifted my hand to brush his away, but he captured it in his, pulling me closer. I finally looked up at him.

"And your eyes. Those gorgeous dark brown eyes are so intense. Sometimes I think you see right through me." His blue eyes were pleading and fiery at the same time and they made my insides twist uncomfortably.

"My future here . . . and Kari, she has a new . . ." I was losing my courage.

"I know," he said. "A career-destroying idea."

Wait, was that in reference to me or to Kari?

He smiled his thousand-watt smile. "Did she request that you soften me up?"

Kari. He was talking about Kari.

I nodded because that's all I could do at the moment with him so close. The heat from his body was making me claustrophobic, like I couldn't breathe.

He chuckled. "Little does she know the ways you plan to do that."

"No," I said, shaking my head, which seemed to give me a little clarity. "I'm not trying to . . . I just want to talk. Her idea isn't bad. Authors genre-hop all the time. If she markets it right, it could be good."

"It could be good," he said in a silky voice, stepping closer. "*Really* good."

The backs of my thighs hit his desk. When had I traveled that far into his office?

"Yes," I said. "It could be."

My hands went to his chest, to push him away. He must've thought it was an invitation because he was suddenly pressed against me, his hot breath on my neck, his hands at my waist. My palms went back on the desk, to stabilize myself, but that really just opened me up even more. He stepped a foot between my legs, his thigh hiking up my skirt.

"Yes?" he said.

"Yes," I muttered.

Then he covered my mouth with his.

My body melted against him as his hands moved up, brushing the sides of my breasts.

I hated that I missed this. Missed feeling wanted, desired.

I missed being touched and kissed. I wanted to be someone to somebody.

His tongue slipped past my lips.

No. The word entered my mind forcefully.

I didn't want just anybody. I wanted the right person. And that wasn't Rob. Everything in me was trying to remind me of that—my twisty stomach, my sweating palms, my stiff back. Why had I let him get close again?

I pulled back as far as I could, considering the desk behind me. "I can't do this."

His forehead sank to my shoulder and his arms wrapped around my waist. "What's wrong, sweetheart?"

I somehow managed to untangle myself from him, sure that when I was free and standing on my own, I would be grounded in reality again. "I just . . . this didn't . . . this is wrong . . ."

I rushed out of the office.

CHAPTER 7

Sloane was sitting on the couch with Miles, her boyfriend, when I got home. Sloane had met Miles when we'd gone to a Dodgers game and the kiss cam thought they were a couple. The first three times they had just laughed and waved it off, mouthing *strangers* to the camera. The fourth time they'd kissed. The crowd went wild. He'd asked her out at the end of the game. It was perfect.

I stepped inside and shut the door behind me. They were watching some reality television show, but I couldn't tell which one at just a glance. Two empty wineglasses and half-full boxes of Chinese food sat on the coffee table in front of them. Sloane was wrapped up in a fuzzy blanket, her feet pulled up on the couch with her.

I made a show of taking a twenty-dollar bill out of my purse, walking over to the bookcase against the wall, and placing it into the Bad Decisions jar.

"Twenty?" she asked, her chin going down to denote that she knew this was serious. "Tell me it's not what I think it is."

"I don't want to talk about it," I said, hanging my keys on the hook in the kitchen, ready to escape into my bedroom to spend time with a guy who could do no wrong—Lord Leopold from the book I was currently reading. He would ease the pit in my stomach.

"If you didn't want to talk about it, you wouldn't have done that." She pointed to the jar. "You would've just lied. Or at least waited until tomorrow."

"I'm ashamed and that was my penance so I can sleep. Hopefully."

"You should've slept with flat-earth guy so that you weren't so susceptible to you-know-who and his wiles."

"I matched with twenty people in the car just now." Another part of my penance.

"*Twenty?* Wow, you really do feel bad."

"I also ordered at the counter instead of the drive-through at Jack's." I held up my bag of food.

"But there wasn't a hot bad boy with a heart of gold waiting for your inside?"

"No," I said with a pout.

"What is happening?" Miles asked, pausing the television. "I don't understand a word of whatever secret language you two speak."

I shot her a warning look. Sloane was the only person on the planet who knew my history with Rob and I hoped she hadn't shared our best-friend secrets with her boyfriend of the moment. That was an unfair thought. They'd been together at least four months and she seemed to really like him. I was just jealous. So jealous. But still, I hoped my secrets were safe.

"Margot is horny," Sloane said.

"Thanks," I said.

Miles opened his mouth to speak and Sloane held up her hand in his direction. "I swear if you make a three-way joke right now, I'll show you the door."

He pantomimed zipping his lips closed. "Hadn't even thought it."

She laughed. I headed toward the hall, thinking I'd gotten the worst of my shame out of the way when Sloane said, "This is sabotage, you know. Either on his end or yours, and I can't decide which is worse."

. . .

An hour or so later I set my book aside right in the middle of a steamy scene. How dare my mind ruin my ability to appreciate Lord Leopold's roaming tongue. Apparently, twenty dollars, twenty matches, and one opportunity for a random meeting weren't fooling anyone into forgiving me of my shortcomings.

Thoughts on self-sabotage, I typed to Oliver.

I stared at my phone for at least five minutes, and just as I went to put it aside in exchange for my book, a message buzzed through.

Am I pro or anti? was his response.

Yes.

I guess it would depend on the context, but generally speaking, anti.

Any self-respecting person would be. But as I lay in bed, trying to read, I had decided that Sloane was right. Intentional or not, me walking into that office and kissing my boss not even a full day after telling him we needed to talk about my future with the agency was . . . self-sabotage, self-preservation, self-hate? It was definitely something.

My phone chimed with another notification. Oliver had followed up his statement with: You? For or against?

I thought I was against but my subconscious seems to be all about self-sabotage. It's a flag waving, pin wearing, dues paid in full member of the self-sabotage club.

That sucks.

I couldn't help but laugh at that simple yet completely accurate statement. So much, I responded.

Do I get actual context to this line of questioning because I'm dying to know?

I smiled at his word choice. Most guys in my dating history would've played it cool, pretended it wasn't a big deal either way. But not him. He was *dying to know*. I knew his openness with his emotions and questions was because we were chatting like friends.

And yet, still, could I tell Oliver, the most consistent guy in my life (according to Sloane), about my less-than-stellar life choices? A wave of shame washed through me again. No, I couldn't. But I could tell him part of it. So I responded with: I should've been promoted at my company about three years ago, after paying my dues in the assistant and junior agent pool, but I haven't. For many reasons, most of which consist of me holding myself back. I should've taken my resume and experience to another agency if my boss wasn't willing to give me a chance but I haven't.

I thought it was because I was loyal, but really it was because I was holding out hope that something would develop between me and my absolutely-wrong-for-me boss.

Why haven't you? he asked.

I think I'm afraid of rejection. Of failing at this. That was true too, I thought as I typed.

And what would happen if you failed?

I knew that was supposed to be a motivating thought. It was supposed to make me think of the worst thing that could happen and realize that the worst thing wasn't all that bad. But from where I sat . . . well, from where I lay at the moment, my bedside lamp creating a soft glow in my room . . . the worst thing was a complete derailing of my future. I'd have to figure out all over again what to do with my life, and I was worried that I'd have absolutely no idea.

. . .

Somehow, despite my brain being unable to turn off, I managed to fall asleep. I didn't feel much better in the morning, though. I wanted to pull the blankets over my head and fake a sick day. But Rob would see right through that after the way I'd fled his office.

I groaned and opened my phone. Several messages waited for me. Not surprising with how many matches I had pushed through the night before. Some of those matches were questionable, considering my state of mind. I scanned through them quickly. Most were the fairly typical "Looks like we're a match." But then I came to a guy named Riley.

Riley at three A.M.: Hi, how are you?

Thirty minutes after first message. Riley: Hello, are you someone who doesn't answer messages right away?

"Can't answer messages in my sleep, Riley," I said to his little profile picture on my phone.

Thirty minutes after second message. Riley: Whatever. I'm a 9/10 but sometimes I message a 4/10 because I value personality over looks, but I don't wait around forever for fours.

Such a gentleman. Thanks for taking the trash out, I messaged back before unmatching him.

Despite my snarky response, his comment stung. "This is your penance," I reminded myself.

I scrolled further and came to a message from Oliver. Relief poured through me and my mood immediately lifted.

What did you really need to hear last night, my texting teacher? Because it wasn't what I said.

I chuckled and typed back: Failing sucks? I understand why you might be paralyzed in fear, feeling like your whole life is on the line? I've never failed in my life so I don't get it? One of those would've worked.

He didn't immediately answer and I got up and padded to my bathroom to brush my teeth. When I was done, a one-word answer was there.

Sorry.

I returned to my room, shut the door, and sat on the end of my bed to respond. Yes, please read my mind next time. You can make it up to me by telling me your worst failure. That might help as well.

Easy. My engagement.

What? How did I not know this?

We didn't talk much on our date.

True. How long were you with her?

Two and a half years.

You still talk to her at all? I stood to open the blinds on my window, letting the light stream in.

Occasionally, but not much.

What happened? I asked, settling back onto my bed. I mean, if you want to tell me. It's really none of my business.

She cheated on me.

I scrunched my nose. Sorry.

It happened a while ago.

How long?

About three years.

I furrowed my brow. Three years? I sat up. Wait . . . I typed.

Yes, you were my first date after the breakup.

Oh my god, Oliver. Why didn't you tell me?

That would've been an appropriate first date conversation?

Probably not. Fonts was much better, I responded. Could this explain why he was so distracted, so awkward, so seemingly uninterested in actually getting to know me on our first date? Or had his recent breakup let me see the real him?

Ha! You're never going to let me live that down.

Never. But really . . . I'm so sorry.

Don't feel sorry for me.

I heard someone recently gave you a carrot, so you're right, I don't feel sorry for you.

I didn't get the carrot!

Well, you should've. We need to know what it means. Will you text her back and ask?

I unmatched her.

I paused. *Interesting.* He was quick to unmatch people too, apparently. Another reason we were on and off each other's radars. Have you unmatched anyone today?

A woman whose first message was asking me what size shoe I wore.

Is that third message talk?

That's wait and find out talk.

I smiled. That was one thing I *hadn't* found out. My hands never made it that far. An image of me unbuttoning his shirt, sliding my hands across his abs, his body reacting to my touch, flashed in my mind and sent a thrill through me. I cleared my throat, surprised. To him, I only typed: Noted.

I'm sorry, he typed back quickly. I don't normally . . . if that made you uncomfortable . . .

I laughed. Pretty sure I started it. Doesn't bother me at all. In fact, I found that I was enjoying the innuendos very much. But again, this was never our problem.

What about you? he asked. Unmatch anyone today?

A man who told me I was a four.

You are NOT a four.

A knock sounded at my door and I jumped, nearly dropping my phone.

"I know you're awake," Sloane said through the door. "If you're staying in there to avoid me, it's not going to work."

"I'm not!" I called.

She opened my door, then jumped onto my queen-sized bed beside me.

"Twenty matches last night? I bet that made for some interesting messages to wake up to," she said.

I pulled my blanket around my shoulders and crossed my legs under me. "Someone called me a four out of ten."

"That person obviously wouldn't know a ten if it slapped him in the face. Which, you should. I hope you go out with him just so you can march up, slap him in the face, and then leave."

"I unmatched him."

"Probably a less-unhinged option." She took my hand in hers, then said, "Spill. What happened yesterday?"

And so I did. She sighed heavily throughout the retelling of the events of the day before. I understood. Telling it again, in the light of day, made it even more obvious how stupid I'd been.

"Rob is a manipulative jackass," she said when I was finished. "Are you okay?"

"Okay?" I asked. "What do you mean?"

"It sounds like he kissed you when you didn't want him to."

"No, I mean, I didn't at first but then I did. He asked," I said.

She lowered her brows, angry. "He did all that because he doesn't want to give you a promotion. You think the timing of him *missing you* is a coincidence?"

"You think?" I asked. I'd been quick to beat myself up about the situation but I didn't think Rob had ulterior motives, aside from the obvious one.

"I *know*. You do *all* the work on your junior agent splits and at least half the work as his assistant on all his other clients. He doesn't want to lose you. You're damn good!"

He just wanted to get laid. It was as simple as that as far as I was concerned.

"Turn him in to HR," she said, hugging her knees to her chest.

"We're too small to have HR," I said.

"Then turn him in to the other agents."

"And tell them what? I propositioned Rob two years ago, he took me up on it, and we've been sleeping together off and on ever since. And now that I want a promotion, I want him to get in trouble for not giving it to me?"

She rolled her eyes. "You're making it sound stupid on purpose because you know I'm right. He shouldn't have been sleeping with you to begin with no matter who started it. He's your boss, Margot. And a lot older than you."

I knew this. It ate at me often. "Let's stop talking about me. How was your night? Is Miles going to steal you from me?"

"You're stuck with me for a while longer. He's nice but it's only been six months."

"Six months? I thought it had been four. Is that a record for you?" I asked.

She shook her head. "No, it's a record for you. For me, it's pretty average."

"Really? Huh. Well, if I get a vote, I say keep him. He seems low on drama."

"Unlike you? I need balance?"

"Rude," I said, shoving her arm. "But probably fair. I swear, I'm working on minimizing the drama."

"Just in time for our quarterly brunch this weekend? The women are going to be so disappointed."

"I don't think I'm going to that. As another part of my penance for kissing Rob I have to go to my nephews' T-ball game."

"How does that make any sense?"

"Believe me, it does."

"Well, try not to let your sister take over your life."

"I think at this point, I'd be better off handing it over to her."

CHAPTER 8

"Excuse me. Sorry," I said, stepping in between a couple on the bleachers as I tried to make my way up to my family on the top row.

"Go Kaylie!" a man yelled to my right as I worked my way past another group. "Run! Run! No, other way!"

"You made it!" Mom said as I sat down next to her. She squeezed me into a side hug.

I leaned forward and waved at my sister, her husband, Chase, and my dad at the very end of our group. Audrey reached across my mom and squeezed my hand.

"Sorry I'm late. There was an accident on the 101," I said as I settled back into place.

That was sort of true. There had been an accident, but it was already moved off to the side of the freeway. People still liked to gawk, though, so it slowed things more than I was expecting. The full truth was, I'd gotten up later than I intended.

This week had not been my favorite. Facing Rob after the kissing session had been just as awful as I'd expected it would be. He asked me if I was okay and apologized for "letting his feelings get the best of him." After what Sloane had implied about his intentions being less than honorable, I hadn't told him everything was fine, like I normally did. I had said something that felt like it made sense in the moment, but the more I analyzed it, the more I realized it made zero sense. I had said, sitting at my desk, hair pulled up in a messy bun and lack-of-sleep circles under my eyes: "We're just on a merry-go-round, and I'm going to have to either puke or get off."

It wasn't: *Give me a promotion or I'm going to need to look at other job opportunities.* It wasn't: *Read Kari's damn book, Rob. She's writing it with or without you.*

Thinking about what I'd actually said again now, surrounded by happy parents watching their kids play T-ball, made my stomach flip.

"I wish you lived closer so you weren't always the one having to travel so far," Mom said, pulling me back into the moment.

"Then I'd have to commute to work every day."

"True." Her eyes went to my empty hands. "I'm surprised you didn't bring a book today."

"I only did that the *one* time." I had been twenty pages from the end when I had to leave. And I only read it during the slow times of the game.

Mom examined my face. Her expression turned to one of concern. "I'm worried about you."

I smiled. "I know, I know, I look terrible." When I'd rolled out of bed that morning, I pulled on a wrinkly T-shirt, some ratty jeans, and a baseball cap. It was a kids' T-ball game; I figured I'd be fine. But my sister was wearing a flowy patterned blouse, dark jeans, and a pair of ankle boots. We did not look like we belonged at the same event.

But both me and my sister were my mom's daughters. It was like she had split herself in half and given Audrey all the best parts—her impeccable sense of style, her mind for business, her follow-through. I got the leftovers—her loud laugh, her impulsiveness, her messy nature.

"No, you look nice," Mom said. "But . . ." She didn't finish. She was obviously talking about my face, not my clothes.

"I'm fine. Just tired." I turned my attention to the field and searched for my nephews. "Have they been up to bat yet?"

"No." She pointed to the outfield, where I could see Jack and Samuel standing shoulder to shoulder, looking at something in Jack's hand. A dandelion, maybe? *Some* sort of flower or weed. In the midst of their inspection, a ball came rolling between them and Jack dropped the weed and chased after it, Samuel close behind.

I cupped my hands around my mouth and yelled, "Go, Jack and Sammy!"

Chase let out a holler as well.

Audrey sat on the edge of her seat as if there were scouts in the crowd ready to promise her kids futures in the majors. Or maybe she was just worried they weren't going to be able to retrieve the ball. I'd noticed over the years that the boys weren't exactly athletic.

"They're doing so good," Mom said, patting my sister's leg after Sammy picked up the ball, only to have Jack reach into his mitt, snatch it up, and begin running toward the infield as their coach shouted, "Throw it! Throw it!"

I sucked in my lips to keep from laughing.

Chase stood up and cheered along with my dad as the ball was finally thrown and chased around by a couple other kids. I stood as well and clapped.

When I sat back down, I leaned forward to get my sister's attention. "Look this way. I want a pic." She tapped her husband and my dad and everyone turned toward me so I could take a selfie of the group.

"Don't post that online," Audrey said.

"Of course not," I teased. Any picture I'd ever posted online with my sister in it had to go through ten steps of approval. Not really, but it felt that way. The downside of a curated life, apparently.

My phone chimed in my hand. All the dating apps had notifications waiting. I had been trying to ignore them, but they had been blowing up all week from my post-makeout self-hate matching session. And now that it was Saturday people were trying to fill their social calendar.

The first message read: I see you have a job. Are you willing to give that up when we start a family? I'm an alpha looking for my beta.

I couldn't hit unmatch fast enough.

I looked around the bleachers. Maybe there was a cute single dad here ready to save me from an errant ball, who I would then need to repay with lunch.

"Are you swiping?" Mom whispered from beside me, leaning close.

"No, I'm not. Just putting my phone on silent."

"Show me some choices," she said with a conspiratorial smile. "I'll tell you who to swipe into the trash. I'm a good judge of character."

I nudged her leg with mine playfully. "You're a bad influence. And nobody is getting trashed."

"There's not a trash icon? I think that would be a good idea."

She might've been onto something. "No, I swipe left if I'm not interested and right if I am."

"And then?"

"And then if they swiped right too, we match."

"Huh," she said.

"What?" I asked, curious what she thought about all this. Mom and Dad had been married for thirty-five years. Met at a B-52s concert. Mom couldn't see the stage very well from her spot in the middle of the general admission pit. She asked a complete stranger if she could sit on his shoulders. He said yes. That stranger was my dad, who always added "I couldn't believe my luck" to the story. I smiled every time I thought of what an epic meet-cute my parents had.

"It's so . . ." Mom paused, her eyes still glued to my phone screen.

"Cold?" I finished for her. "Boring? Unromantic?"

"I was going to say 'interesting.'"

"I want to see possible matches too," my sister said from the other side of Mom.

"I don't know what *you* two are doing," I said. "But *I'm* watching my nephews play T-ball."

Audrey smiled, her eyes still on the field.

Mom leaned closer to my phone. "Ooh, who's that?"

A new message had buzzed through with Oliver's face next to it.

"Nobody," I said, scanning the message.

Is complimenting someone's looks before having been on a first date a red flag?

"Well, *Nobody* is cute," Mom said, even though the thumbnail picture was too small for her to see much of anything.

I turned my phone over in my lap so she would turn her

attention back to the game. Then, covertly, several minutes later, when she was distracted talking to my sister, I responded to Oliver, Someone complimenting your looks or you complimenting someone?

Me complimenting someone.

A feeling started in my chest, like a rubber band being twisted tighter and tighter. I rubbed at it until it released. My coffee, the only thing I'd had that morning, must've been giving me heartburn. I responded: I guess it depends on the compliment. Generic, blanket compliments are only meh for me. They don't feel sincere. But not necessarily a red flag. Use at your own discretion and try to be creative.

Thank you for your service.

Curious, I asked, What about you? Do you like compliments early on?

Call me a sucker, but yes. And they can be any old generic, overused compliment. A copy and paste job.

I smirked, then sent, You're so tall, dark, and handsome. Oh, wait, that was on my clipboard. Hold on. You're so average sized (are you? I don't remember your height), sandy haired, and friendly-faced.

Friendly-faced?!

You're right, that wasn't generic. That was very specific. Sorry, I'll do better next time.

I feel my ego crumbling.

I smiled. I'm positive you get more than enough compliments to keep that intact.

Apparently, I've only been getting generic ones. I request those from now on.

I stared at his thumbnail picture, and even though it really was too small to make out many details, I remembered his face perfectly. His big brown eyes bordered with thick lashes. His wide contagious smile. His slightly crooked nose. I bit my lip, but as I contemplated typing out any of those things, the rubber band in my chest was back. So instead, I typed: I'll keep that in mind.

"What are you smiling about over here?" Mom asked, leaning her shoulder against mine.

"Just chatting with a friend."

"I'm glad you have good friends, sweetheart."

"Me too." Even if it was all I had.

· · ·

Forty minutes later and two times up to bat for the boys and the game was over.

"I'm in charge of snacks this week," Audrey said. "Will you help me pass them out?" She looked at me with the question, leaning around Mom.

"Yes, of course. Let's do it." I stood and brushed off the back of my jeans before following my sister toward the parking lot and her car.

"How are you?" she asked. "Mom's worried."

"Mom's always worried," I said.

"Should she be?" She opened her trunk to reveal a medium-sized ice chest.

How could I tell my super successful sister that my execution of all her stellar advice over the years was very poor and I was stalled in both my career and my dating life? How could I ask for her advice about self-sabotage and things with Rob when I knew how much she would judge me? Rightfully so. "No, I'm fine."

We lifted the ice chest out of the trunk and headed back to

the picnic area next to the field, me holding one handle, her the other.

After a dozen steps, I adjusted the handle in my grip, the weight of the ice chest causing it to slip. "Are you feeding these kids a nine-course meal or something?"

She laughed. "They're growing kids and they're always hungry after playing."

"So yes? Your answer is yes?"

"It's not a nine-course meal."

"I'm sure whatever it is, it's the best."

"Is that an insult?"

My brows shot down. "Did it sound like one? It wasn't supposed to be." A group of kids shrieked as they ran by us.

"Speaking of meals," Audrey said. "I want to take you to brunch after this."

"What?" I asked.

"Brunch," she said. "I know you missed the one with your friends for this. Chase offered to take the boys home and I could really use some time away."

"Yes, sounds good."

Kids gathered around us before we even had time to set the ice chest on the newly stained picnic table beside the bleachers.

"You played good, guys," I said, rubbing my nephews' sweaty hair.

My dad joined us and gave me a hug. "Hey, honey. Haven't seen you in a couple weeks. Glad you were able to come."

"It was fun. You should come to my side of LA for dinner sometime."

"That would be nice," he said.

Audrey was pulling string cheese, carrot sticks, apple sauce pouches, and a bag of what looked like rolled salami with toothpicks out of the ice chest. "One of each until everyone has had some," she said, then gave me a pointed look, which made me realize I wasn't helping at all.

"Yes, one each, everyone," I said, then set up shop by the string cheese and handed them out as the kids went by.

A little girl stopped in front of me, snatching the string cheese I held. She looked me up and down, then said, "Your shirt is ugly and wrinkly."

"You know what else is ugly?" I asked.

My sister, obviously hearing me, elbowed me in the side.

"My shoes," I said, raising my dirty sneaker in the air.

"You're right, they really are ugly," she said.

A person who I assumed was her mom had just come up behind her, and she gasped. "Jasmine, say you're sorry. That wasn't very nice."

"Sorry," she sang in a *not sorry at all* voice, and skipped away.

"I'm so sorry," Jasmine's mom said in a *very very sorry* voice.

I shrugged. "In her defense, my shirt is ugly."

The woman looked at my shirt, and I could tell she was trying to think of something nice to say, but when she couldn't, she rushed after her daughter.

Once the only kids left around the table were Jack and Samuel, I turned to my sister and said, "You thought I was going to insult that little girl, didn't you?"

My mom and dad were helping my nephews pry open cheese and peel oranges.

"I could tell you wanted to," she said.

"I was just going to tell her baseball uniforms are ugly." She was right; had she not elbowed me, I would've.

"Glad you held your tongue."

"Unlike her," I said under my breath.

"Kids are honest."

I smiled. "So you're not a fan of my outfit either?"

She let out a trilling laugh. It was one I heard on her YouTube channel often. I wondered if she rehearsed it along with the rest of her script.

"Who was that little girl, anyway?" I asked.

"I'm not sure. She must've been on the other team. Sometimes they wander over and we share snacks and vice versa."

"She was on the other team?" I asked. "Then I'm glad we beat them."

Jack and Sammy looked up. "We beat them?" Samuel asked.

"No," Audrey said. "You know we don't keep score."

"You don't keep score?" I asked. "What kind of madness is that?" Then, quietly so only my sister could hear, I added, "I was keeping score in my head and we won."

She laughed again. Ditching friend brunch to be here with my family was the right choice. I needed this family time.

CHAPTER 9

"Then Sloane says, we should write a book titled *Good Morning, Beautiful, and Other Things You Shouldn't Text Because Every Dude Bro Does*. Or something like that. Maybe she said one of the other common phrases. I don't remember, but it was funny." I laughed and Audrey gave me one of her courtesy chuckles.

The sun was shining bright as we drove down the street toward Eat and Be Merry looking for a parking space. The shops and restaurants were crowded today and so far parking was unfindable.

"I don't get it," she said after a moment. "*Good morning beautiful* seems sweet. Wouldn't that be a pro, not a con?"

"Ah, my *never had to do dating apps because she met her husband in college* sister, it would be sweet if I knew the guy at all. If I'd met him or even exchanged more than a handful of words. But in most cases, I haven't. And the first time it happened, I thought it was romantic. The fiftieth time? I'm kind of over it. I want real effort, you know?"

"So what should they say instead?"

"There's this guy who sent me a pic of him with a dog that was kind of an inside joke—"

"Hold on." She lifted her wrist, read something on her watch, and then giggled.

"Don't read and drive!" I said, smacking her leg.

She pointed at the stopped car in front of her. "I'm not driving."

"Who was it?" I asked, nodding to her watch.

"Chase. He says the boys refused a bath so he threatened to spray them down with a hose and they thought that sounded fun."

I smiled. "They're so funny. So did he?"

"If he did, I hope he rewrapped the hose and made them dry off before going inside."

"Structure, the catalyst for fun," I said, sarcastically.

The car in front of us was now trying to back into a spot along the curb. "Just hop out and get our names on the list. It's right up the street," she said, acting like I didn't grow up in this town.

I looked in the side mirror to ensure no cars were coming and opened the door.

"Patio seating!" she yelled as I shut the door.

I stepped onto the sidewalk and headed up the street. Of course, patio seating. It was too nice a day not to sit outside. It was a gorgeous patio with potted flowers and vines crawling along the surrounding fence.

The air smelled like garlic and butter and salt. As I passed by the patio on my way to the host stand, my eyes scanned the wrought-iron tables and matching chairs topped with lime-green cushions and people enjoying the sun. That's when I saw Oliver, sitting across from a woman, eggs and fruit on the table between them. Like in a movie, his head seemed to be turning my way in slow motion.

"Shit!" I hissed as I ducked. I squat-walked until I was past the fenced-in area and safely behind the redbrick building.

A girl behind the check-in podium eyed me suspiciously as I straightened to standing. "Hi . . . uh . . . table for one?"

I adjusted my baseball cap. "No, two. My sister is parking."

"It will be a little wait for the patio," she said.

"No, not outside," I snapped. My pounding heart seemed to think this was a life-or-death situation. I took a deep breath, trying to calm my flight instinct, because it definitely wasn't . . . a life-or-death situation. It was something slightly below that. "Sorry, I mean, we don't want to sit on the patio. Inside is fine. In a corner . . . away from the windows."

Her brows shot down. "Um, sounds good. There's no wait at all for inside. Follow me."

I shot Audrey a text about seating choice, and when she joined me, she said, "What happened to outside? Did the hostess give you trouble? I'll go talk to her."

"No! Please don't. I know someone out there," I said.

"Ohh-kay . . ." She pulled out the chair across from me and sat.

I tugged on my wrinkly tee. "He does not need to see me like this."

"He?" she asked, craning to find a window, but there was no direct view to the back seating area from here. "This could've been a fun meet-cute," my sister said. "You all grungy, him . . ." She trailed off because she obviously hadn't seen him to fill in any details.

"With another woman," I finished for her. I wondered if

this was the woman he was asking advice about. If, based on my feedback, he had ended up complimenting her in some fun, unique way before their date.

"Oh, yeah, not ideal," she said.

I opened the menu, my heart still several beats faster than normal. Why did it care so much? This was Oliver. My sister was right. I should've just waved hi and smiled big and said something like, *You do still exist outside the apps.* "Besides, it wouldn't be a meet-cute. We've already met. Years ago." And it went terrible. So bad.

"What's your favorite meet-cute?" she asked. "Out of all the books you've read or movies you've watched."

That was one of my favorite questions. "I'm a fan of the trapped together somewhere with a stranger. Or fake dating. Like in *The Proposal.*"

Audrey scrunched her nose. "But they already knew each other in the movie too."

"True. So it would have to be more like if we showed up here today and there was a hot guy waiting outside and he grabbed me by the hand before we went in and said, *I need your help. I haven't seen all my college buddies for years and they're all engaged or married and I'm still sad and single. Will you pretend to be my girlfriend for the morning?*"

Audrey raised her eyebrows. "A bunch of guys are meeting for brunch? Not believable."

"Guys can meet for brunch."

"They can, but do they?"

"They should. Besides, they brought dates, remember?"

"Oh, right. The dates. So you'd ditch me for this handsome college kid?"

"No, he hasn't seen them in a long time. He's a grown man now."

"You'd ditch me for this grown man?"

"Absolutely." I smiled. "You'd want me to, right? The universe would basically be dropping my future husband in my lap. You wouldn't deny me that."

"Never," she said, putting her hand on her heart in a dramatic fashion.

"Thank you for your support."

"But thank goodness that didn't happen because you look like that. The guy would've waited for his next option."

I grunted and she laughed. "You're not wrong," I said. "I wasn't planning on brunch today. I was planning on T-ball and home."

"Home by way of the Ripped Bodice?"

She knew me well. The Ripped Bodice was an indie romance bookstore I loved that just happened to be a good stopping point between my house and hers. I tugged on my ugly shirt. "There is only love there. No judgment."

She smiled, her eyes taking in my outfit again. "I should've prepped you for brunch. It's just been awhile since we've had time together without the kids or parents."

"True." It had been at least a few weeks. "Speaking of meet-cutes, you have a great one. A costume party, Chase thinking you were someone else because she was also supposed to be dressed up as hot Rapunzel."

"I was not hot Rapunzel," she said. "I was normal Rapunzel." My sister looked a lot like Rapunzel. She'd inherited light hair and eyes from my dad, while I'd inherited dark hair and eyes from my mom.

"Well, either way," I said. "The story finishes the same. You both talked into the night and forgot whoever you were supposed to be meeting that night. Who was your Flynn Rider that night anyway?"

"I actually had a boyfriend when I met Chase."

"What? How did I not remember that part of the story?"

"You were too busy imagining a hot Rapunzel."

"So whatever happened to the boyfriend?"

"Chase was charming and relentless and I couldn't resist."

"Sounds stalkerish," I said.

"It wasn't," she said. "You had to be there. It was sweet."

The waitress came to our table. "Can I start you with something to drink? We have dollar mimosas today."

"Um, yes, please," I said. "That's a bargain."

"Just water for me," Audrey said.

"You're off the clock," I teased. "Alcohol is required for the occasion."

Instead of smiling and saying *Fine, just one*, like I expected her to, she nodded at the waitress. "Just water."

"Guess I'm partying alone this morning," I said.

After the waitress brought back our drinks and we put in our food orders, Audrey sighed and met my eyes. "So what's going on with work? Have you talked to your boss yet?"

Here it was, the Audrey motivational speech. My body instantly went on high alert, straightening my spine and grounding my feet. A memory of us sitting at the kitchen table and her poring over the college classes I'd signed up for, helping me switch out two, came to me. "We're speaking soon," I reported now. "About becoming a full agent and dropping the assistant responsibilities."

"Soon, Maggie? That's not specific enough."

"I know, I'm working on it."

"What's the holdup?"

I've been sleeping with him! I screamed inside my head, but regardless of how much I shared with her, I couldn't share that. She'd never look at me the same again.

She straightened the fork and knife on the table so they aligned perfectly with the square pattern on the tablecloth. "How does your savings look? Are you going to be able to handle a straight-to-commission type job? You've been putting some away from every paycheck like we set up years ago, yeah?"

"Yes. I think I could survive for about a year. I do have some reoccurring commission from our shared clients that will help too."

"And if you made a few good sales right away, I'm sure that savings could stretch out for longer," she said.

Tiny beads of sweat formed along my upper lip. I wiped them away. "It helps that I'm with a well-known agency that gets dozens of submissions a day. I should have free rein with the authors the other agents aren't interested in. Plus, once my name and picture are added to the agency website, authors should start emailing me directly. Then I won't have to wait for the other agents to pass. I'm hoping for several new clients as soon as Rob says go." At least I hoped my transition happened that smoothly, because even though I had some contacts and some success, I knew it would take a couple more years to get a good footing in the industry.

Audrey nodded, approving my plans. "Remember when you talk to him to lead with your head, not with your feelings. Cool and collected. Show him you have the upper hand."

"But I don't," I said. "He has all the hands."

"The key is to make it seem like you have more options than just him."

I stared at the water droplets on the outside of my glass. "I really don't. All my real options outside of the agency I'm at are in New York."

"So make him think you'd go there. He needs you, not the other way around." She pointed to her chest. "You have to believe it in here. That you have a lot to offer." She'd donned her "on-camera" voice. The one she reserved for her podcasts and her YouTube channel, where she gave this very advice to thousands of people. "Because you do have a lot to offer." I could see why her viewers liked her. She was good at pep talks.

"I do."

"Head first," she reiterated. "You tend to lead with emotions, then actions, then get your brain involved."

If only she knew how true that was when it came to Rob. "What?" I asked in faux shock. "I do?"

She shook her head but had a smile on her face. "It's backwards."

"I'll work on it." This was my constant mantra when talking to my sister.

"Practice what you're going to say the day before with Sloane, I'm sure she'll help you. She's a fighter."

Was that her way of saying I wasn't? I didn't want to know. "Enough about me. How are you?"

"I'm pregnant." She said it as if she was showing me an example of how to lead without her emotions.

"What?" My eyes shot to her water glass. "Oh! Wow! Congrats, Audrey."

"I waited as long as I could, but the gap between the boys and her was getting too big. I want them to be close."

"Her? You already know it's a girl?"

"Yes," she said.

"That's exciting. I'm so happy for you."

She nodded slowly, her eyes not leaving mine, like she expected me to say more. I wasn't sure what else there was to say.

I decided on: "I'll plan a shower. It will be fun. Just get me a list of who you want to invite."

"Oh, no, you don't have to. I have a vision. And my friend Janine is going to help me. It has to be a certain vibe for the socials. You know."

I did know. "Right, of course. I can help, at least. Just give me a job. I'm sure Mom will help too. Wait, do Mom and Dad know yet?"

"Yes," she said. "I'm twenty weeks."

"Twenty . . . weeks? That's like halfway." My eyes traveled down, but the table was covering her stomach. I tried to picture her earlier at the T-ball game as we walked with the ice chest, but my mind did not remember a baby bump. Twenty weeks? I couldn't believe she'd waited this long to tell me. A wave of hurt washed over me.

"Don't be mad," she said. "I wasn't sure how to tell you. I know you wanted our kids to grow up together."

My eyes went wide. "You waited to get pregnant because of *me*? Audrey, you . . . shouldn't . . . you . . . Why would you do that?"

"Because it was part of the five-year plan I helped you put together years ago," she said. "Career advancement, marriage, then baby. But . . . ."

"Not everything happens on a schedule," I said, taking a swig of my mimosa. "I know you married young, but I'm only twenty-seven. I have time."

"It's not that. It's just you don't know exactly what you want. You're a bit directionless, unfocused." She held up her hand, perhaps reacting to my shocked expression. "And that's not terrible. You've always been that way. Like you said, you're young. You have time to progress in your career. You have time to search for this perfect guy that you'll meet in the perfect way. Or time to realize that perfect only exists in books and to stop being so picky."

"Wow," I said.

"Please don't take this the wrong way."

"I think there's only one way to take it, Audrey."

"I'm not trying to offend you. I love that you have this dream guy that you're building in your mind, pieced together from all the media you've consumed. It's romantic, and sweet. And maybe you'll find him. After you get the single fun aunt who travels and parties out of your system."

"Parties? Audrey, having a social life doesn't mean I party. Having actual relationships with friends is a good thing." I almost added, *How many of those do you have?*

"Of course it is," she said. "It's part of my ideal life goal sheet I have people fill out."

"I'm glad they're somewhere in the mix of living an optimal life."

"Balance is the key. You can't let that one aspect outweigh other things."

"I know I'm not exactly where I want to be in my career right now, but I do work."

"You're a glorified intern," she said, softening her words with a smile.

I sucked in some air, but all the words seemed to vanish

from my head. My eyes stung hot and I blinked until I had the tears in check.

"I shouldn't have said that. I just get so frustrated with you sometimes. You have so much potential." She reached across the table and took my hand in hers. "We'll figure it out, okay?"

I nodded but refused to let my emotions take over, since she'd accused me of doing just that.

This was the moment the waitress arrived with our food. She set it in front of us with a cheery smile, asking me if I wanted another mimosa. I think I shook my head no. Then my sister and I ate and we moved on to different, less charged topics. By the time brunch was over, we were mostly back to normal.

CHAPTER 10

"My sister called me 'directionless and unfocused' today," I said to Sloane from the couch when she walked in the door. I'd gotten home earlier from my brunch than she had from hers, even with the additional driving time. I'd been so distracted that I'd forgotten to stop by the bookstore.

"Sounds like Audrey. Did you tell her she was bossy and overbearing?"

"No, I said nothing." The entire drive home I'd thought about her comments. They hurt, but they really were the story of my life. Reacting to things instead of acting. Letting life take me on whatever path it decided instead of pursuing what I wanted. "But maybe she's right."

She dropped her purse on the coffee table and sat next to me. She smelled like fresh air and a little like bacon from brunch. "Don't you think she gets enough affirmations in her comments section? You should've told her she was wrong."

"So you don't think I'm directionless and unfocused? Easily distracted by . . ."

"Rob's penis?"

I knew she was kidding, but that comment felt like a punch to the gut. "Among other things."

"Compared to her, everyone is unfocused," Sloane said, not necessarily denying the accusation. "Why did she say this? Was there a point?"

"She wants me to talk to Rob, demand a promotion. And she's pregnant."

"You're blaming this on pregnancy hormones? How very feminist of you."

"No, not the hormones. Although hormones are real. *Should* I blame it on the hormones?" I thought about that, then shook my head. "No, not hormones. But maybe it came out a little harsher than normal because she's pregnant. I'm sure she meant well."

Sloane slid the cell phone she'd been holding onto the coffee table like she now planned to stay awhile. "I hope you told her you were already planning to talk to Rob about a promotion, without her advice."

"I actually did."

"Good," she said. "Because you did."

Yes, I did and I would. I'd show her I was capable of more than she gave me credit for. "How was your brunch?" I asked. "Better than mine?"

"You're calling a T-ball game brunch now?"

"No, Audrey took me to brunch after."

"Well, at least you got a meal with the insults."

I snorted out a laugh.

"Oh!" She grabbed my arm. "Guess who else announced a pregnancy today?"

"Hopefully not you," I said.

"I would tell you first, for sure."

"Before Miles?"

"Is this Miles's child?"

"I don't know. Is it? Or is there someone else in the running for the title? Are you cheating on Miles?"

"I'm not cheating."

"Then why are you questioning the paternity?"

"I'm not pregnant."

"But in our hypothetical situation, you were. Maybe you need to analyze that reaction."

She laughed and shook her head. "Cheryl. Cheryl is pregnant."

"Aw. That's nice. Does *she* know who the father is?"

"Hopefully her husband."

"You have me questioning everything."

My phone buzzed with a notification, and I picked it up to see a message waiting in a dating app. I really wasn't in the mood to chat with random strangers today, but when I opened the app, the most recent message was from Oliver.

Did I see you today?

The blood seemed to drain from my face.

"What?" Sloane asked. "Something bad?"

I showed her the message.

"Did he?!" she yelled.

"I hope he didn't." I pointed to my outfit.

"Ew!" she said.

"I know."

"For someone who expects to meet her future boyfriend organically, out in the world, in some random cute way, you sure do dress like a slob more often than you should."

"If my future boyfriend can't love me looking like this, he doesn't deserve me when I look like a goddess."

"You say that with so much confidence for someone who hid from a guy today."

"How do you know I hid?"

She nodded toward my phone. "His message." When I didn't protest, she chuckled, then stood, pointing to her outfit—some orange cropped corduroy pants, a white boho-style V-neck, and some black strappy sandals—and turned in a slow circle. "This is how you dress to meet someone. Take note." With that, she picked up her phone, blew me a kiss, and headed toward the hall. "I have some work calls to make."

"On a Saturday?"

"I know. I'm such a dedicated boss."

"If that's what you want to call it."

After she left, I stared back at the cryptic message. Had he seen me? I thought I'd ducked in time.

Maybe? I texted back.

Perhaps the question should be: did you see me?

I grunted. He wasn't going to let this slide. If you saw me then you know why I would make sure I didn't see you.

No . . . actually, I have no idea why.

I let out a breathy laugh. That's nice, but three people today told me I looked like garbage so I know you're lying.

What kind of friends do you have?

One was a little girl. And they are known to be the most honest demographic on earth.

Are there actual studies supporting this?

I adjusted the throw pillow that was digging into my lower back and typed: If there aren't, there should be.

So the lack of acknowledgment had nothing to do with me and everything to do with you in a cute baseball cap?

I sighed, then typed: You did see me. But you were on a date. I wasn't going to interrupt your date.

I really wish you would've, he responded.

That bad?

Yes.

I had a bad date today too.

Oh yeah?

Yes, with my sister. The second person to tell me I looked terrible.

And the third? he asked.

My roommate, Sloane.

And to think if I had seen you for more than half a second, I could've been the fourth. You took that privilege away from me.

I snapped a quick selfie—hat, wrinkly shirt, and all—and sent it to him before I changed my mind.

His response: Terrible. I can't believe you left the house like that.

Right?

No, but in all seriousness, you look gorgeous.

My heart fluttered in my chest. "Down, girl, down," I said. But to him I wrote: Didn't I tell you no generic compliments before a first date?

We've already had a first date.

If a second date doesn't follow within a year, the dating history gets reset.

Not sure I want a reset on all my first dates.

I cringed, sure that was his nice guy way of saying, *Yeah, we don't need a reset on our terrible first date.* And I agreed . . . didn't I?

Do you live in Thousand Oaks? I typed back. That's where I grew up and where my sister and my parents still lived. And it's where I'd gone today for the T-ball game and brunch afterward.

No, I live in Glendale. Do you live in Thousand Oaks?

I live in Glendale! It was weird to me that we didn't know this very basic information about each other. One of the first things we should've known, it seemed. Well, not that weird; he had asked me next to no questions on our date. And I'd matched his energy.

That's probably why the apps keep matching us, he responded.

Yes, that must be it. They don't care about our compatibility, they just care that we can easily make late night house calls.

Why are we making late night house calls? I could practically hear the sarcasm in his voice.

I put my socked feet up on the coffee table in front of me. Oh, you know, borrowing a cup of sugar, or a toilet or something.

A toilet?

In this scenario my plumbing would be backed up and I wouldn't be able to find a twenty-four-hour service to fix it at such a late hour.

Oh, right, the backed-up plumbing. I should've thought of that. Well, my toilet is yours if you ever need it.

Is toilet code for something else? I asked.

No!

I laughed. Sorry, you're right. Toilets and carrots are completely different.

Entirely.

Why was your date bad? I texted.

We just didn't connect, he responded. The older I get the more I realize I don't want to settle. Alone isn't the worst thing to be.

Is that how I sound when I say that?

How's that?

I took two breaths and typed, Like I don't mean it.

CHAPTER 11

Rob had "taken a personal day" on Monday and "had appointments out of the office" all day today. But I knew what was happening. He was avoiding me. As I thought back over the past three years, I realized this was a pattern. I brought up the promotion, he promised we'd talk about it, then he'd wait me out. I couldn't believe I'd let him get away with this so many times. This time, I would outmaneuver him. I was his assistant. I filled in his schedule all the time with appointments and calls. I would add myself to his calendar. I'd even have another agent sit in so we both kept our hands where they belonged.

I pulled up his digital calendar for the week on my computer. He had an opening on Friday at eleven. Without giving away that it was going to be a meeting with me, I added myself to his calendar with the words Meeting in office. I even put my phone number after as the contact because I knew he didn't have my number memorized. It wouldn't set off any alarm bells. It wasn't that I didn't want him to know it was our talk I scheduled, but I didn't want him to prioritize something else over me.

Then I walked down the hall to the cubicles where I used to sit. Cole sat at his desk. If I were to guess, Cole was twenty-three. I knew he had literally just graduated the year before and had been here at our agency for six months. He was nice and eager, but we didn't talk much.

"Is Rebecca available for a two-minute ask?" I didn't do this. I didn't march around the office demanding agents' time. I did the opposite, did my best to help them have more time in their day. Even though I worked for Rob, I often filled in when the other two agents were between assistants. Answered phones, filed paperwork, scheduled appointments. I had earned some time.

"Let me check." Cole picked up the phone on his desk and dialed. Into the phone he said, "You have a minute for Margot?" He listened for several beats, then hung up. "Go on in."

"Thank you."

Rebecca's office was slightly bigger than Rob's, but she didn't have the corner windows like Rob did. She did have a wall of bookcases that Rob didn't. I could always tell Rebecca got into this field for the love of books while Rob for the love of sales and contracts and numbers.

I once googled Rebecca. She was in her late thirties, had started her career in New York, and had moved out here when her husband got a promotion at his company. She also liked to say, *I did it for the sun.* "Hi, Margot. How can I help you?"

"Hi, Rebecca. Friday at eleven, I'm having a meeting with Rob about my future here at the agency. I was hoping you could sit in. Give your advice and opinions. If you have time."

"Really?" she said, a smile lighting up her face. "That's

great news. He's always said you were happy with your current responsibilities."

"He . . ." At one point in the past Rob had told me he discussed my promotion with the other agents and the three of them thought I wasn't ready. Either she had misremembered their conversation or he'd been lying. They seemed equally likely to me. "He has?"

"But things change, right? I'd love to sit in on a meeting."

"Gr—great. I— Thank you," I finally spat out.

"Will you have Cole put that in my calendar?"

"Of course."

I did just that, and after Cole added me to the schedule I went back to my desk, reeling with this added information that once again proved Rob was holding me back, sabotaging me. *You sabotaged yourself*, Audrey would've said. I felt so stupid.

I swiveled my chair back and forth, trying to bring my anger levels down. I'd been a willing pawn in his game for too long. I was taking charge of the narrative. Friday. Everything would be better on Friday.

Speaking of anger . . . I pursed my lips and tapped my phone to life. I hadn't talked to Audrey since brunch. I had thought she would reach out, smooth things over even more after calling me a glorified intern. She hadn't. I typed a message to her: You hurt my feelings Saturday.

I erased the words that sounded juvenile and instead typed: I set a meeting with Rob for Friday about a promotion. That wasn't at all what I needed to say to her, but maybe it was what she needed to hear—that I could take charge of my life.

That's awesome! Remember to practice.

I grumbled a "Don't tell me what to do" under my breath and reminded myself it was Rob I was actually angry at, not Audrey.

The office phone rang and I answered it with my normal greeting.

"Margot, how did it go? Any progress?" It was Kari.

"Rob is avoiding me," I said, then clamped my mouth shut. I shouldn't have said that.

She just laughed. "That makes two of us."

"I'm sorry. I haven't given up."

"Can I send you some pages? Help you understand what I'm fighting for?"

"Yes! Please! I'd love to read some."

"Great! I'll send along my first fifty by the end of today."

. . .

"Romantic thriller with a horror-style ending."

Miles paused the television. *Love Island.* That's what he and Sloane were watching. A reality show where they threw twenty hot people together in a house, made the women wear bikinis twenty-four seven, and hoped anyone fell in love by the end. I checked up on all the past contestants on social media. Very few of them had stayed together. Having to wear regular clothes must've broken the magic spell.

"Genre-bending?" Sloane asked.

I'd been reading in my room for the past hour and came out, head buzzing. "Kari Cross's newest manuscript."

"Kari Cross? The romance queen?" Sloane asked. "Pass."

"You'd pass if you heard the concept?"

"I love her romance. Horror-style ending?" Sloane said,

sitting forward on the couch. She always did that when she turned on her work brain, like she was ready to spring into action. "Isn't that the exact opposite of a happily ever after?"

"What's considered a horror-style ending?" Miles asked.

"Basically everyone dies," I said. "Or at least are horribly maimed."

Sloane shook her head. "Says the girl who doesn't watch or read horror. It's true, a lot of times the main character dies or is hinted at dying. Or sometimes, the monster we thought was defeated rears their ugly head at the last second, promising a return. But what I mean by the opposite of romance is that the horror genre as a whole doesn't try to leave the watcher happy. Its goal is to disturb and its ending is often just as uncomfortable as the journey it took to get there."

I smirked and waved my tablet that I'd been reading from at her. "I should've known better than to try to tell a film agent what a horror ending entails."

"Yes, you should've." She pointed at my tablet. "And Rob should know better than to encourage Kari Cross to write anything but romance."

I rolled my eyes. "Rob does know better."

"Wait, *you're* encouraging her?"

"It's good," I whined. "Like, really good. There's this family, the parents on the brink of divorce, that moves into a town where everyone has pledged to live by a certain set of rules designed by AI to keep everyone safe. If you break one of the rules, you're kicked out. No second chances. But everyone is happy because the AI designed it perfectly to maximize happiness, so everyone follows the rules willingly."

"Until?" Miles asks.

"I don't know. She only sent me fifty pages so far. I need to ask her for more."

"Horror ending, Margot," Sloane said. "You'll hate it. You're all about the fun meeting and the romantic tension and the big bow tying everything together."

I let out a grunt, then headed back toward my room while grumbling, "You don't know what I'm all about."

"Yes I do!" she called after me. "Love! And so are all of Kari Cross's readers!"

"Don't pigeonhole us!" I called back and shut my door.

I knew Sloane had a point. I knew Rob had a point. But I also knew why Kari couldn't just walk away from this book.

I opened the laptop and signed in to my work email.

> Kari,
> I understand why you love this book so much. I do too!
> Have you thought about a pen name? It might solve
> the problem Rob has. Also, my only note so far is
> your setting is a bit weak. Why California? The writing
> makes me feel like you haven't been here before. Can
> you set it somewhere you're more familiar with? Also,
> I'm ready for more pages.—M

I shut my laptop and slid it off my lap and onto the bed.

My phone buzzed beside me. Kari was fast. But when I picked up my cell to check, it wasn't an email notification waiting; it was a voice memo from Oliver in the dating app. That was new.

I hit the play button. "Hi. Thoughts on a funeral for a first date?"

The shock of what he said battled with the shock of hearing his voice for the first time in three years. It was warm and comforting. And as if my body remembered exactly what he'd been doing the last time his low, raspy voice was in my ear, my lady parts clenched while the rest of my body was flooded with heat. It was kind of annoying that just his voice could bring back such a visceral memory. As I thought about how to respond to his question, I started analyzing *my* voice. Was it going to do the same thing for him? Did he remember what I sounded like when his hands were on me? It was only fair that he got back some of the same feelings he was dishing out.

I rolled out of bed and flung myself down the hall. "Do I have a sexy voice?"

Both Sloane and Miles gave me matching perplexed faces.

"Hello," I practiced. "My name is Margot."

"Well, don't use *that* voice," Sloane said. "You sound like a sex line operator."

"That's good, right?"

Miles nodded. Sloane smacked his chest.

"What? I just answered her question," he said.

"Who are you trying to impress?" she asked.

"Nobody. I'm just practicing phone etiquette."

She threw a throw pillow straight at my head and it actually connected.

"Ouch!" I snatched it up, ready to fling it back.

She held up her hands in defense. "Don't lie to me. And don't fake your voice for your boyfriend. There's no way you can keep that up. Just be yourself, dork."

"You have a boyfriend?" Miles asked. "Since when?"

"They're three years strong," Sloane said.

"You're the worst." I threw the pillow, which completely

missed her, then shut myself back in my room. "I do *not* have a boyfriend." I just had someone I needed to make hot and bothered for sport.

"Hello," I practiced again, trying to be normal. "Hello." I walked over to my window and watched a man in the parking lot disconnecting the battery in his car, a new one waiting on the sidewalk behind him. "Hi."

As though the man could hear me, he looked over his shoulder. I stepped back quickly, then closed my blinds.

I took a deep breath and messaged Oliver my phone number. My phone rang several minutes later.

"Hey," I answered. My voice was definitely not sex-line operator. The lack of air in my lungs made it sound squeaky instead of sultry. "Hi," I tried again. Better.

"Hello," he said, like he was the audiobook narrator of a romance novel.

"You're inviting a woman to a funeral for a first date?" I asked. "Probably a bad choice. Better to just bring your best friend or distant cousin for support. Also, are you okay? Who died?"

"No, not me. A woman invited me to a funeral. Not sure how to respond to that. It feels cruel to say *Too much, too fast* or to just ignore her. She's obviously grieving."

I would probably feel the same way if someone invited me. I sat on my bed to answer. "I see your dilemma. But how would the rest of the family feel having a stranger at something so very personal?"

"True. That's a great response. How come we haven't been each other's coaches for all these years?"

"Because we've been trying to wash the taste of our first date out of our mouths," I said.

"I thought the *taste* of our first date was the only good part," he responded.

It was validating to hear I wasn't the only one who thought the makeout was exceptional. "You're right. We really should've just been each other's booty calls for all these years."

He strangled out a choking laugh.

"Too much?" I asked, laying back on my pile of pillows.

"From you? No."

I narrowed my eyes. "I'll take that as a compliment."

"It is," he said. "What was *your* weirdest message from the apps this week? Does it beat my funeral one?"

I tried to remember any message I had gotten this week. The truth was, I hadn't opened the apps in days. "Um . . ."

"You're still on the apps, right?"

"Yes, of course," came my defensive reply. "Pimple popping."

"What?"

"Someone asked me if I watched pimple popping videos." That was a message from last week, not this week, but it answered his question.

"Huge red flag," he said.

I snorted out a breath. "It's stress relief!"

"Oh, your response was yes."

I smiled. "Mostly I read for stress relief, but those videos are mindless and kind of great and if you haven't watched any, I don't want to hear it."

His laugh was low and settled in my belly. My hand trailed a slow path along the strip of exposed skin between my silky pajama shorts and tank top. Back and forth. My eyes fluttered closed as every nerve ending in my body hummed to life. Why *hadn't* we revisited our physical connection before? Because I'd walked away frustrated that first night?

"What do *you* do to relax?" I asked, my voice huskier than I intended.

"You okay?" he returned.

"Just . . ." *Imagining your hands on me, that's all.* "Where are you?"

"Where am I?" he asked.

"Yes."

"In my bedroom. You?"

"Same. In bed." God, we'd been good together in that car. How much better would we be in an actual bed. Maybe just one session would get him out of my head for another three years.

He cleared his throat. "Are you tired?"

"Not at all." Goose bumps formed along the path my hand trailed. "Has anyone ever told you that you should record audiobooks? You have the perfect voice for it."

"Nobody has ever told me that."

"I have a book you can practice with."

"Oh yeah? What kind of book?" Was it possible for his voice to get even sexier with that question?

"The kind where the main characters do really bad things to each other," I said.

"Like a psychological thriller?" he teased, a smile in his voice.

"There are definitely head games involved."

He let out a low chuckle. "I would like to read this book. To you."

Heat poured through my body. I feared the only person getting hot and bothered by this conversation was me. "Okay," I breathed.

"By the way, I run to relax," he said, answering my previous question.

I pulled down my tank top and sat up, trying to shake off

the obviously one-sided physical responses happening. "Huge red flag," I said, parroting his earlier sentiment. "My sister is a run-when-stressed person."

"Is it a good thing or bad thing to be compared to your sister?"

My sister was a work of art in all ways, in how she dressed, how she kept her house, how she mothered, how she ran her businesses.

"Running is a pretty innocuous thing to have in common with someone. I won't hold it against you," I said to Oliver.

He let out a low hum. "Interesting. So it's a bad thing."

"What? No. My sister and I are just very different, but I love her. Now, if you have a regimented schedule, like her . . ."

"Schedules are good for anxiety."

I laughed. "You totally do! Let's hear this schedule."

"It's a perfectly normal schedule. Wake up. Run. Work for a couple hours. Gym. Lunch. Work. You know. Normal."

It was good to be reminded, once again, how very different we were. "I sense it's much more detailed than that, but we can pretend you're not super strict with it for now."

"You have no schedule?" he asked.

"I have organized chaos." That's what my sister always called my life. "Do you have any siblings?"

"I also have an older sister."

"Does she run?" I asked.

"Yes, actually."

"Looks like we've discovered why we're incompatible. We don't agree on running."

His voice was low when he said, "We're hopeless."

CHAPTER 12

"The book can't be set anywhere else. It needs to be California and it needs to be a more sleepy, less populated area of California. You'll see why later," Kari said to me on the phone the next day at work. She'd called me almost immediately when I sat down at my desk, iced tea in hand.

"I trust you," I said. "Maybe do some more Google Earth searches, then, because I want to feel like I'm there but I don't."

"Have you been to Paso Robles before? Near the central coast?" she asked. "It's wine country, but the place I'm setting it is just outside there but similar terrain: rolling hills and farmland."

"I haven't," I said. "I'm a Southern California girl. You should book a flight. It's a good excuse for a vacation."

"I wish I could. I don't have the time right now. Maybe this summer. My son is about to graduate and it's all-consuming."

"Congratulations! I didn't realize Bryce had gotten so old. I swear he was a freshman yesterday."

"You're telling me," she said.

"This summer works. You have time to get it right."

"If I can get Rob's eyes on this, I don't want him to have any excuse not to love it. I'll work on setting. And, Margot, thanks for the suggestion. You're not wrong."

"No problem." I woke up my sleeping computer. "Do you have more pages for me? I'd love to read more. It really is amazing, Kari."

"Let me apply your notes to the next section so you can tell me if I'm succeeding, and I'll send it soon."

"Sounds good." I hung up the office phone, then checked my cell phone. No notifications or texts. Not even from Oliver. A tinge of disappointment settled in my chest and I tried not to read into it. We'd decided we were hopeless, after all.

I got to work on my daily tasks. They seemed more mind-numbing, more tedious than they ever had before. Now that my goal was in reach, it was hard to focus on building someone else's business. I was ready to get to work on my own.

It felt like I had been in the office all day when the bell on the front door jingled at ten A.M. I looked up to see Rob walking in. It was the first time he'd been in this week, and by the way he avoided my eyes, I could tell he wouldn't be in long today.

Following close behind him was Rebecca. They rarely arrived to work at the same time. Had someone asked me if they were close, or even friends, before today I would've said, *No, just business partners.* But there was something about the way she looked at him, about the way her hand brushed along his arm as he held the door open for her, that made my stomach lurch. He said something under his breath and she laughed. Not some polite chuckle or airy sound of amusement but a full-on laugh.

They both practically floated through the lobby. The only form of acknowledgment was a nod from Rebecca in my direction. I froze, staring after them. Was I being paranoid? They were coworkers, after all. Maybe they'd almost hit each other in the parking lot or run into each other at the coffee shop and were recounting the story.

Or maybe Rob is screwing her too.

Those words came to me in Sloane's voice, but my brain had come up with them all on its own. Just because I thought the words didn't make them true. It wasn't that I was jealous. I actually found I wasn't. At all. But I was worried. Had Rebecca told him about the meeting? What kind of support would she give me Friday if Rob had prepped her with his opinion?

I scooped up my purse from beneath my desk and carried it outside, freeing my phone and dialing a number while I did.

"Go for Sloane," she said, answering.

"You're a dork."

"I should answer my office phone like that."

I stepped around our brick building and leaned against the wall. "You really shouldn't."

"Guess what happened today?" she said.

"What?"

"My favorite director is interested in one of my scripts."

"Cindy Farrow?" She'd only talked about wanting to attach her to one of the scripts she repped for years.

"Yes!"

"That's amazing!"

"Wait, you called me," she said. "What's your news?"

I looked over my shoulder even though I knew nobody had followed me outside. "I think Rob is sleeping with Rebecca."

She gasped audibly. "I thought she was married."

"She is," I said.

"That asshole. Did you catch them doing something?"

"Walking into the office laughing together."

There was silence. "Tell me that's not the end of your sentence."

"There was a vibe."

"You're projecting."

"There was a shared look."

"You're overreaching."

"There was a lingering arm brush."

"Margot, you're killing me."

"Should I tell her never mind about backing me up Friday? Should I ask Mr. Maxwell instead?" A car passed by the street to my right, its radio blaring.

"Crusty Maxwell? Isn't that what you call him?"

"Only behind his back!" His name was Dusty Maxwell and he was really old, like, *he should've retired twenty-five years ago* old, so it made sense.

"You will not ask Crusty Maxwell, who only reps nonfiction. And you will take a deep breath and start putting positive vibes into the universe. All this negativity is going to make the universe angry. It's going to grant your wish to fail."

"I don't wish to fail." I closed my eyes, the brick wall behind me rubbing against the back of my arm.

"That's not what you're telling the universe."

She was right. If the power of positive thinking was real, the power of negative thinking was too. I squared my shoulders and opened my eyes. "Okay, positive thoughts starting now."

"Not just positive thoughts; you need positive actions to undo this damage."

"Okay . . . let's do a celebratory lunch after my meeting and subsequent promotion to agent on Friday."

"Better! Yes, do that."

"Put it on your schedule."

"Oh, you meant with me?" she said. "Sorry, I'm out on Friday. I have a meeting with the previously mentioned director."

"You suck."

"But I'll get together a group for Friday night at Pinky's."

Pinky's was our favorite bar that often hosted karaoke and trivia nights and poetry slams. It was where we went when Cheryl got engaged and when Laurel broke up with her boyfriend. It was our celebration spot.

"Deal," I said.

"You should double up on positivity, though, and go out for a celebratory lunch as well. I'm sure you can think of someone who would be willing to *celebrate* with you."

Oliver's face immediately came to my mind. I knew that was who Sloane was implying I ask as well.

"You're right," I said. "It's time to defuse the three-year bomb. My brain has been building up our car makeout into far more than it was, I'm sure of it."

"So you'll make out with him again to test this theory?"

I laughed. "It wouldn't hurt. I mean, the best celebrations involve makeouts, right?"

"Maybe it won't be as awkward this time and you'll see that you have both chemistry and compatibility. The perfect combination."

I rolled my eyes. "We don't. He's too uptight for me, I think."

"Opposites attract?"

"Too regimented." I shifted on my feet and almost stepped on a piece of chewed-up gum on the asphalt.

"Maybe that's why he's so good with his hands," she said. "His regimented study of the art of sex."

I gave a sarcastic laugh. "You really want the universe to deliver me everything on Friday. The perfect job, the perfect man."

"So you admit Oliver is the perfect man?"

"Stop," I said.

"If you had met him in any other way but on the apps, you would be giving him a real chance."

"I gave him a chance!"

"*Past* Margot gave him a chance."

"I would trust Past Margot with my life."

"Fine, fine. Keep looking for your meet-cute, and in the meantime, get yourself a fun makeout partner because, yes, I do want the universe to deliver you everything. You deserve it. Do you hear that, Universe?" Sloane yelled. "It's the era of Margot!"

"Are you alone at work today?" I asked.

"No," she said. "And my coworkers agree."

I heard a couple whoops ring out behind her.

Then she repeated, "The era of Margot."

. . .

The era of Margot. The era of Margot.

I had repeated that phrase multiple times throughout the day. And now, home again, changing out of my work attire and into my lounge attire, I repeated it again, hyping myself up for the phone call I was about to make.

Positive vibes. "I'm going to celebrate big-time on Friday, Universe, because I'm getting this promotion," I said out loud.

I didn't know why I was nervous to call Oliver. Maybe it was just that I was proposing a change in our dynamic. We hadn't tried to meet each other again for three years. He had been on the same date I was; what made me think Oliver even wanted to hang out? I had my complaints about him, but I was sure he had some about me too. After all, he'd had every opportunity to initiate something like this. He hadn't.

I moved the stack of clothes off the overstuffed chair in the corner of my room and onto my bed and took a seat. These weren't positive thoughts. These were the exact opposite.

I shook out my hands but my nerves stayed firmly intact. I pushed the call button next to his name and held my breath. His phone rang several times before it went to voicemail. I disconnected the call and typed out a text instead. I need a midday celebration partner Friday. You in?

I paced my bedroom for several lengths, then picked up the book on my nightstand and carried it back to the chair. I turned to my spot near the back and read the same line a dozen times but still had no idea what I'd read.

"Lord Leopold, do your job," I muttered to my book.

My phone buzzed from where it had settled between my thigh and the chair and I let out a surprised yelp. In my attempt to pick it up, my book tumbled to the floor. "Hello," I answered as I scrambled to rescue the lord from his page-bending, open-faced landing.

"Hi," the deep voice of Oliver sounded. "You okay?"

That was the second time he'd sensed my distraction from just my voice. "Fine, yes, just dropped my book, hello."

He chuckled. "I got your text. What are we celebrating?"

"Does that make a difference?" I asked, curious.

"Sure. Puppy murder, house fires, cavities. Out. Anything else, probably in."

I laughed, but responded, "Cavities are on the same level as puppy murder and house fires?"

"I didn't rank them."

I pulled my feet up onto the chair with me, my nerves from before squelched. My eyes narrowed in on my work shoes, laying sideways by the bed where I had just discarded them. "Shit. I stepped in gum earlier."

"That doesn't seem like something to celebrate."

"Well, then I guess I'll have to find someone else to celebrate with me."

"I hear ice and/or peanut butter works for removing gum."

"Did you minor in gum-removing techniques in college?"

"Yes, UCLA is known for that program."

"You went to UCLA? My sister went there. Maybe you knew her," I deadpanned. "You probably ran together."

"It's true, all the people who ran at UCLA knew each other," he said, returning my sarcasm.

"I wouldn't be surprised. Oh, and real celebration: I'm getting my dream job on Friday! Apparently, the universe requires positive energy or it takes things away . . . according to Sloane."

"You did it? You faced your fear?"

I had forgotten I'd told him about being afraid to go after the promotion. "Almost. Friday."

"This is way better than animal cruelty or house fires."

"What about cavities?"

"Slightly better than cavities."

I laughed but then realized he hadn't actually committed to lunch. "So? Can you come celebrate with me then? Friday. Noonish?"

"Yes," he said.

"Okay, cool."

"Margot?" he said.

"Yes?"

"I'm excited to see you again. Finally."

My heart galloped to life in my chest. "Me too."

CHAPTER 13

I knocked on Rob's office door while glancing down the hall toward Rebecca's. She'd join us when she got off her phone call. That's what Cole had said when I stopped by on my way here.

"Come in," came Rob's muffled reply.

I took a deep breath. This was it. The moment my life was going to change. Or at least the moment it was going to take a massive step forward.

Two hours ago, I'd arrived at the office, completed my morning tasks, and immediately started reading author queries from the email slush pile. The very first email was amazing: the story interesting, the voice fun and refreshing. I read the five sample pages she'd included. Those were even better! The first email of the day! That never happened. I took it as a sign. Sloane was right. Positive energy was in the air. The universe was providing.

I opened the door and stepped into Rob's office. He was sitting behind his desk. A book was open on top of it, but his attention was on the computer.

"Hi," I said.

"Margot, good morning again." He'd said good morning on his way into the office thirty minutes earlier. It was weirdly formal, but that's where we were at this point.

"Yes, good morning."

"Could you grab me a cup of coffee? I haven't had a chance to get to the lounge yet."

The agents called the break room "the lounge." They probably thought it sounded fancier than what the break room was: a couple tables and chairs, a microwave, a fridge, and a coffee maker. A break room.

When I didn't move, he said, "I think my mug is in the sink. If not, I have one in the cupboard as well."

"Don't let him play any head games," Sloane had said that morning during our practice session.

Was this a head game? Either way, I didn't want to start on his bad side, so I left his office and rushed to the break room. I should've worn flats today. I'd put on my heels for confidence but I felt like I was going to fall flat on my face.

"Hey, Margot," Cole said from his seat at a table.

"Oh, hey. How are you?" I went to the sink. Rob's dirty mug was in there from the day before, unwashed. Ironically, it said *world's greatest boss* on the side. I'd given it to him two years ago when that sentiment was truer.

"Living the dream," Cole said, raising a carrot stick to me. The carrot made me think of Oliver and the woman who'd told him he was rideable. I had to stifle a laugh.

I rinsed out the mug, then filled it, and left Cole with a "Keep dreaming." It sounded more sarcastic than I meant for it to.

I was forced to walk slower on the way back. I'd filled the

cup too full. Rookie mistake. In my left hand, I held a handful of creamers and sugar packets. Rob didn't take either in his coffee, but if this was about control, I was prepared.

I slid the coffee onto his desk.

He gave it a quick glance. "Oh, can you—"

I dumped my handful of additives next to the mug.

"Always one step ahead of me," he said with a wink.

I smiled when what I really wanted to do was sigh. Then, without waiting to be asked, I sat in the big rolling chair opposite him and clasped my hands together.

"I noticed on the schedule—"

"It's me. Your eleven o'clock is me."

His eyebrows popped up. I sensed with his coffee stunt that he already knew it was me. Had put two and two together with the phone number I'd added next to the appointment. He must've known my number after all. Or maybe Rebecca had told him. But with the expression on his face now, I second-guessed myself. Maybe he really did want creamer in his coffee today.

When he picked it up without adding any, however, and took a sip, he had me confused all over again. This was the story of our whole relationship.

It's going to go well, I reminded myself. *The amazing first query this morning, my celebration with Oliver later, the party tonight. All good vibes.* I tried to channel my inner Audrey for this encounter: cool, calm, confident.

"You said we could talk," I said. "I put myself in your schedule so we could do that."

"I said we could talk?" His eyes shot to the open door behind me.

Now I really did sigh. He thought I wanted to talk about us. "About becoming a full-time agent, Rob," I clarified.

"Oh!" he said, and relief washed over his face. "Today isn't the best—"

"I scheduled us an hour. You have an hour."

An amused smirk came on his face, then he held his hands out to his sides as if to say, *The floor is yours.*

Nobody in our little office had moved from assistant to agent in the time I'd worked here. Most assistants lasted a year or so and moved on to positions outside the company (it's what I should've done. Except . . . I was screwing my boss). I thought he'd tell me the steps to make it happen. But obviously he was waiting for me to lay out a plan. I looked over my shoulder for Rebecca, but she wasn't here yet. "I was thinking we could start by giving me full ownership of the clients I'm a junior agent on." That would mean I wouldn't have to split commission.

"We sold them on you by promising me. That won't work."

"I have a strong relationship with all of them."

"Knock knock," Rebecca said from behind me, and my shoulders relaxed a degree. It felt like I suddenly had backup. "Sorry I'm late."

"Rebecca," Rob said. "Margot and I are about to have—"

"I know!" she said, coming in and sitting in the chair beside me. "She asked me to join. I'm surprised you didn't ask me since this involves the agency."

"It's just a preliminary meeting," he said. "Of course I intended to have an agency meeting once I assessed her readiness."

They met eyes and I could've sworn a little smirk came

onto Rebecca's face, making me question the nature of their relationship all over again. No, I was just imagining it.

Rob turned back to me with a hardness behind his eyes I didn't recognize. He was angry I'd invited Rebecca. Or angry I hadn't told him I'd invited her. Or angry about the meeting. He was angry about *something*. "Is there more to your plan?" he asked.

I swallowed, sat up straighter, and tried to remember the rest of the speech I had practiced with Sloane that morning, but my mind was blank after his rejection of what I thought was a given. I grasped at the first thought that came to me. "I found a manuscript in the slush this morning that I'm really interested in. I thought maybe . . ." *Be confident, Margot.* "It would make a great manuscript for me to solo on."

"You want to offer solo representation to a person who emailed *me*?"

A lump rose in my throat as embarrassment took over and I swallowed it down. I inhaled a calming breath. "Yes. It's the type of story you typically pass on. But you're welcome to look at the query to make sure."

His eyes went wide. "I'm *welcome* to look at a query written to me?"

I bit the inside of my cheek, realizing my misstep.

Rebecca stepped in with a save. "And you think this aspiring writer will accept your proposal? It's not what she'll be expecting," Rebecca asked.

I was confused. I thought sharing the slush pile was a standard practice. Maybe it wasn't standard for this agency.

"I think I'm good at selling myself," I said, even though I wasn't proving it in this particular moment.

Rob templed his fingers. "You'll need to start by putting yourself out there as *yourself* and wait to see if writers email you. You post on your socials, you announce yourself in Publishers Marketplace, you go to conferences and then you start sifting through the emails that come in hoping for one that shines."

"I can definitely sift through emails," I said. "I've been doing it for four years. I think I found half your current list. And I found all the writers we coagent on." I offered Rob an innocent smile with my very true statement.

He brushed over the fact as if it wasn't a big deal. "You won't have quite as big a selection, which will make the standouts few and far between. Nobody knows who you are."

"But I could have my face and bio on the agency website?" I suddenly wished I hadn't invited Rebecca. I couldn't say the things I wanted to say. Like: *You owe this to me, Rob.* Or: *I'm not making this up; this is how you told me it would work in the past.*

"If Rebecca and Dusty are okay with that."

Rebecca nodded. "We can have a more in-depth meeting, the three of us."

"Sounds good." He clapped his hands together like the meeting was over.

Rebecca stood as if the clap dismissed her as well. "This was fun. Thanks for inviting me."

"Thanks for making the time," I said, staying firmly in my seat.

She lingered in the doorway before Rob winked at her and she exited the room. My breath caught in my throat. I hadn't imagined that.

When she left, Rob picked up the phone.

"Wait," I said.

He raised his eyebrows.

"You're going to make this happen." I stared at him.

He stared back.

"Right?" I added. I shouldn't have added that. It weakened my statement.

"Hopefully."

My chest was tight with anger now. It clawed its way up and wrapped a hand around my throat. I didn't want to let my emotions take over, so I tried to push it back down. "I don't expect you to hand over clients you're passionate about, but if there's one that isn't a fit for your list, you can suggest me as an alternative."

He let out a hearty laugh. When I didn't join him, he said, "Oh, you're serious?"

My eyes stung. Shit. I was going to cry. I could not cry. I sucked in a breath and stood.

Before I even took a single step, he said, "Margot, don't do that to me again."

I paused, not understanding what he meant.

He looked toward the hall. "Inviting another agent without informing me first, putting yourself on my schedule. It was unprofessional and immature. Proves exactly why you're still where you are."

"Are you sleeping with her?" I asked in a low voice.

His face paled before he recovered with a slimy smile. "Of course not. Is that what this is about?"

"You're an ass," I spit out, and whirled around. The chair I'd been sitting in shot across the room with my sharp movement. I didn't return it to its place, I just marched toward the door. So much for keeping my emotions in control. When I had almost made my escape, my ankle rolled to the side, my heel not supporting my angry gait. I nearly tripped, but caught myself by the door handle and finished my walk out.

CHAPTER 14

Did I just quit? No, no, no, no, I didn't. Right? I couldn't afford to quit. I had a year of savings but with zero prospects, that's all I had. I could not start over at the bottom again. And I especially couldn't make a move to New York now to find a place to do that. My money would last half as long there.

I made it to my desk, out of breath. I leaned onto my palms and sucked air into my lungs because my eyes were still stinging and my ears were red, burning beneath my hair. I could feel the blood pumping through my veins, heavy in my limbs and loud in my ears. I waited for several long minutes, thinking maybe Rob would come out, smooth things over. After all, he *was* being an ass, despite the fact that I shouldn't have pointed that out.

When he didn't come, I retrieved my purse from beneath the desk and left. If I was fired, I'd come back after hours and clean out my station. "I can't be fired," I pleaded under my breath as I opened the door and stepped out into a perfect Southern California day. How dare it be so nice today. "I will smooth things over. I have to."

The first thing I did was kick my feet, one at a time, up behind me to take off my heels. Then I walked around the building toward the small lot in the back. A rock dug into my bare foot halfway to my car and I sucked air between my teeth before continuing on with a limp.

The buzz of my phone sounded in my purse and I stopped in the middle of the parking lot to look. Maybe it was Rob telling me to come back.

It wasn't. It was a text from my sister: *How did your meeting go? I'm sure you did great! I'm proud of you. Call me later so you can tell me how you plan to grow your client list.*

I groaned.

Then I gasped.

My celebration lunch with Oliver.

No. That couldn't happen. Our first time together was a disaster. This would be even worse.

I shot off a text: I know this is last minute and I'm so sorry, but today isn't going to work after all. There is nothing to celebrate.

Once inside my car, I threw my shoes and purse onto the seat behind me and stared at the message from Audrey again. My heart thudded heavily in my chest as I responded: It went great! You were right, using my brain instead of my emotions was the way to go.

I pushed send, put my head on my steering wheel, and cried.

I wasn't sure how long I'd been sobbing like my body had been saving it up for an eternity when there was a knock on my passenger-side window. The sound startled me to a sitting position. I glanced over while wiping my face. All I could see was a torso. It wasn't Rob's. It wore a steel-gray button-down shirt, sleeves rolled up to quarter length.

"No, thank you!" I called out. I wasn't sure what this person needed but it was nothing I could give at the moment.

"Margot! It's me," came a muffled reply.

"Me who?" I could not think of a single person who would be standing outside my window right now. Sure, my brain was on overload, but that alarmed me.

"Did you forget my name again?"

My mouth fell open and Oliver squatted down. Suddenly his handsome face with his thick, wavy hair and beautiful brown eyes was smiling at me through my closed window. I could only imagine the image that greeted him: mascara down my face, smeared lipstick, snot. Was there snot? I dragged the back of my hand across my upper lip. It was wet, but it could've been tears. Please say it was just tears.

I covered my face with my hands. "I sent you a message!"

"I didn't get it until I parked my car!"

I hadn't realized I'd texted him so close to our meeting time. "I didn't tell you to meet me here!"

"You told me to meet you at *that* restaurant!" He pointed across the street. He was right. That's exactly where I told him to meet me. Since he worked from home, he offered to drive to my restaurant pick. And I selected a place close to work so I could have the full hour. He must've recognized my car, the same one I had driven to our date last time, parked here across the street.

"I'll call you later! I'm sorry!" I was being weird. I knew I was being weird. At this point, he probably didn't want me to message him later.

"Margot! Unlock the door!" He placed his hand flat on the glass. "Please." He didn't yell that last word and I could barely hear it, but his whole expression softened.

I clicked the unlock button. He climbed in the car and shut the door behind him. Suddenly my whole car smelled like soap and cedar and cinnamon and I breathed it in, remembering the scent. Remembering him.

I hiccupped through another sob.

"Come here." His voice was low and husky.

"You don't have to . . ." I tried to object but he pulled me into his arms, our cheeks brushing in the process. Then I was sobbing onto his shoulder. He smelled even better up close, and the deep timbre of his voice speaking soothing words— "It's okay . . . I have you . . . let it out . . . I'm here"—rumbled through my chest, calming me. I wasn't sure how long we stayed that way, stretched across a center console once again, but under much different circumstances than the first time.

Eventually, I took one last quivering breath, then sat up and wiped my face. "I'm sorry," I said. "Thank you."

"Don't be sorry," he responded.

The wet mess that his shoulder had become was not helping his statement.

I flipped down the visor and hesitated before sliding open the mirror. Did I want to know how bad I looked? I steeled myself and slid.

It was bad. So much mascara. I had gone all in that morning to look good for my meeting. "I'll dry-clean your shirt for you."

"It's fine, really."

I rummaged through my center console until I found a fast-food napkin, then scrubbed at the mascara on my cheeks with it. There was lipstick on one side of my mouth and not the other. I wiped at that as well.

"Do you want to talk about it or do you want me to go get you some takeout and bring it back here? Or both?" he asked.

"I don't think I can eat right now. My stomach is . . . I don't know. It's off. Might be missing entirely." I did the best I could with my makeup, which was better than when I started but not great, and shut the visor.

"That doesn't sound pleasant."

"It's not." I scrunched up the napkin and deposited it in the compartment under the door handle.

"If you really want me to leave, I will," he said.

I grabbed hold of his arm without any forethought, as if out of instinct, and shook my head no. Why was I going to cry again? How was there any liquid left in my body? I turned sideways and leaned my head against the headrest, my hand not leaving his arm.

He mimicked me. "Hi," he said, placing his hand on top of mine. It was warm and a little rough. It made me feel cozy and dizzy at the same time.

"Hi," I said.

"It's been awhile."

"Has it?" I asked.

"What have you been up to today?" he teased back.

"I think I just quit my job," I said.

"There was some ambiguity to it?"

"I called my boss an ass."

His eyebrows popped up. He was so expressive in person, I'd forgotten. "Was he being an ass?"

"A huge one."

"And did you want to quit?"

"No?"

He didn't say anything, just waited.

"What I wanted was a promotion, but once I realized he was talking in circles around that, making vague suggestions about how it would work, I don't know, maybe I did want to quit. He treated me like I shouldn't have expected a promotion. Like I had no idea what I was talking about. Like I made up scenarios we'd discussed in the past. He acted like I was being unreasonable or naïve. It didn't feel good."

Oliver squeezed my hand. "I'm sorry."

"You have nothing to be sorry for."

"I'm sorry someone made you feel that way and I wish he was sorry."

"Thank you."

We fell into silence and my body became hyperaware of where I gripped his arm. His muscle tight, his skin warm. Goose bumps sprang to life across my skin and my eyes traveled his face. He was even more handsome than I remembered. The way his energy vibrated through the car. Several days' worth of unshaven hair lined his jaw and upper lip. It was a good look on him, something he hadn't had last time or in any of his pictures. I wanted to rub my hand along it.

"I'm sorry this event isn't as advertised," I said.

"As advertised?"

"A celebration," I said.

"Hey," he said, lowering his head to look me in the eyes. "I'm glad I'm here. Besides, I told you the only celebrations I didn't want to be a part of. This isn't one of those." His smile was sweet. "Would a speech about fonts help right now?"

For the first time since leaving Rob's office, a weight lifted off my chest. "No, please."

His eyes were steady as he stared at me, searching. They were a golden brown and were making my insides feel light as air. His mouth was soft and inviting, a small smirk lifting the corners. He must've known I was staring at his mouth. My eyes popped back to his. There was no humor there, though, only intensity. We really did have an insane amount of chemistry.

"What?" he asked, his voice low and gravelly. His thumb, whether he realized it or not, was making lazy circles on the back of my hand.

I moved first, my mouth colliding with his, but he didn't stop me. He answered me with just as much intensity as had been in his eyes. I parted my lips and his tongue was urgent yet deliberate as it explored my mouth. He tasted so good. His hands cupped my face just below my jaw and I grabbed a handful each of the sides of his shirt, pulling him as close as the confines of the car allowed. My right hip rested on the console and my feet were searching for purchase against the ground.

I hadn't built this up at all in the last three years. If anything, I'd *underplayed* it.

My hands slid down his firm sides and were on his waistband, feeling for the button of his pants before he covered them with his and pulled back. I let out a disappointed huff of air.

"Probably not the wisest location for this," he said, slightly breathless.

I looked around, seeming to come to my senses. He was right. We were literally in the parking lot of the job I still needed, in broad daylight. I flopped back onto my seat. "Right. There is something about you in a car that does it for me, apparently."

He barked out a laugh. "And me outside a car?"

I smirked at him. "We'll have to see. I don't live far from here if you want to—" My stomach let out a large grumble, cutting me off, and I covered it with my hands.

"Your stomach has returned." He gestured toward our originally planned destination with a questioning eyebrow raise.

"Yes, let's go eat." I opened my door, then went to my trunk, where I kept a set of gym clothes that rarely got used. I took out the sneakers, shut the trunk, and leaned against it to pull them on. "Can you be seen with me in a pencil skirt and sneakers?"

He'd joined me at the back of the car. "If I knew that was an option, I would've worn it myself."

"That I'd like to see."

We walked across the street in silence, my lips tingling from his scruff. His hand brushed along mine and I grabbed hold. My insides still bubbled from our kiss and our now-clasped hands sent warmth up my arm. He smiled at me as we reached the door.

Inside, I pointed to the restrooms. "Give me five minutes?"

"Take your time. I'll get a table." He squeezed my hand, then didn't let go as I walked away, which resulted in our arms stretching until their forced separation.

In the bathroom, I shut myself in a stall and called Sloane.

"Is this a happy call or a venting call?" is how she answered. "And be fast because I'm on my way to my lunch meeting."

All the giddy feelings of making out with Oliver rushed out of my body as the stark reality of what happened before that came crashing back. "I accused Rob of sleeping with Rebecca to his face, then called him an ass."

"Oh no, I'm torn," she said. "Because in my book, calling him an ass is cause for celebration, but I think in your book, that's . . . bad?"

"Yes! It's bad. Very bad. I'm jobless." My leg bumped into

the toilet with my exclamation and I recoiled, standing as close to the door as possible.

"He fired you?"

"No, but do you think I can go back after that?"

She gave a single laugh. "I can think of many different walks of shame that you went back after."

"Ugh. I hate you."

"You hate yourself."

"I need to fix this." I sniffled, my tears from before ready and willing to come back.

"Are you *crying*? I didn't mean that! You shouldn't hate yourself."

"I know," I said. "But right now, I do. I'm in a bathroom stall."

"Oh, Margot. Please don't hate yourself. Get out of the bathroom and direct your anger where it belongs. At your stupid boss."

"Ex-boss."

"Do you even *want* to go back?"

"I have no other options. I need to." I ripped off some toilet paper from the roll and blew my nose. "I better go. Oliver is waiting for me at my celebratory lunch."

"That's right. Oliver. How was it? Seeing him again after all this time?" she asked.

"Wet," I said. "And not the good kind."

"The universe really screwed you over on your celebration."

"Can you cancel the thing tonight?"

"No, let's turn it into an angry party. You're going to need it."

"I just want to crawl in bed and sleep for years."

"Exactly why you need tonight. Now go celebrate being

with a hot man and we'll fix all your other problems tomorrow."
She hung up the phone.

On the stall door in front of me someone had written *Men
Suck*. The solidarity I felt with the author of those words in
that moment was much more than the situation warranted. I
closed my eyes, tried to think of some words of affirmation to
give myself, but when my mind remained blank, I walked out
of the stall. Some woman was standing by the door, staring at
me with a look of disgust.

"Emergency," I mumbled, and went to the sink to wash off
my face, then used my purse makeup to make myself present-
able. Maybe I could still salvage this time with Oliver.

CHAPTER 15

I sat down in the chair across from Oliver. "I lied to my sister," I said.

Oliver blinked once. "You are turning out to be the most interesting person I know."

"Is that a nice-guy way of saying that I'm a mess?"

"Not at all. You lied to your sister?" he asked. "Is this the sister that runs?"

"Yes, she's my only sister. And she's perfect. Everything she touches turns to gold, so when she asked me how my promotion went today, I told her it went great." I sighed. "I'm going to get struck down by lightning for lying to my pregnant sister."

"What does her being pregnant have to do with it?"

"I don't know, it feels worse lying to pregnant people."

He laughed, but then seemed to realize that now was not the time to laugh, so he quickly changed it to a cough. "Is this her first pregnancy?"

"No. She already has five-year-old twins. You'd think she

was ten years older than me with how much she's accomplished in her life, but no, she's just three." I cringed. "I sound jealous, don't I? Maybe I am."

"Hi! Welcome," a peppy waitress appeared at our table. "Can I start you with something to drink?"

For a second I had forgotten where we were, what we were doing. "I'll just have some ice water," I said.

"Are you sure you don't want something stronger?" Oliver asked. "This was supposed to be a celebration, after all."

"I've already embarrassed myself in front of you enough, completely sober. I should stick to water."

"Me too," Oliver said, and the waitress left.

The menu sat on the table in front of me. I didn't need to look at it. Since it was across the street from the office, I'd been to this restaurant a million times over the last four years. And yet my eyes scanned the food options like I needed to memorize them.

"Ugh, I'm sorry," I said. "I'm usually so much better on dates. Funny and witty. Not that this is a date, but I feel bad that after all this time, this is the person you get to hang out with."

"Please stop apologizing, Margot. I already know you're funny *and* witty. Also . . . is this *not* a date?" he asked.

My eyes shot to his in surprise.

"Oh . . . it's not," he said. "You *did* use the words *celebration partner*. I should've realized you were just wanting to . . ." He tilted his head as if piecing together my thoughts and how I had jumped him in the car.

I *had* jumped him in the car, and my body wanted to again as I sat here under his intense gaze. But my thoughts were all over the place. "No, that's not . . . It's just our last date was . . ."

"Terrible?" he said. "Despite my epic souvenir."

"Yes," I said. "Exactly."

"With your talk of resets, I thought you were giving me a do-over."

"You *want* a do-over?" I asked. He had seemed like he hadn't when I'd brought it up.

"Yes," he said. "Very much."

My heart raced to life and flutters twirled around my stomach. My body and brain seemed to be in two different hemispheres.

"But you just wanted . . . ?" He looked out the window toward the car.

"No, I mean, I just wanted to hang out and maybe . . ."

"I think we have too much chemistry to not give ourselves a second chance at something more. I was out of practice last time."

"You didn't seem out of practice," I said with a smirk.

Before he could respond, the waitress returned with our waters. "You ready to order?"

I nodded. "I'll just have a summer salad with grilled chicken."

"I'll take the California burger, lots of avocado, and fries, please," Oliver said.

When she left I picked up my water and took a drink. The cool liquid slid down my throat. Oliver wanted a second chance. Did *I*? This date, if we were calling it that, was already going a million times better than the last one we'd had. And considering what had happened today, I was surprised by how good it felt to be here with him. "So you still have my panties, then?"

Oliver, who had been taking a sip of water as well, must've sucked some down his lungs with the question, because he started coughing. When he regained control of his breathing, he shook his head with a smile.

I shrugged. "Is that a yes?"

"No comment."

I laughed and his expression softened, like he'd been waiting for me to laugh since he'd stepped into my car. My chest expanded, but then I remembered that aside from the red flags of our first date, which I could easily chalk up to him being out of practice or nervous, or whatever, another reason I didn't think this would work was because we were so different. I didn't have a filter and he seemed to have all of them. "Can you handle a girl who asks you about panties in the middle of a restaurant?"

"How am I doing so far?" he asked, his handsome face only slightly pink.

"You almost choked to death."

"But I *didn't*."

I laughed again. He was right, we had a lot of chemistry. But did we have anything else? "Tell me about yourself. What was younger Oliver like?"

He smiled. He really did have a great smile. "First-date questions. I didn't ask you any of those last time. I didn't ask you much of anything."

"Because of your recent breakup?"

"Yes. I had pushed myself to get on the apps. A friend told me it would be a good way to get over everything."

"But you saw me and immediately knew it was a mistake?" I asked, remembering his first words to me, about how, despite how good the apps were, they couldn't replicate an actual meeting.

He shook his head. "No. God, no. I saw you and my brain left me. You're gorgeous."

Why did he keep saying things that made me want to kiss him again? "Well, I'm glad your brain is back."

"Only halfway."

"Yes," I said, leaning forward, my elbows resting on the table.

"What?"

"I want a reset. A do-over."

He leaned forward too, the small table between us feeling even smaller now. "Let's see . . . Younger Oliver," he said, answering my question from earlier. "I grew up in Northern California, but came down here for college."

"Where you majored in gum removal," I teased.

"Did my techniques work? For the gum?"

"Yes, actually, a little bit of ice and a butter knife did the trick."

"You went off script, I see."

"I'm creative like that." I looked down at our hands that were inches apart on the table. "What did you really major in?"

"Engineering."

"I figured."

"What about you?" he asked. "Where did you go to school?"

"Not UCLA. That's where I wanted to go. I wasn't the best student in high school, so my sister encouraged me to apply to Santa Barbara instead. In high school, I had my head in the clouds a lot, planning out how I was going to become a world-famous screenwriter."

"What happened with that dream?"

"I guess I listened to all the people telling me I needed a backup plan, just in case," I said. "Because the truth of the matter is that it's a hard market to break into. But it worked out. I was always better at seeing the flaws and strengths in other people's stories than in my own. Agenting is a better . . ." I trailed off as it hit me that this dream might be dead too. "The publishing world is small. I just hope my boss doesn't trash my name."

"Why would he?"

Through the window I could see our building across the street, sitting there, innocent in my day's drama, Rob inside possibly plotting my destruction. "I don't know," was how I answered Oliver. Another lie. I turned the subject back to him. "What about you? Was software engineering always your dream?"

"From the time I was five."

"Really?"

"No," he said. "At five I told my mom I wanted to be Spider-Man."

"Solid superhero choice. How *is* your mom?" I asked.

"My mom?" he returned.

"Years ago, in one of our early rematching chats, you told me you were worried about her. I think . . ." Maybe I was remembering somebody totally different.

His hands slid over mine. "Yes, I was. You remember that?"

Tingles scurried up my arms and down my back. I wished we were somewhere more private. Even just back in my car. "I do."

"She's doing better. She moved down here, not too far from me. It's nice to be able to help her when she needs it. My dad left when I was fourteen and it was hard for her."

"Have you seen him since?"

"No. Don't want to," he responded, then changed the subject fast. "You close with your family?"

"Very. I feel like I'm disappointing them all . . ." Emotion rose in my chest. I'd already displayed too much emotion in front of him today.

He squeezed my hands. "Everything will work out. You'll make sure of that."

"You barely know me," I said softly. "You have no business making that statement so confidently."

He smirked. "I think we know each other better than we realize." There was something about his presence that calmed me, grounded me. I liked that.

The bell on the front door rang, drawing my attention as Rob stepped inside. His large frame filled the space. His dark hair, normally neat and tidy, was disheveled. And his bright blue eyes searched the room, landing on me with an instant expression of relief. But then his eyes shot to my hands in Oliver's and his hard look was back.

The hostess stepped in front of him and said something, but he shook his head and pointed at me. Then he was walking toward our table.

I pulled my hands into my lap. "Rob," I said.

Oliver looked over his shoulder just as Rob reached our table.

"I was worried," Rob said. "I saw your car still in the lot." He didn't even glance in Oliver's direction. "I thought you'd come back so we could finish our discussion."

"I need time to think," I said, surprising myself. From how desperate I'd been not even an hour ago to keep my job, I thought hearing those words would bring me relief, but they only made me panic more.

"Can I just have a minute?" he asked.

Oliver stood now. He was nearly as tall as Rob, but he was broader. "You heard her. She needs time," Oliver said.

"Who are you?" Rob asked, finally acknowledging Oliver's existence.

I stood, not wanting this to turn into . . . well, anything . . . in the middle of a restaurant. "It's fine," I said to Oliver. "Give me a minute?"

His Adam's apple bobbed in his throat, then he nodded.

I walked past Rob toward the front door without waiting to see if he'd follow. Then I stepped outside and past the outdoor tables all the way to the alleyway between the restaurant and the dry cleaner's next door (another place I'd been to a lot).

I turned around and waited for him to join me. When he did, he looked toward the agency windows in full view across the street.

"Should we stand behind the dumpster or . . ." I had been kidding, but he gave a curt nod and headed that way.

This time *I* joined him, and when we were out of sight, he pulled me into a hug. "I'm sorry. Forgive me. We'll figure something out. Something that works for both of us." He nuzzled his face into my neck. The air smelled like rotten food and chemicals and stung my nose. The hug felt uncomfortable, unnatural, wrong. "There's nothing going on between Rebecca and me. It's kind of cute to see you jealous, though."

I took several steps back until my shoulder blades collided with the metal of the garbage bin. It startled me. An overwhelming aroma of rotting meat filled my nose. I pushed against Rob's chest until he released me. "I'm not. No. None of this has worked for both of us. It's only worked for you."

At my words, he folded his arms across his chest in a defensive manner.

"You know that's true, Rob. I'm good at my job. You made

me feel like a child today who was asking for something she didn't deserve. I deserve this."

"I don't think you're ready. You haven't been proactive about going to New York and conferences, making the in-person connections in the industry that you need to succeed at this job."

My eyes went wide. "You think I can afford that with what you pay me? I thought you'd take me with you, that the agency would pay. You always said you'd take me with you."

"And how would that have looked? You and I traveling together?"

"It would've only looked like something because it *was*!"

Rob's eyes darted over my shoulder. "Keep your voice down."

When his eyes were back on me, I screamed, "I quit!"

"Margot, wait!"

I didn't wait. I didn't stop. I went back inside and sat down at the table again, my breath coming in short angry bursts.

Oliver seemed . . . cold? His eyes were shadowed, closed off. "Are you sleeping with your boss?"

CHAPTER 16

I squeezed through a group of people standing near the entrance of the bar, either coming or going—whichever the case, loud and in the way. I reached a high-top table where Sloane, Becky, Laurel, and Cheryl (our brunch group) were already standing. A round of shots were in front of everyone but Cheryl.

"Ahhh!" Becky screamed when she saw me. "She's here! Congratulations on finally asking for a promotion!"

"Yes, it's the first step," Laurel agreed. "He'll come around. He knows how much you do."

"I quit," I said. "In a very loud, official manner." As loud and official as standing next to a dumpster could be.

Sloane slid her shot in front of me, her eyes asking me questions that didn't make it to her mouth.

I threw back the shot and sucked in some air as it burned a path down my throat. The others followed suit.

"I'll get started on another round," Sloane said, heading toward the bar.

"Oh, Cheryl, congrats on the pregnancy," I said. Cheryl

had met her husband at this very bar four years earlier. He'd dumped the handful of drinks he was taking back to his table all over her. He apologized for ten minutes, then offered to literally give her the shirt off his back. She accepted. He took it off right there and she changed into it in the bathroom. He stood around shirtless, talking to her until the bouncer kicked him out for not being properly clothed. But not before he got Cheryl's phone number. *That* was a solid meet-cute, an adorable story that could be told for the rest of their lives.

"Thank you," she said to me now, rubbing her flat stomach. "You all have a built-in designated driver for the next seven months."

"That is good news," Becky said.

Sloane came back, carrying four more shots, which she expertly placed on the table. She held one in the air. "To the future."

I lifted one as well. "If the universe won't provide, we'll do it ourselves." As much as I didn't want it to be true—in fact, for the last six hours I'd been trying to convince myself it wasn't true—I knew that the only way to keep my dream alive right now was to start my own agency. With no backup, no name recognition, not enough money, no potential clients.

"For real?" Sloane asked. She must've known what I was implying with that declaration.

"It's my only option at this point," I said. I'd cut all ties with Rob and, by so doing, probably with the rest of my Los Angeles agency connections. I definitely couldn't survive alone in New York. I needed to stay here, where I was surrounded by family and friends. This was the only way.

Sloane downed her drink and I did the same. "That's cause to celebrate."

I wasn't sure if it was, but I could pretend, at least for

tonight, before reality set in. "How did *your* meeting go?" I asked.

"I'm not going to yum your yuck," she said.

"You got the saying backward," I said.

"In this case, I did not."

"I'm happy for you," I said.

She pointed to the bar and left again.

Three more shots and a plate of boneless wings later, I started to think my own agency was not just some far-fetched dream but the best idea ever. I was listing all the pros to Sloane while the others were trying to choose which songs they wanted to sing for karaoke. It was an important decision that they didn't take lightly.

I counted the benefits off on my fingers. "I don't have to share any of my commission. I don't have to answer to anyone. I can rep whatever books I want to rep."

"If you want to rep a romantic thriller with a horror ending, you can," Sloane said, slapping her hand on the table to emphasize her point.

"Exactly," I said.

"Did Oliver . . . this dec . . . today? If s . . . tell . . . amazing."

"What?" I leaned a little closer. It was loud in the bar. Getting louder by the second, it seemed. Or maybe I was just getting more drunk by the second.

She spoke directly into my ear. "Oliver. Did he influence this decision?"

"No. I made it all by myself, thank you very much. The only thing that came out of lunch was Oliver asking me if I was sleeping with Rob."

"You aren't sleeping with Rob, so I hope you said no."

"I said, 'Not currently.'"

She groaned. "Less is more, Marjorie. Those are conversations you have when you know someone better."

"Probably true. You should've seen the way he looked at me." It had hurt, sitting there in the restaurant after loudly quitting my job in the alley, to have Oliver close himself off, become overly polite, asking generic questions and barely answering mine with no more than a word or two. But maybe it was better this way. Our second chance proving just as much as our first one that we weren't right for each other.

Becky called out from across the table, "What do you think about Celine Dion?"

"Wildly ambitious," Sloane said. "But go for it!"

"Yes!" Laurel agreed.

Back to me, Sloane said, "Did words accompany his look?"

"He said, 'Oh.'"

"Oh? And then what?"

"And then our food came and we ate and he asked me if I'd ever been to Seattle."

"Seattle? Why?"

"Because that's what you do when you're done trying to get to know someone. You ask them generic questions like if they've ever eaten crab legs or been to Seattle."

"I didn't think Oliver would be so judgmental," she said.

"Because you know Oliver so well?"

"He's been your online boyfriend for three years. That's as long as I've known you! I've seen him with at least one bad haircut and a plethora of questionable clothing choices."

I laughed. "Oh, and remember that time he posted only pictures of him blinking?"

"That was funny. Exactly! I thought he was chill and funny. But he's actually judgmental and . . . judgy?"

A snort burst out of me. "You judge me for sleeping with Rob too," I said. Just like my sister and parents would.

"I judge Rob for Rob and . . . okay, I judge you. But I'm your best friend and I know the whole story. I don't deflect with questions about Seattle." She let out a short breath. "You should've stalked Oliver online. Then you would've found *all* his red flags."

"He didn't have any social media attached to his dating profile and I just barely got his phone number. I still don't know his last name! I reverse-image searched his pictures last week and nothing came up."

"You *did* stalk him online. How dare you do that without me." It was one of our traditions to research my app matches online. Mainly to make sure they weren't on any of the lists that women put up after scary dating encounters. But also to feel them out, see the kinds of things they posted.

"I found nothing."

"Maybe he doesn't exist," she said, her eyes wide.

I doubled over, laughing. "You're drunk."

"So are you," she said.

"I am! How am I so drunk already?"

"You drank," Sloane said as someone bumped into her from behind. She reclaimed her space by widening her stance. "Wait, *have* you been to Seattle?"

"I haven't. Is that a bad thing? Is this a question I should be asking people? Does it answer a question without having to ask the question?" I wanted the answer to be *yes* because maybe that meant Oliver wasn't done trying to get to know me.

"What?" Sloane asked, not keeping up.

"You know what I mean," I said. Someone onstage was

singing "Open Arms" very poorly. "It's a question that reveals things about someone without being overly invasive."

"Invasive, like asking them if they're sleeping with their boss?"

"Yeah, like that." Shame washed through me. Oliver was done. And why wouldn't he be? The feeling must've been accompanied by a change in expression because she pulled me into a hug.

"You've had a hard day," she said. "I'm sorry."

I just let out a muffled whine against her shoulder.

"What you should've said to Oliver's question was, *No, but I can be sleeping with you tonight if you want.*"

I gave an ironic laugh. "Believe me, after the look he gave me today, he doesn't want to. It will probably be another three years, at least, before I see him again." That thought twisted my insides.

"Call him. We'll tell him he's being judgy and to get over it."

"The only thing I want to do now is drink until I don't remember any of my problems."

"Deal."

• • •

Sharp stabs of pain radiated behind my eyes. Like the sun's rays were slicing through my eyelids, trying to blind me. My mouth felt like someone had been filling it with cotton balls all night only to empty it this morning, leaving my throat scratchy and my tongue stuck to my bottom teeth. I tried to enable my spit glands but they had been emptied as well.

"Sloane," I groaned, wondering if she was up yet. Even if she was, she probably couldn't hear me. I rolled over and the knives inside my head ricocheted around in my empty skull.

Empty, because I certainly didn't have a brain anymore. A brain would've given me thoughts and memories, would've reminded me how I ended up in this terrible state, but there was nothing. No thoughts. No memories.

I stumbled out of bed and to the bathroom, where I stuck my mouth under the faucet and sucked down water for several minutes. "This is why we don't drink, kids," I said to the nonexistent children in the room. My nephews immediately sprang into my mind, watching me with their innocent eyes, asking me if I was sick, telling me that their perfect mom never drank. I knew that wasn't true, but hungover Margot was extra hard on me. She was super judgy.

Judgy. A thought rattled around in my brain with that word but refused to produce any actual memories.

"Sloane," I said again, and beelined it out of the bathroom, heading for the kitchen and aspirin. On the floor next to the couch was the Bad Decisions jar. It was empty, turned on its side with two five-dollar bills on the carpet nearby. Weird.

A note was waiting on the counter next to the bottle of aspirin. *I hate you. How dare you get to sleep in while I have to go to lunch with my family and face the consequences of our actions. Also, I love you. Sorry about your job. But remember, you're a rock star.*

Ugh. My job. I hadn't forgotten that trainwreck. But a rock star? She'd never called me that before. I was sure there was context there, but again, my brain wasn't filling me in. My phone started buzzing in my hand even though I didn't recall picking it up.

Mom. I hadn't talked to her since the T-ball game a week ago.

The clock on the microwave said it was just after noon.

Before I answered the phone, I opened the bottle of aspirin

and took three. An open bag of potato chips was also on the counter, probably another way Sloane was trying to smother her hangover. I stuffed a couple in my mouth, begging the grease to ease the nausea in my stomach. My phone stopped buzzing, but before I could even finish chewing another chip, it sprang back to life.

"Hey, Mom," I said.

"Honey, hi! Congratulations! I'm having something sent over. Did you get it?"

I cringed at the volume of her voice. "What? Did I get what? Why?"

"Bill!" Mom called to my dad, yelling in my ear. "Did you send it? Did it work?" Back to me she said, "I thought the bugs were finally ironed out."

"Bugs?"

"On the food app."

"You sent me food?" Did she somehow know I'd need food this morning? Had I drunk-texted my *mom* the night before?

"I thought it worked. It says delivered on my screen. Is it delivered?"

"Let me check." I slowly walked to the door, trying not to anger my pounding head any further, and opened it. I let out a surprised yelp when a man was standing on my front porch holding an In-N-Out bag. He was backlit by the sun and I squinted against the light.

"What's wrong?" Mom asked.

"Nothing. It's . . . it's here. Thank you." To the man, I said, "Hold on." I spun around, walked to the couch, and plucked the two five-dollar bills off the floor.

"Glad you got it," Mom said. "Enjoy."

"Mom, wait."

"Yes?"

"I'm sorry I haven't been to see you more lately. You were right, I have been . . . unhappy. But I'm working on things. I'm going to visit soon." I walked back to the door and held out the cash for the delivery guy.

Over the phone, Mom said, "Yes, I heard about how you're working on things. Audrey told us! We're so proud. Call me after you eat so you can tell me all about your new position."

I was stunned silent. Before I had time to respond, the phone went dead. The bills in my hand were still extended in front of me. Only now that my eyes were adjusted to the sun, I could see that it wasn't a delivery guy at all.

It was Oliver.

CHAPTER 17

Oliver was on my porch. Even after that look he'd given me at the restaurant yesterday. Even after I was certain he wouldn't want to see me again.

"I've decided that somehow you know when I look my worst and magically appear," I said, stepping aside and opening the door wider for him to come in. Unlike me, he looked amazing.

"On two out of the three occasions you're referring to, you invited me. So *magic* isn't really the right descriptor." He handed me the bag of food.

I raised my eyebrows at the money I still held out for him.

He shook his head with a smile and took the cash from me, only to pull me forward by the pocket of my sweats and tuck the money inside. The way my downstairs region reacted to that simple, yet intimate, gesture surprised me.

I gripped the In-N-Out bag tighter and tried to say as casually as possible, "I invited you today?"

He chuckled, stepping inside.

"I'm scared to know."

"You were really drunk."

"Don't hold it against me. Yesterday was a bad day and Sloane is a bad influence." I closed the door and locked it.

"That isn't from me, by the way." He pointed to the fast food in my hands. "It was on the porch."

"My mom."

"Nice mom," he said.

"It's not a hangover gift." I peered in the bag to see several orders of fries and at least three burgers. "It's a promotion gift."

"I see," he said.

"She thinks . . ." *I was actually promoted* was how I should've finished the sentence, but I didn't. The lie I'd told my sister had now spread to my mom. My head hurt too much to think about the conversation I needed to have with her.

He walked past me to the living room, his scent filling my senses. He looked at the empty Bad Decisions jar on the ground.

"You smell good," I said.

He chuckled again. "So I've heard."

"Ugh. I don't want to know." I swiped up the jar and placed it on the coffee table. Then I gestured toward the table in the kitchen. "Are you hungry? My mom ordered me too much food."

"Yes, actually."

We settled in at the table, him on the end by the window and me to his right. I passed him a burger and the smirk that had been on his face since he'd arrived slipped off as he opened it. "I wasn't judging you, Margot. I promise my reaction had nothing to do with you and everything to do with my history.

My face sometimes has a mind of its own and it was obviously giving off dick vibes."

"What?"

"Yesterday. Your boss. I was surprised and shouldn't have asked."

"Spill. Did I call you last night or something? How do you know that I thought you were judging me for Rob? You didn't talk to Sloane, did you?"

"Your roommate? No. You left me a message."

I put my face in my hands. "I didn't."

He laughed. "It was amazing and I will save it forever. You don't remember?"

"Not even a little bit."

He took a bite of his burger while simultaneously pulling his phone out. I let it happen. I let him pull up his voicemails and push play while I slowly ate my burger, hoping that the aspirin or the grease would take away the pounding in my head and the twisting in my stomach because I knew the sound of my voice ringing out over his speakers wouldn't.

"You probably didn't think it was a booty call," was how the message started.

He paused it. "You sent me a text before this message asking if I was awake, followed very shortly by a text that said 'that was not a booty call.'"

"Thank you for the context," I said, a spotty memory coming back to me with his explanation.

He smiled and pushed play again, and my voice continued: "But I just got a booty call text from someone. So that's on my mind. From someone on the apps, I mean, not from someone in my life. I said no, of course. I could've said yes if I wanted to. I'm a single woman who actually likes sex."

My real-time self groaned in embarrassment.

"And, by the way," my very drunk voice continued, "my boss was single when I slept with him. I know he's older and he's my boss, but it's not like I slept with him the first second I saw him. I knew him. We have lots of things in common. Unlike us. You really shouldn't judge people. My boss is dreamy. You saw him. Maybe not as dreamy as you but not everyone can have amazing hair and a killer smile. Also, you have nice arms. And you smell like soap and wood and cinnamon. Why do you smell like cinnamon? I didn't think I liked the smell of cinnamon. Well, I mean, everyone likes the smell of cinnamon, but in hot chocolate or on cookies or whatever. I didn't think I liked it on a person. You make it work. Like, really make it work."

I met Oliver's eyes then and he raised one side of his mouth in a half smile.

I narrowed mine as I continued to listen to myself drone on: "Also, is Seattle code for something? Do I need to add it to my first-date questions? I should sleep. Not with you. Not that I wouldn't. I mean, I would. I totally would. We should. You want to, right? Let's just do it and get it out of our system. We should've three years ago and then we wouldn't be here now pining, thinking about how hot it was. You were hot in that car. You really had no right to be when your dinner conversation was so terribly one-sided. You hardly knew me. *And* you were rude to our waitress. Why aren't you responding to my texts? It's late, I guess. Oh shit, it's two A.M. Shhh, I'm sorry. Go to sleep. But come over tomorrow so I know you're not a judgy jerk with a stick up his ass. Sorry, I don't think you have a stick up your ass. I'm drunk. Really drunk. But come over. My address is . . ."

He pressed stop halfway through me relaying my address.

"Wow," I said. "I'm never drinking again."

"I am here to prove I'm not a judgy jerk with a stick up his ass." He didn't comment on all the sex talk.

Neither did I. "Drunk Margot is ridiculous. I'm sorry. The stuff about my boss, it was my shame talking. I have all sorts of . . ." I blew out some air because my throat tightened with emotion. "I'm not proud of sleeping with him."

"I wasn't trying to make you feel bad at all. And besides, it's really not my business. I shouldn't have asked. *I'm* sorry. Also, was I rude to our waitress that first night?"

I covered my face with my hands. "No, I mean, sort of, but it's fine."

"What did I do?"

"You just ignored her when she tried to take our order. Didn't stop talking."

"Wow. I'm sorry. Like I said, I'd just broken up with my fiancée and I really had no business being there."

"And your reaction at lunch yesterday, you said that had to do with your history too?"

A fry was halfway to his mouth when a questioning look took over his face. "I said that?"

I leveled him with a stare. "Yes, you said that, earlier. And since nothing can be more embarrassing than that"—I pointed at the sleeping screen of his phone sitting on the table—"you have to tell me what you meant."

He seemed to struggle with himself for several minutes but eventually said, "The whole thing yesterday reminded me of how I found out my fiancée was cheating on me. We were sitting in a café and her ex came in and her face went pale because apparently he'd given her some sort of ultimatum about telling me or he would. He marched up to our table, much like your boss yesterday, and demanded to speak to her. And she asked me to give her just one minute."

"Like I did yesterday."

"Yes, like you did. And it . . ."

"Triggered you?"

"A little. It shouldn't have . . . but it did." He wadded up the wrapper of his finished burger.

"I get it. I'm sorry. Are she and her ex still together?"

He nodded slowly. "It's not the first time I've been cheated on either."

"Oh yeah? When was the first time?" I reached into the bag, pulled out another burger, and put it on the table in front of him.

"In college. Also, I can't eat another one."

"I believe in you." I nudged the burger closer to him. "Were you two serious?"

"Yes. We were good friends for about six months then dated for about six months."

"Shit. Sorry."

"It was a long time ago, but I obviously still have trust issues."

"What?" I asked in faux shock. "There's a valid reason why you're single?"

He gave a breathy laugh. "Yes. I overthink everything. What about you? Do you have a valid reason for being single?"

"Apparently, I *underthink* everything, lead with my feelings, and end up in terrible relationships. You met the main one yesterday. My emotionally unavailable and completely wrong-for-me boss, who has been keeping me on the hook for the last several years in more ways than one. And now my life is . . ." I waved my arm around to indicate the mess my life had become.

"Right," he said.

I picked up a fry that was already half-soggy. "Have you ever cheated on anyone?"

"No. You?" he asked.

"No. But I've turned into a liar, I guess."

"You haven't told your sister you didn't really get promoted?"

"No. And now she told my mom. So now I need to tell both of them. A conversation I'm not looking forward to."

"Maybe you texted her. You seemed to be sending all sorts of messages last night."

"I hope not. Like I said, drunk Margot is not exactly tactful." I tapped my phone to life. "By the way, you will delete that voicemail."

"Never," he said.

I clicked on my text app and scanned for my sister's name. Before I could find it, I was stopped cold by Rebecca's name. She never texted me. We only talked in the office or over the office line when her assistant was out.

Congrats on taking some steps forward, she said. Let me know if there's anything I can do to help.

I had actually answered her with the words: I quit. Rob is an asshat.

"Ugh," I said and scrolled past that mess to see if I'd made any other ones.

The most recent text from Audrey read: Not sure that's the right call. Let's talk it out.

Her message was a result of me texting her: I've actually decided to start my own agency instead of accept a promotion. How's that for directionless and unfocused? This wasn't even close to the five-year plan. Guess there's more than one way to be successful.

I cringed.

"Bad?" Oliver asked.

I read it out loud to him.

"Ouch."

"Just add that one to the list of things I need to fix when my head isn't pounding."

"Aside from the pounding head, how are you feeling today about quitting your job?"

"Terrible, free, scared, hopeful, overwhelmed."

He nodded. "All completely valid. What's next?"

"You have your own business, right? Any advice?"

"You really are going to start your own agency?" He nodded to my phone, indicating the text I'd sent my sister stating that.

"I'm going to try my hardest."

"Give yourself grace and at least double the time you think it will take."

"I have no time at all."

"Then give yourself ten times that long."

"Zero times ten is zero."

He laughed. "I sense patience isn't your strength."

"I've been waiting years for this."

"That's a long time to wait for something," he said, his eyes meeting mine. Despite what he'd said about not trusting people, his eyes were soft and open and genuine. I wanted to lean closer.

Instead, his phone caught my attention.

It sat between us on the table and the voicemail replayed

in my mind like some slow-motion horror sequence. I lunged forward, but as if he knew exactly what I was thinking, he pulled it out of my reach.

"Seriously," I said, standing. "Will you delete that message?"

He stood as well, turning his back to me. "It's epic. I don't want to delete it."

I stood on the chair he'd just abandoned and tried to reach around him but, because I couldn't see, just ended up hugging him from behind. With my body pressed against his back, his laughter vibrated against my chest.

He turned to face me and I released him. But because I was still standing on the chair, I lost my balance, teetering backward. He caught me before I fell off, pulling me forward by one hand, causing me to crash into him. He wrapped his arm around my thighs and we both went still as I steadied myself.

His chest was hard against my stomach, and his cheek brushed against my chest. His arm felt firm and comfortable, like it had been wrapped around me many times before. Like I wanted it to be wrapped around me many times in the future. I rested my arms on his shoulders, my whole body relaxing.

"You smell good too," he said.

My heart increased its speed. "I'm sure I smell like vodka and sweat."

"You smell sweet. Like citrus or something."

"Um . . . pomegranates. My lotion." I could feel my blood pulsing in my neck and in places much lower.

He met my eyes and his hold tightened around me.

I ran my fingers through his hair, then leaned down, my eyes closing in anticipation of the kiss.

"You don't think we have anything in common?" he asked, his lips millimeters from mine.

My eyes flew open. "What?"

"In your message, you said you didn't think we had anything in common."

"Don't listen to drunk Margot. She rambles."

"So you *do* think we have things in common?"

I hesitated. "We probably do . . . um . . . We're both funny."

He laughed.

"Do *you* think we have anything in common?" I asked.

"We both have our own businesses."

"One of us does. The other has a very long road ahead of her."

"It's something," he said.

"We are both very attractive," I said.

He smiled, lifted me off the chair, and spun around, setting me on the ground. I looked up at him in surprise.

"We're good at this," he said, a single finger running from the inside of my elbow to my wrist, showing me what he meant by *this* as waves of pleasure sang through me.

"So good," I agreed.

"We need to make sure we're good at *not* this."

"That sounds like a terrible plan," I said. Aside from today, we'd only hung out two times in real life. The first time was catastrophic and the second time, in the end, not much better. "You want to keep trying?"

"I *want* to throw you on this table and taste every inch of you."

"Okay."

He chuckled. "And god, I want that feeling in a relationship. It's been awhile since I've had that. But I also want something real. Something more. We need to see if we get along outside of apps . . . and cars."

I stepped closer to him, our chests almost bumping. "So you want to ignore the physical stuff for a while and . . . be friends?" Why was this man insisting on keeping the only thing we seemed to be good at together away from us?

"If that's what you want to call it." His voice was barely above a whisper and his eyes were steady on mine.

"Right. Okay." I took a step back, breaking our connection. "I . . . I need to shower. Alone," I added for some stupid reason. "I mean, of course alone. You already made that clear. I'm an idiot. I'll-I-I'll be back."

I left him in my kitchen, and it wasn't until I was locked in my bathroom standing under a steaming hot shower that I realized I should've given him the option to leave. Maybe he did.

"I hope he left," I whispered to the white tiles in my shower.

"Liar," they would've whispered back if they could talk.

CHAPTER 18

I got out of the shower feeling much more clearheaded. Maybe Oliver was right. This was really only the third time we'd hung out. The first time was directly following a major implosion in *his* life and the second followed one in mine. We hadn't given each other a real chance, outside the physical stuff. And the physical stuff was mucking up our judgment, our ability to see if there was something beyond that. Despite how little we had in common, we seemed to get along over messages. That could transfer to real life. I chuckled when I thought about the first thing Oliver ever said to me: not even the best programmer could replicate human interaction. Maybe his self from three years ago knew what he was talking about.

It took me ten minutes to put on a minimal amount of makeup and some casual yet cute clothes. Then I rushed out of my bedroom, feeling bad about leaving Oliver alone.

Only he wasn't alone.

I rounded the corner to see him and Sloane sitting on the couch together, talking.

"Look who I found in our apartment, Margot. Your boyfriend," she said.

"Not my boyfriend," I blurted at the same time Sloane said, "Your boyfriend is even cuter in person."

"Sloane," I scolded. "Stop calling him that." To Oliver, I clarified, "It was just a joke because of how long we'd been messaging each other."

He smirked my way like he appreciated that joke.

She stood from the couch and collected a Styrofoam box from the coffee table. "I'm going to put these delicious leftovers, that I let not a single man in my life take, in the fridge and then I'm going to come back over here and be filled in on how you ended up here. Because last I heard, you were a judgy jerk."

I sighed and sat in the seat she had just abandoned, next to Oliver. "My roommate has an oversharing problem. Seriously, Sloane, I'm never telling you anything again."

After several moments of Sloane grumbling about space in the fridge and how we needed to save only exceptional leftovers from now on, she finally shut the door and joined us, sitting in the love seat to our left. She leaned forward, elbows on knees, as if ready to take in all the gossip we were willing to share.

"Oliver, Sloane," I said. "Sloane, Oliver."

"We already met," she said, waving a hand through the air like I was wasting time. "While you were showering."

"Right."

"I see you came to your senses," she said to him. "We both know Rob is an ass and not deserving of our girl here."

"Actually," I said, cutting her off before she got too far, "Oliver came over because I left him an unhinged voicemail." I narrowed my eyes at her to assess if she had been present while that choice had been made.

She cringed. "Oh, that."

"How dare you let me leave that."

"You told me you're a grown-ass woman."

"I'm obviously not." My eyes found the empty jar on the coffee table. "And what happened with our jar?"

"You don't remember?"

"I remember very little of last night."

"Probably for the best since you performed a very poor rendition of 'My Heart Will Go On.'"

"What? *I* did Celine? I would *never*."

"You did."

"Tell me someone recorded it," Oliver said.

"You don't need another recording in your possession," I shot at him.

He laughed.

"Sadly, nobody recorded it as far as I know. Maybe it will show up online at some point in the future, posted by some stranger who found it as funny as we did. As for that"—Sloane pointed to the jar—"you paid half of next month's rent with it, telling me how you were going to be broke in a year if you weren't extra careful with money and how we should Airbnb your room while you sleep at your parents' house."

"I claimed all the money in the Bad Decisions jar as my own?"

"To be fair," she said, "most of it came from you, so I accept it as payment."

"How magnanimous."

"I reject the Airbnb idea, though," she said. "I'm not trying to get murdered."

"It could make a good meet-cute for you," I said.

"That's what you said last night," she reminded me. "And

like I told you last night, I already have a boyfriend and I'm not hung up on meet-cutes like you are. And like I also told you, we'll be fine. You're going to be a rock-star agent."

"Rock star," I said, the last missing puzzle piece of the night finally clicking into place.

Sloane pinched the bridge of her nose. "Considering I still have a hangover, we will resume this conversation tomorrow." She stood and, as she reached the hall, turned and said, "Oliver, my brain has been too foggy to get to know you properly. So you get to come to coffee with us tomorrow."

His lip twitched into a smirk, then he nodded.

"Also," she said, pointing to both of us, "don't eat my leftovers."

I gestured to our pile of half-eaten burgers and fries in the kitchen and she grunted her acknowledgment.

"What exactly are her leftovers?" Oliver asked after she was gone. "Her passion for them is admirable."

"Trust me, it's just an omelet or something basic. When she's hungry she thinks everything was more delicious than it actually was."

"You two have a fun dynamic."

"Do you have roommates?" I asked.

"I do not."

My eyes narrowed. "Don't you get lonely?"

"Yes, very," he said, his husky voice sending tingles skating up my spine. "Also, what's a meet-cute?"

I smiled. "It's what we call the first meeting between the love interests in a book or movie. It's usually something adorable. Like a mixed-up drink order or a mistaken identity, a kiss cam or a concert shoulder ride."

"What about a *u up* on a dating app? Does that qualify?"

I laughed. "Never!" Another memory came to me from the night before. "I deleted my apps last night. Right after that guy texted me those words, which prompted my unhinged message to you."

He didn't seem surprised. "I delete mine every few months."

"Me too."

"That's why we keep matching," he said.

"That and your toilet." I pulled my knee onto the couch with me, hugging it to my chest.

"Oh yes, the proximity of you to my toilet is important, I forgot."

My eyes shot down to his crotch even though I really knew *toilet* was *not* code for his penis. My cheeks went pink and I quickly averted my gaze. "How many people are you chatting with this round?"

"On the apps?" he asked.

"Yes."

"Like five or six."

"Any standouts?"

His eyes met mine again. "Yes, this woman who only wants me for my body."

I raised my eyebrows. "You *do* have a nice body."

"She thinks we're incompatible because we have nothing in common. Any advice for me?"

I let out a sharp breath. "Tell her to give you time. You seem like the type who grows on people."

"I am," he said, a sly smile coming onto his handsome face.

I needed to get up, move. Not sit so close to him, absorbing all his energy, making me wonder why I let any sort of line be drawn in the sand about our relationship status or lack thereof. "Do you want a tour?"

"A tour?" he asked.

"Of the apartment."

He scanned the room. From where he sat, he could see that there wasn't much to our apartment. He'd been in our modest kitchen and now sat in our small living room. He probably thought he'd already had the tour.

"Your books," he said after his scan. "I'd like to see your books. You said you had a bigger collection than at your office. You need to back this up."

My books were in my bedroom. No big deal. I could take this man into my bedroom. We were friends now. Friends who weren't going to have sex anytime soon.

"Yes, you must see my collection. If I'm going to brag about size, I better be willing to prove it."

He chuckled. "You're good at that, you know."

"At what?" I asked, feigning innocence.

"You know what." He stood.

"I'm sorry," I said. "I'll stop."

"Don't stop on my account."

I smiled, then led him down the hall and opened my bedroom door.

He hesitated at the threshold. "I didn't realize they would be in your bedroom."

"Is that a problem, *friend*?" I teased.

"Not at all," he said, stepping in first.

I shoved him playfully with a laugh and he stumbled forward, laughing as well. I pointed toward my bed, the comforter balled up at the bottom, my sheets twisted and messy. "I blame that on my night. Normally I make my bed every morning."

"Do you?" he asked, curious.

I cringed. "No, but I'm starting that habit tomorrow. And that's my clothes chair." I nodded to the stack of clothes piled high on my overstuffed chair. "Worn once but not dirty enough to need a wash."

"You have a system," he said.

"Organized chaos."

Across from my bed, on the opposite wall, were my bookcases. I'd bought them from Ikea and they fit almost perfectly across the length of the wall, giving the appearance of built-ins. And like my bed and my clothes chair, the books that lived there were a mismatch of stacks and rows, organized in a way that only I understood.

"Oh wow," he said. "You're right, you *should* brag about size. You should even pull out a tape measure." He took several steps closer and ran his hand along some spines. He might as well have been running his hand up my spine based on how my body shivered in reaction to his words and action.

"You want to borrow a book?" I asked too loudly.

"Sure, will you pick one out for me? Your favorite."

"I don't have a favorite," I said, which was mostly true. I couldn't pick. I liked lots of books for lots of different reasons but some did rise to the top. The problem was the top was always changing. "Do you like romance?" I stepped up beside him, examining my books along with him, our shoulders bumping as I did.

"I've never read a romance."

I crinkled my nose. "Deal-breaker."

"Above or below the *Dirty Dancing* requirement?"

I smiled. "I mean, if I say, 'I had the time of my life,' I need someone to be ready and willing to respond with, 'and I owe it all to you.'"

He closed one eye in thought. "I take it that's a *Dirty Dancing* reference?"

I let out a fake sigh. "All my hopes and dreams going up in flames."

We shuffled a few more steps forward.

"Do you meet a lot of men who read romance?" He angled toward me, his breath mingling with mine now.

"No, it's why I'm still single," I said.

His lip curved into a crooked smirk. "Understandable."

I continued along the shelves, him following until I came to a stop on one I thought would be tame enough not to scare him, but spicy enough to give him ideas. Ideas of what he could do to me if . . . *Stop, Margot.* I pulled it out and presented it to him.

"Is this the kind of book you wanted me to read out loud?" He took it from me and opened to one of my colorful tabs near the middle.

I nodded. "Yes, actually."

His eyes scanned the page and his eyebrows rose higher and higher as he read.

"What's it say?" I teased, knowing exactly what the pink tabs marked in my books. They weren't the red tabs, but they were good.

He took a resolute breath, then surprisingly cleared his throat and read aloud, "'His finger drew circles around her sweat-slicked navel and he longed for a salty taste of her. She whimpered, goose bumps forming under his touch. He wasn't sure he could last another second without his mouth, his tongue, on her. Her top covered her breasts, but just barely, and the evidence that she wanted him just as much was visible through the thin material.'"

I want to throw you on this table and taste every inch of you. Oliver had said those words to me earlier and now the words coming out of his mouth were reminding me of them. The throbbing between my legs wasn't helping either. I wanted to forget everything we had just agreed to about friendship and abstinence.

Oliver stopped and closed the book. "I get the gist."

I took a breath, my head light, my legs weak. "I wasn't lying when I said that you should narrate books for a living." We were close. So close I could feel the heat from his body on my bare arms. Had we inched closer during his reading? His eyes were stormy when he looked at me, like he was trying to hold back. I wished he wouldn't, but he seemed to have all the willpower in the world.

I tapped his chest. "It's good we're just friends, Oliver. Because I think you might be too nice for me. I could wreck you."

He closed his eyes for a moment. When he opened them again, they were even more intense. And his voice was husky when he said, "Maybe it would be good for me."

The bathroom door shut across the hall and I jumped.

Oliver seemed to snap out of his daze as well. "I better go," he said. "If I've proved my ass is stickless, that is."

"You have *definitely* proved that."

"Coffee tomorrow?" He jerked his head toward the hall, reminding me that Sloane had invited him.

"Yes, that would be . . . yes. We go to Java. Do you know it?"

"Yes, I've been there."

"Okay, see you tomorrow." I play punched his shoulder, not sure why. Every word out of my mouth sounded the opposite of sincere right now.

He looked down at where my fist had connected with his shoulder and smiled a full smile. My heart melted a little.

"Bye." He took a step toward the door, but before he took another, I grabbed his hand that wasn't holding my book and pulled him into a hug.

"Friends hug," I said. "Right?"

"Friends hug," he answered, holding me tight, his lips resting on my temple. It wasn't a friendly hug between friends. But a tight desperate hug of people who had just agreed to stop touching each other but still wanted to. I wondered if he could feel my heart pounding heavy against his chest. He pulled back first, then rushed away.

CHAPTER 19

"Is his car here?" I hissed from the passenger seat, my head between my knees. The place it had been for the last several turns.

"What's his car look like again?" Sloane asked.

"A black BMW."

"He drives a Beamer?"

"Yes, is it here?"

"Rob's car is not anywhere in the vicinity."

I took a relieved breath and sat up, pushing my hair back and letting the blood return to its normal places in my body. I made Sloane drive so he wouldn't recognize my car if he happened to be at the office on a Sunday morning. Rare, but not unheard of.

Sloane shifted her car into park and turned off the ignition. "What if they changed the locks or the alarm code?"

"It's only been two days." I unbuckled my seat belt. "Wait, do you think they did?"

"Probably not. It's not like you threatened to destroy the place . . . did you?"

"No!"

"Just checking. I wasn't sure how much badassery you released on Friday."

We got out of the car and headed toward the back entrance to the office. Both my key and code worked to admit us.

"What do you even leave at work?" Sloane asked. "I'm trying to picture my desk and I don't think there's anything I would save in a fire."

"For someone who's been at her job for three years, it sounds like you haven't committed," I said.

"There's only one person with a fear of commitment here and it's not me."

"Whatever," I mumbled. "I signed a one-year lease with you. How's that for commitment."

Sloane laughed, then spun a circle as we came to the lobby and my desk. "It's been forever since I've been here." She walked to the bookcases while I beelined to my space. "Can I take some books?" she asked. "I want some books." Before I answered, she pulled one off the shelf.

I plopped the empty box I'd brought on my desk and looked around. Was Sloane right? What did I really want or need from my life here? I had a single framed picture of my family from the last vacation we'd gone on together—a posh cabin by a lake paid for by my sister. I'd recently graduated from college, and in between swimming and paddleboarding I'd spent half that vacation recording videos of my sister for her channel and the other half poring through English major–related job opportunities in the Los Angeles area. "I thought you wanted to be an editor," my sister had said when I found the assistant-to-a-literary-agent job. "Agents are sharks."

I set the picture, along with the memory, in the box, then

placed my potted heartleaf philodendron on top, as if to hold it there. The middle desk drawer had a few snacks: a couple KIND bars and a half-empty bag of Goldfish crackers. I added them to the box. The other drawers were mainly pens and stationery, envelopes and stamps. I took it all to aid in my justification for coming here.

Then I sat in my high-backed, ergonomically correct rolling chair that I would miss more than anything (and knew I could never afford to replace) and picked up the office phone. I'd tried calling Kari Cross twice from my cell phone but she hadn't answered. I was going to send her an email, the main way we communicated, but thought I'd try here first so I could explain things in a more personal way.

She picked up on the second ring. "Working on a Sunday?" was how she answered. "That's dedication."

"No, I'm cleaning out my desk."

"Cleaning out your desk? Are you moving?"

"I wanted to call and tell you how much I enjoyed the latest fifty pages you sent me. Amazing. The AI government is creepy but also I can completely understand why the community trusts it."

"Thank you. What about the setting? Was it better?"

"It was better," I said.

She sighed. "Don't bullshit me, Margot."

"It could still use some work."

"I was afraid you'd say that. Have you made any headway with Rob? Has he read any pages?"

"That's what I'm calling to tell you." I paused, squared my shoulders, then finished with, "I quit."

"You quit? Did you get a job somewhere else?"

"No, I'm starting my own agency."

"Oh." She sounded less than pleased with this development. "I guess it makes sense. Your timing couldn't be worse."

"I'm sorry about that. I tried to convince him about your book. He wasn't open to discussing it with me," I said, remembering how he was only open to kissing me at the time. My anger reignited in my chest.

"Guess I'll have to convince him myself. You quitting doesn't have to do with my book, does it?"

"No. Nothing like that. He didn't see the same future for me that I saw for myself."

"That sounds like a theme for him."

"I'd love to read the rest of your book," I said. "if you still want feedback. And"—I gave a nervous chuckle—"if Rob ever retires or croaks or something and you find yourself in need of an agent, think of me."

Across the room, Sloane's eyes went wide, like she didn't think I'd ever have the guts to say that to Kari Cross, queen of romance.

Kari gave a sharp laugh. "Call me in a few years when you've gotten your feet wet and we'll see if Rob is still screwing me over."

My stomach clenched with her words. The words I was afraid every potential client was going to say. I had relationships with editors, had sold a couple books myself, even, but I'd done it all under the supervision of Rob. "Yes, of course."

"But I might take you up on the reading," she said.

"Please do. I'll send you my personal email."

"Sounds good. Talk to you later, Margot."

I hung up.

"What did she say?" Sloane asked, her arms full of books.

"That I don't have enough experience."

Sloane rolled her eyes. "What does she call the last four years?"

"She calls them me being a glorified intern," I said, remembering my sister's words.

"Maybe she's not as smart as I thought," Sloane said, adding her pilfered books to my box.

"No, she's smarter."

Sloane put a finger under my chin. "Buck up. You got this. Don't let one author rejection bring you down."

I slapped her hand away. "It's a little bit more than one rejection that's bringing me down."

"I know. But we're going to solve all your problems at our business brainstorming session with Oliver after this."

With Sloane's books, the box was heavier than I'd anticipated. I lifted it and my groan turned into a grunt. "Let's go. And by the way, I'm not sure you made it clear that a brainstorming session was what you were inviting Oliver to. From what I recall, you invited him to judge his worthiness."

"I said that? Huh. Even when I'm hungover, I'm still so witty."

"Is that what we're calling *annoying* these days?" I said, moving the box to my hip to reset the alarm.

"Maybe a good grilling *is* more important than the brainstorming sesh after this whole friendship nonsense thing he initiated."

"Don't, Sloane. If we need to be friends so we stop touching each other and actually get to know each other, it's not a bad thing." At least that was the logic I'd been talking myself into for the last twenty-four hours.

The alarm beeped with its activation and I relocked the door.

She sighed. "Whatever. I think the real problem is that he's not the meet-cute you've been attempting to manifest so you're keeping him at arm's length."

"Not true." When I whirled around to walk to the car, Rob's BMW was pulling into the parking lot.

"Shit," I said. "Just keep walking."

"What?" Sloane hadn't noticed, but as soon as she did, her fists clenched into balls.

"Don't do anything stupid," I said.

"But I want to really bad. Do you think there are cameras in the office? Is that how he knew you were here?"

There were cameras in the main lobby of the office, but I didn't think he sat there and monitored them.

Rob stepped out of the car. He was wearing workout shorts and a fitted blue tee. He must've been at the gym, which was literally three blocks from here.

"Just cleaning out my desk," I said.

He joined us just as we reached the trunk. His eyes went to the box and the handful of books Sloane had stolen. I shot her a look and she had the decency to appear penitent.

I thought Rob would beg me to stay again or maybe even say he'd been wrong and that he'd talked to the other agents and they all agreed I deserved a chance. He didn't. He said, "I need your key."

"You really are an ass," Sloane said, and I wasn't mad about it. She must've thought I was, though, because she sucked in her lips and then got in the car and shut the door.

I placed the box in the trunk and then struggled to free the office key from my key ring.

"It doesn't have to be like this," Rob said as I finally got the head of the key wedged beneath the first layer of metal.

I twisted it around the circle. Everything in me wanted to say, *You're right, it doesn't. We can figure something out. I need this job. I need you to help me succeed at the next stage of my career. My life.* But I swallowed down that fear and that anxiety and accepted the truth. "I think we both know it does." I held the key out to him.

He took it from me. "Thanks for not . . ." His words trailed off.

Not what? I almost screamed. *Not telling the other agents that we slept together? Not making a scene? Not demanding better? Not slapping you right now? Thanks for not* about covered everything, didn't it?

"Yeah," I said. "The Margot that doesn't is over. I'm ready to."

"To what?" he said, obviously confused.

"To everything."

CHAPTER 20

"I can't fail at this," I said from my seat at the coffee shop we went to after driving away from the office, leaving Rob standing in the parking lot. For all I knew he was still standing there, still confused.

"You want to stick it to him now, don't you? Become the biggest success ever so you can rub it in his face," Sloane said. "I'm not mad at that motivation."

Oliver hadn't joined us yet. It hadn't taken as long at the office as I thought it would, even with the interruption from Rob. "Yes, that is one of the reasons I want to succeed now. But it's way down the list. And I have a few thousand steps to take before success."

"You're right. We need a plan of action. How do you feel about ethics?" she asked.

"What about them?"

"Are you for or against?"

"I mean, I was sleeping with my boss, so . . ."

"That says more about *his* ethics than yours, but sure. With that answer, I'm going to assume that your ethics are questionable."

"Okay. Thank you. Are you kicking me while I'm down or is there a point to this?"

"How would you feel about stealing potential clients?"

I choked on the sip of chai I'd just taken. "What do you mean?" I said through the coughing fit that followed.

"You know what I mean. Go through the queries authors send to Rob and poach some of his potential clients."

"He's going to disable my access. That's why I gave Kari my personal email."

"Then sign into his email from home. You have his passwords, right? Because you literally did everything for him."

"I have his passwords."

She shrugged. "It's a good plan."

"I can't steal his potential clients. Did you see Rob's face when he saw those books you took? How do you think he'd feel if I took his clients?"

"I don't care about Rob's feelings," she said.

"I can't do that . . ."

"But . . ." she prompted, obviously seeing my mind working.

"But maybe I can reach out to the ones from the past that I thought had potential but he ended up rejecting and see if they've found agents yet. And . . . what about our shared clients? I did all the work for them anyway and they love me. The commission on their past projects is lost to me, stays with the agency, but what if I convinced them to come with me for their next projects?"

"Yes!" she said.

This could be the jump start I needed. But before I could

even think about approaching clients, I needed to take the proper steps: make a *Publishers Weekly* announcement, change my online profiles, make a website, contact editors. "I need to get a business license, don't I? This is going to take time. I don't have time. I already feel the clock ticking on my savings."

"Can your parents loan you some money in the future if it takes you longer than you think?"

I cringed. I didn't want to have to do that. "I haven't even told my parents what's really going on yet. I'll call them today. And my sister . . . I need to tell her that I have no choice but to start my own agency because I quit after not getting a promotion . . ." I really should also tell her *why* I had to quit, what had led me down that path. But the thought of her face after learning I'd slept with Rob sent icy shivers through me. I was moving on with my life, leaving him behind; it was a nonissue now. I didn't need to tell her that part.

"What's worse? Facing Rob today or having to call your sister?"

"It's a draw," I said with a laugh. "My sister is just—"

"Perfect?"

"Yes. And Rob is maddening."

"Yes, he is, but you look hot, and the fact that Rob had to see what he is missing one last time is making me happy right here." She placed a hand over her heart.

I let out a breathy laugh.

"But we all know who you really dressed up for." Her gaze was over my right shoulder and I turned to see Oliver come through the door. All wavy-haired, chocolate-eyed, chiseled-jawed, six-foot-something of him.

Even though my cheeks were now warm, back to her, I said,

"I wouldn't call jeans and a button-down shirt *dressed up*." I wiped my palms against said jeans.

"We both know what your normal Sunday coffee outfits consist of and it's not a shirt with buttons."

I ignored her and stood when I realized he hadn't seen us in the back corner yet. My movement caught his eye and he had the nerve to smile at me. His smile made my insides squishy. It really was going to be hard to ignore the physical connection we had.

"Hi," he said. "You two look like you are fully functional today." He slid onto the bench seat next to me. I picked up my tote that was between us and put it on my opposite side. His scent immediately clouded my senses.

Sloane was in a chair across from us. "*Fully* is up for debate," she said.

"Shhh!" A guy at the next table over hissed in our direction. He was on his computer typing away.

"This isn't a library, dude," Sloane said.

"Are you a writer?" I asked, disregarding his annoyed face. "I'm a literary agent if you're looking. Tell your friends."

"I'm taking a test," he said, like we should've known that.

"Again," Sloane said. "A library would've been the better choice. Or noise-canceling headphones. Do you have a pair of those?"

His bushy brows went down and he turned his attention back to his computer screen.

I tried not to laugh, but I did lower my voice when I said, "I need business cards."

"So you can hand them to anyone typing on a computer? You need to learn the talent of discernment. You want clients, but not just any clients." She nodded disgustingly toward the test taker. "Good ones."

She wasn't wrong. "I need a website," I said. "And online posts. Lots of posts. Do I need TikTok? I'm not good at TikTok."

"Stay off TikTok," Sloane said. "You'd be addicted to that in hours and become completely useless."

"Rude," I said.

"I know someone who can help you with a website," Oliver said.

"Who?" I asked.

"Someone who designs things on computers for a living," he prompted.

"Oh! You? You'd help me?"

"We're friends, right?" he asked in that sincere voice of his.

"Yes, you're *friends*," Sloane said, emphasizing the word way more than one should emphasize any word. When I'd told her our decision the night before to slow things down, get to know each other a little better, become friends first, she'd given me the most perplexed look and said, "Friends with benefits?" I had responded with, "I wish."

"You're a terrible person," I said to her now. To Oliver, I said, "Thank you. I'm just desperate enough to take you up on the website thing. Wait, how much do you charge?"

He laughed a warm throaty laugh that made my heart gallop. "Only the friend rate."

"Which is?" I asked.

"A coffee."

"Sold," I said, and stood, ready to march to the register that second.

He stood as well, after me, as if he had just remembered we were sitting in a coffee shop and I could pay my half of the bargain that second. "Not now," he said. "After the work is finished and you decide if it's worth a coffee or not."

"If it's not worth a coffee, we're both in trouble," I said, and stepped around the table.

He cut me off, his fingers brushing down my left arm as he did, hovering just short of my hand. "Just wait. I don't want to . . . I can't . . . Just wait."

I raised my hands in surrender and said, "Fine, I will not buy you coffee today. But if you don't let me buy it after you complete the work, due to however those half sentences you just uttered ended, we will have beef."

"Beef?" he asked.

I narrowed my eyes at him. "Don't pretend you don't know what that means."

He smiled that killer smile of his at me again, then whispered, close to my ear, "Don't pretend anyone still uses that word." With those words, he left me standing there, the back of my neck prickling to life, as he went to order the coffee he refused to let me buy.

"Oh," Sloane said as I sat down again. "I see now."

"What?"

"You two have a lot of chemistry."

I laughed. "I know. But do we have anything else?"

Her eyebrows popped up. "If you ever want to find out, you have to actually let him in. I know Rob hurt you, made you wary, made you think you only had one thing to offer, but—"

A lump sprung to my throat. "This has nothing to do with Rob."

She pursed her lips and stopped talking.

Oliver came back to the table a few minutes later carrying an iced coffee with some sort of drizzle—caramel? Brown sugar? He sat down, then let his shoulder bump into mine, as if greeting me again.

I smiled up at him.

"Did you bring a book?" He nodded toward my book at the corner of the table. I had pulled it out earlier when digging through my tote for my wallet.

"It's her emotional support book," Sloane said.

I shoved it back into my bag. "Downtime is a real thing."

"It's true," Sloane said. "I carry scripts around. I once read an entire screenplay while stuck in standstill traffic."

"What do you carry around, Oliver?" I asked.

"The entire internet," he said, patting his phone in his pocket.

"Boring," I said with a smirk.

"Speaking of boring," Sloane said. "Time to brainstorm Margot's new business venture. Have you thought of a name for your agency yet?"

"Rude transition," I said.

"I thought it was brilliant."

"And yes. I *have* thought of a name. Love Lit." My last name was Hart. It seemed like the perfect fit.

"You're going to pigeonhole yourself into only representing romance authors?" she asked.

"It's what I'm passionate about."

"I saw some pretty insane passion when you were talking about Kari's thriller/horror the other day."

"Thriller/horror?" Oliver asked.

"Yes," I said. "One of my ex-boss's client's works in progress. And speaking of, Kari sent me the next fifty pages." I held up my phone, the notification I'd gotten for the waiting email earlier still up on my screen.

"For someone who rejected you so handily today," Sloane said, "she sure didn't waste any time sending those."

"She didn't reject me," I said. "I wasn't asking her to be my client."

"Pages? Work in progress?" Oliver asked.

"Yes, she's writing this book about an AI-run city. In the last installment I read, the AI is starting to give questionable rules to a woman named Ana and her husband, Alan, but they have to follow them if they want to stay. And so far, the town has proven to be basically heaven on Earth, so they are desperate to stay."

"So they are following the AI's questionable rules, then?" Sloane asked.

"The reader sees them as more questionable than the characters. They've all but shut off their decision-making skills, the whole town has."

"Sounds unrealistic," Sloane said.

"*You* would totally let an AI dictate your love life," I said.

She shrugged. "If it had a high success rate."

"Might be more reliable than a human programmer," Oliver said.

"Yes, we all know how shady those people are," I said, smirking in his direction.

"The shadiest," he agreed. "Also, an AI making decisions for me sounds way easier than the apps."

"Apparently you would also let an AI dictate your love life," I said. "No computer is going to figure out love for me."

"It could be romantic," he said. "Have you ever read about AI-generated dates? The bots have been trained and they learn way faster than the average man."

I laughed. "Maybe we could implant a chip at the base of

your neck and you could be fed romantic ideas all day long. Because what you just said is not romantic. At all." The words gave me an excuse to reach out and touch his neck, and when I did, a zap of electricity shot through my body as if I were the one being touched.

"Is this book coming out soon?" Oliver asked, goose bumps forming under my fingers despite the fact that he otherwise seemed unaffected. "It sounds good."

I put my hands on my knees. I needed to keep them to myself. "It hasn't even sold yet."

"Hello," Sloane said. "Less about a book you don't even represent and back to the business you're actually trying to start. Still not sure Love Lit is the right choice."

"Hart Lit? HEA Literary?" I asked.

"I like Hart Lit better," she said. "It makes more sense."

"Maybe." I shook my head. "I need time to think." The idea of having to come up with the permanent name of my agency was making my palms sweat. This would be on business cards and in website announcements. "It needs to be right, perfect, because it's going to be forever."

"Commitment issues," Sloane coughed.

"You're the one who said you didn't like Love Lit."

"I changed my mind," she said. "Because we're allowed to do that." She looked between me and Oliver like she was making a point. "Love Lit. It's perfect."

CHAPTER 21

"Hey, Audrey. I've been trying to call you," I said, leaving a message for my sister. "I'm sorry for the snarky text I sent you the other day. It's not an excuse but I was drunk. Okay, maybe it's a little excuse, but probably one that solidifies your thoughts about me." I sighed. "That sounded snarky too. I mean, your thoughts about me are mostly right is what I'm trying to say. I am unfocused, or have been. I'm working on it. Also, I'm not drunk now even though I sound like I am. Anyway, call me, I need to clarify what happened Friday. Bye." I disconnected the call.

"That was a mess," Sloane said.

It was Wednesday evening. I'd spent the last few days applying for a business license and ordering business cards and creating a new business email.

"I know! I'm more nervous to talk to my sister than I've been informing editors that I've started my own agency." The truth was that I missed her. This had been the longest I'd ever gone without talking to her and I wanted us to be okay again.

I hated that I had lied to her. And I could really use her help. She would be so good at this.

"You've been killing it the last couple days. Who knew running into Rob in the parking lot would light a bigger fire under your ass."

"It was more the quitting thing that motivated me, but sure, seeing Rob just reconfirmed my commitment."

"Have you told your parents yet?"

"I talked to them yesterday. I don't think they quite understand exactly what I'm doing because they kept saying that they were so happy Mr. Bishop gave me this opportunity. Once I have my website up and running, I'll give them the link. That will help."

"When did Oliver say he'd help you with the website?"

"Friday night."

I pulled up my phone to review our exchanged texts over the last several days to double-check that I was right.

Me: Hey, Website Designer, when should we do this? Considering how much I'm paying you for this service, I have a very long list of demands.

Oliver: Demanding clients are my favorite. Friday night?

Me: You don't have a hot date?

Oliver: If you're calling it a date, then yes, I do.

Me: I'm calling it a business transaction.

Oliver: Then I have a hot business transaction.

"Oh my gaaaawwwd," Sloane groaned, pulling me out of my phone. "Good luck keeping horny Margot at bay."

"What?" I asked, confused.

"The look on your face right now while you're reading texts from Oliver. Good. Luck. Keeping. Horny. Margot. At. Bay."

I pointed to my face. "This isn't horny Margot. This is

mildly amused Margot. Horny Margot has been suppressed, replaced by getting-shit-done Margot."

"If you say so."

"Me and my self-control will be perfectly fine."

. . .

I have self-control, I told myself as I walked the path to Oliver's front door Friday evening. More than a moderate amount. I didn't slap Rob in the parking lot, after all. That had to count for something.

But when Oliver answered the door with wet hair, my mind immediately pictured him in the shower even though he was fully clothed, and that didn't help at all. Tonight was about my agency, my future. I could not lose sight of that.

"Hi," he said, holding the door open for me. Then his hand went to his face, wiping at his chin and cheek. "Do I have something on my face?"

"What?" I asked.

"You're staring at me with an alarmed expression."

"Sorry, no. I'm just overwhelmed. It's been a long few days."

"Sorry your life hasn't instantly solved all its problems."

"Yeah, me too."

"Come in."

I stepped forward and we came together in an awkward half hug, half cheek kiss. I'd never kissed a friend's cheek in my life; I wasn't sure why that was my instinct. As if I'd suddenly become European. "I finally get to see inside."

"Oh, right. The farthest you got last time was the driveway."

"It was a good driveway." A *very* good driveway.

He smiled.

I took in his living room, where I now stood. It smelled like him but also like sandalwood or leather or something. It smelled good, like I wanted to sink onto the oversized brown couch and wrap myself up in the throw that was draped over the arm of it. "I thought maybe you lived with your parents last time I was here. Nobody I knew lived in an actual house at the time."

"Just me," he said.

The house didn't look like a bachelor pad. The walls were a warm olive green and the television stand and bookcase were a rich chocolate with decorative knickknacks on various shelves. A big gold-trimmed mirror hung on the wall just inside the door. I found myself wondering if this was the house he'd lived in with his ex-fiancée. If she had decorated. "I like your style," I said. A passive-aggressive way to ask the question my brain had just come up with.

"Thank you," was his only response.

"I thought you didn't have physical books." I walked to his bookshelf on the opposite wall.

"Those are mainly for show," he said with a smirk.

I scanned the titles. They were mostly nonfiction was what they were. I turned and my eyes collided with a book on the coffee table. The book he had borrowed from me. A bookmark stuck out from the pages about halfway through. "You're actually reading it?" I asked.

He cleared his throat. "After the excerpt, how could I not?"

"I should've taken out my tabs for you."

"Pretty sure I have decrypted your color coding," he said, picking it up and fanning through the pages, all the colors flipping past his fingers.

Of course he had. With a job like his, how could he not?

I hoped he also took the time to stop thinking and actually enjoy the words. "Which color is your favorite?" I asked with a wink.

"You're trouble, Margot," he said, then nodded toward the hall. "My office is back here. Also, my favorite are the red ones."

I laughed. "Good choice."

We passed through a farmhouse-style kitchen, the colors from the living room flowing through the backsplash and cupboards. "You could have a social media presence with a place like this. Especially if you did the work yourself." I would know; my sister's house and style garnered her hundreds of thousands of followers.

"I'm not big on social media." He paused before we reached the hall at the end of the kitchen. "Would you like something to drink?"

"Yes, please," I said. "And I know. I tried to stalk you. Twice now, and nothing."

He chuckled as he backtracked to the fridge.

I followed him, needing to know if the inside of his fridge was as clean as the rest of his house. I peered inside. Bottles of beer and hard lemonade and water were lined up perfectly. All the food items were stored in uniform containers.

"What would you like?" he asked.

"I'd like to mess up your life a little," I teased, moving a beer to the lemonade row and a water on its side. "This is why you were shocked by the state of my bed and clothes chair, isn't it?"

"I was not shocked."

"Shocked," I repeated.

"I had next to no reaction," he said.

"That's what you think, but your face is very expressive."

He gave me an amused look. "What am I thinking now?"

"You're wondering why you agreed to help me," I said.

He laughed. "You're terrible at this game."

I helped myself to a beer and then raised it in a thank-you. He took one as well and we resumed our walk toward the office. "Do you really not have any social media outside of dating apps?"

"I have a LinkedIn."

"Doesn't count," I said as we stepped into his office.

Unlike the greens and dark woods of the rest of the house, this room was bright white. A long table with silver accents lined an entire wall. Beneath it was a walking pad on one side and a fancy chair on the other. There was an uncomfortable-looking leather couch along another wall. A single potted plant sat in the corner, too small for the space.

"The internet is very permanent," he said, then looked around his office like he was seeing it for the first time. "I know. It's cold and impersonal, but working from home, I had to make my office feel like a different place or I was less productive."

"That makes sense." I'd never thought about it before, but there probably was some psychology behind that. I pointed to the walking pad. "Do I have to walk while we design the website or do you?"

"One of us does, that's how I power the computer."

He said it with such a straight face that for a split second I thought he was serious. But the slight crinkles at the corners of his eyes clued me in to the fact that he was kidding. "I mean, you are an engineer, it wouldn't surprise me."

"You have no idea what I do for a living, do you?"

"All I know is there are ones and zeros involved."

"I take it back, you know exactly what I do for a living."

I bowed like he was being serious.

"I'll grab an extra chair from the kitchen," he said.

When he got back, he flipped the walking pad onto its side, slid it beside the desk, and replaced it with the chair he'd brought back. He pulled out his fancy chair and gestured for me to sit.

"This is amazing," I said, settling into the soft leather.

"A good chair and a good computer are the top two factors of my success."

I spun once then stopped it with my feet. "Maybe you should sit here, then, so you can make me the best website in the world."

He sat on the chair from the kitchen, picked up my beer from the desk where I'd set it, and twisted off the cap. "I'm good here." He handed me the bottle, then pulled his chair closer to mine. So close his scent invaded my space, made me want to lean into him, breathe him in, try out some red tab scenes from the book he was reading.

I picked up a container of cinnamon Altoids that sat next to a wooden box of pens. "The mystery is solved," I said.

"I didn't realize it was a mystery," he returned.

"It was," I assured him.

He smiled. "I already got started on the generic layout. Do you have your business license and tax ID number yet?"

"No," I said. "Probably in the next day or two."

"Okay, I'll change all the info over to you when you have that." He moved the mouse, the black computer screen lighting up with his action. The words *Love Lit* were at the top of the page, a placeholder in boring black font.

"Oh, I decided to go with Hart Lit," I said.

"Really? Sloane talked you out of the name you wanted?"

"It just makes more sense." Not only was it my last name but it could refer to stories with heart.

His eyes traveled down my body and to the small backpack I'd brought with me. "You have ideas?"

I took a sip of beer. "So many ideas."

. . .

"You can't just use anyone's pictures on the internet," he said, leaning back in his chair and putting his hands behind his head. The action made the muscles in both his arms pop. "You have to pay for pictures."

I knew that. Of course I knew that. I worked in publishing, after all. And the amount of times people stole clients' books and posted them on illegal downloading sites was sickening. "If we change them up a lot? Obscure faces?" I asked. We'd been working for two hours and were so close to finishing. We were down to the header. But even as I made the suggestion, I knew I wouldn't feel comfortable taking someone's image without their permission. "You're right, that won't work," I conceded. My mind spun, trying to figure out another solution. It landed on "What about you?"

"Me?"

"Just one pic and you'll be backlit so nobody will know it's you." My idea for the header was an open door with a man standing in it, his arm high on the doorframe in a lean. The room bright behind him. The name of the agency would be spelled out in shadows on the floor in front of him.

It would stand out. It wouldn't be a stuffy, boring website. The right clients would appreciate it . . . I hoped. Besides, attracting readers to my website to check out clients' books was an important part of agenting as well.

"I know you didn't just ask me to model for you," Oliver said. He crossed his arms over his chest. "Stop looking at me like that."

I had been scanning his body, trying to imagine what was hiding under his thick, dark T-shirt. "Have you *seen* yourself? You were made to model. Show me what I'm working with." I tugged on the sleeve of his shirt. "Just a little peek."

He met my eyes with a calm stare, but I could see the teasing twinkle behind it. "Is this how you talk to your friends?"

"All of them," I said.

He couldn't help but laugh.

"Oliver, I promise it will be tasteful and anonymous. Here, let me show you what I'm talking about." I clicked on what I thought would open a new window on the computer only to have a screen from the bottom bar open. A paused image of Johnny and Baby from the cabin scene in *Dirty Dancing* came up. "Are you watching this movie?" I asked, surprised.

"Someone told me it was good," he said, meeting my eyes, his expression suddenly impossible to read.

"It is," I said. "A classic." My heart thudded heavily in my chest as I remembered what I'd told him about this movie. That if someone hadn't watched it, that was a dealbreaker. It had been a joke, but still, he really was trying to get to know me better. Putting in the work. I couldn't remember the last time a man had done that for me. "What are your dealbreakers?" I said, realizing I'd never asked him that question.

"Someone asking me to model shirtless for their website."

I laughed. "Seriously, nobody will know it's you."

"*You* will. And you'll tell Sloane. And she'll tell everyone."

"I swear on my life I won't tell her."

"Margot, come on."

"Yes, come on." I took his hand in mine, always looking for an excuse to touch him—I'd been wanting to all night—and met his eyes.

"Not even with those eyes," he said, squeezing my hand. "But your idea is good. What about a bright room with a messy bed in the distance. It would be less in-your-face. Perhaps a step classier."

I rolled my eyes but smiled. Maybe he was right. A dark hall, a lit bed in the distance? "What's your bedroom look like?"

"I was thinking we'd use yours."

"I want a man's bedroom. Is your bedroom as cool as the rest of your house?"

His fingers tightened around mine as if he was talking himself through all the possible outcomes of having his bedroom posted online. He came to some conclusion, because he stood. "You tell me."

CHAPTER 22

The hall wasn't that long, but the walk from the office to the door at the end seemed like an eternity with my heart thumping heavy in my chest and my skin reacting to every stimulus, even the air, it seemed.

I have self-control, I reminded myself once more. Unless he didn't want me to have it. *No.* I had not come here to ravage Oliver. We were getting to know each other. I had come here to make a website.

The hall was dark. Had it always been this dark? It would be perfect for the photo, but right now my mind didn't need any more excuses to think what it wanted to think. I looked around for a light switch, but we were already to the door. Standing outside of it. He paused as if he understood the story element of a dramatic reveal. He grabbed hold of the handle and leaned his right shoulder into the door. I was next to him, waiting. When nothing happened, I looked up at him.

He smiled. "I can't believe you talked me into this."

"It honestly wasn't that hard," I said. My voice was silkier than I meant for it to be.

He held my stare as if daring me to do something. I broke eye contact first. He opened the door and flipped on the light.

"My sister would love you," I breathed out as I took in the room. The bed had a dark wood headboard. Around that, thin strips of wood formed geometric shapes that were then painted the same color as the wall. The bedding was rich in both color and material. A double row of pillows leaned against the head-board.

"She does interior design?" he asked.

"Yes," I said. "This is why you agreed. You knew you had the perfect bed for this. It's even framed perfectly by the door."

A smile crept onto his face. "It is rather perfect."

"It needs to be messy, though," I said. "Like two people just rolled around in it." I approached the bed and climbed on.

If I thought his house smelled good, his bed enveloped me in a scent that was both him and somehow more as I crawled across it. I flung myself onto his pillows on my back, arms stretched wide. My socked feet pedaled up and down. It was in that moment that my brain caught up with me: I had just climbed onto his bed.

"I'm sorry," I said, pointing to the bed. "May I?"

He laughed. "Pretty sure you already did."

I propped myself up on my elbows to see that he'd positioned himself at the foot of the bed. "Want to help me mess this up?"

"Margot, I . . ."

"With all our clothes on, *friend*. Where did your mind go?"

"You're in my bed. You know where it went."

The air was sucked from my lungs as my heart raced to life. He was having impure thoughts as well. That meant this whole "slow down" thing was hard for him too.

I cleared my throat. "I just meant mess it up with your hands. Like this . . ." I moved to my knees and peeled back his comforter. "I'm guessing you have hotel corners and everything under here."

He stretched over and tugged at one of the bottom corners, freeing it. I used the opportunity to grab hold of the edge of the blanket and roll myself up like a burrito.

"Is that how you do things in bed?" he asked.

My elbows were pinned to my sides, my hands holding the top of the blanket under my chin. "This *isn't* how you do things in bed?" If I kept rolling, I'd deposit myself onto the ground. But just as I went to unroll myself, he rounded the bed and sat down, blocking me in.

"Are you stuck?" he asked in a fake innocent voice.

"You know I am."

He lifted his hands like he was going to free me, then paused and asked, "Are you ticklish?"

"Don't you dare."

"Is that a yes or a no?" His hands moved along my sides.

I squealed and made several empty threats about taking him down.

He stopped and brushed a piece of hair off my forehead. Then he studied my face. I wasn't sure what he saw there, but he met my eyes with an intensity I'd seen before. An ache settled between my legs and I swallowed hard. Then, as if I were made of fire, he yanked his hand away and stood. "We'd better get some pictures. It's getting late."

I nodded but didn't move. The thought of him stretched out beside me, pressed up against me, flashed through my mind. We could keep all our clothes on, I just wanted to lay here in his arms, in his scent, in his life.

"Are you still stuck?" he asked. "Do I need to unroll you?"

I avoided his gaze, worried he'd be able to read all my thoughts. Or maybe I was worried he wouldn't be able to. "Yes, please," I said, even though I didn't need his help. I just knew this might be the only opportunity to feel his hands on me again.

He leaned over, grabbed me by the waist, and pulled. I flopped onto my stomach with an unflattering "Oof."

He chuckled, then flipped me again. I was able to free my arms and sit up. He took in the bed as I climbed out of it.

"Huh," he said. "I mocked you for the execution but that actually worked. It looks like two people *used* this bed."

I laughed, then whispered, "Has it been awhile since it's seen that much action?"

I had been joking, but he said, "Yes, actually."

And because I was nosy, I asked, "Why?"

"Like I said before, I'm kind of over meaningless hookups. I want more."

I nodded.

"And you?" he asked. "Does your bed have stories to tell?"

"I wish it had more because that would mean that my weakness for the past couple years wasn't someone who was completely wrong for me."

"He never went home with you?"

I swallowed. *Let him in*, Sloane had said. It was hard when I'd been keeping this part of my life a secret from most people for so long. When I felt so ashamed about it. "No," I said.

"That might've meant we were committed, and he would never admit to that." I picked at a hangnail on my thumb. "We snuck out of town occasionally like the secret that I was. And I constantly had to lie to my family about where I was going and who I was going with. And then when we got home, it was like it never happened. He usually started ignoring me, until I made him see me again."

"I'm sorry," he said, his hand brushing along my arm.

"Me too," I said.

"I know it's not the same, but both times I was cheated on, it was the secrets that hurt the most. The person you thought you cared about lying to you. I get lies and secrets. They hurt."

My throat felt tight. My family was still in the dark about Rob, obviously. I had decided it was pointless to tell them now that it was over. But maybe that meant I was a horrible person.

"And I get feeling unseen," he said as his other hand brushed along my other arm until both my hands were in his. "It's a lonely place to be."

I nodded.

"Maybe we both have trust issues."

"We're not supposed to touch," I said softly.

"Friends touch," he returned.

I closed my eyes and listened to our breathing sync up. In and out.

"You can trust me, Margot. I see you," he said.

"I think you might. Three years ago, in your car, I would've sworn you had been handed a study guide on my body. It was impressive."

"You know what my study guide was?"

My hands felt weightless in his grip. "No, what?"

"You. The way you moved against me when I hit the right

spot, the noises you made when my mouth was on you. And that was in a car, Margot."

A slow fire had started in my belly with his words and was slowly expanding through all my limbs. "I know. Imagine how much better it would be here, where we have full access to each other."

"I have," he said.

I bit my bottom lip trying to tamp down my desire. "Is this how you talk to all your friends?" I said, mimicking what he'd asked me earlier.

"Yes, all of them," he said, copying me.

We stayed that way for several minutes, holding hands, perfectly still, not looking at each other, just breathing.

Then with the slightest tug, he pulled me forward, into his arms. "We already established that friends hug, right?" he asked.

"Yes." My hands wrapped around him to his back, where they moved up and down it. "I am also known to rub my friends' backs."

He gave a breathy laugh. "Such a good friend." His feather-soft touch traveled from my back to my waist, where he grabbed hold of me. I thought he was going to separate us, be the first to say *uncle*, but he didn't, he pressed me even closer to him. So close I could feel just how much he didn't want to let go.

I sucked in some air as all the little hairs along my arms and up to the back of my neck stood on end.

My hands paused in their exploration of his broad back and, finally, I looked up and met his eyes.

His darted back and forth between mine, probably looking

for hesitancy. He wouldn't find it. My entire body ached for him.

I wasn't sure who closed the distance, just that our lips collided with such force that it was both painful and exhilarating at once.

CHAPTER 23

His mouth moved expertly on mine, releasing some pressure only to reapply it again in a new way.

My hands, which had been resting on his back, apparently shocked into inactivity, finally awakened and wanted to explore every inch of him. They started by traveling his strong arms, feeling his taut muscles holding me tight against him. Then they moved across his shoulders and up into his thick, wavy hair, where they grabbed hold.

His hand drifted from my lower back to my ass to my thigh, which he lifted up so he could lower me back onto the bed, climbing on after me.

He stretched alongside me, my right hip connected to his left as he rested on his side. I pulled his upper half onto mine. He relented, our mouths meeting again. His fingers found a strip of exposed skin at my waist and traced the line until my body was on fire. I let out a whimper. He gathered my hands in his and pulled them above my head, trapping them against the mattress.

I arched against him and his mouth moved from mine to my neck and then lower, his tongue tracing along my collarbone. His hand found my breast, teasing my nipple through my bra until it pebbled.

I wanted him on top of me, to feel the full weight of him. Unable to pull him over with my hands trapped, I wrapped my leg around his waist and tugged. He got the message, propping himself up with one elbow and lowering his entire body onto mine. I could feel his pleasure, hard against the softness of my stomach. I arched again, pressing into him and then grinding against him.

His moan practically brought me to a climax all by itself. His mouth was back on mine, his tongue both soft and urgent. He tasted like mint and beer and lust, all my lust.

"I need my hands back," I said against his mouth. As much as it turned me on that he was in control here, I wanted to touch him. To dig my fingers into his back. To rake my hands through his hair. He loosened his grip and my hands hungrily dove under his shirt. His skin was hot and smooth under my touch.

His hand slid up my back to my bra strap, which he easily unhooked.

"Your friends are so lucky to have you," I said against his mouth.

"So are yours," he said, kissing along my jaw as his hand worked its way under my loosened bra to cup my breast. His thumb circled my nipple until I whimpered in protest and then he pinched it firmly, causing me to gasp with pleasure.

It took me a moment, in my completely high-on-endorphins state, to feel the buzzing against my thigh. It took me another moment to realize it wasn't something he was magically doing and that it was actually my phone. He seemed to come to the same realization at the same time as me because he rolled onto his back with a groan.

"I'll turn it off," I said. I thought I'd left it in my bag.

It stopped buzzing. I pulled it out of my pocket and was about to power it off when it started buzzing again.

"It's Sloane," I said. "She normally doesn't call twice in a row like this."

"You should answer," he assured me, pulling his shirt down and adjusting his pants near his crotch.

I cringed, but I wasn't faring much better; every part of me throbbed with desire. I swiped to answer. "Hello."

"I'm sorry to bug you," Sloane started. "How is the website coming along?"

"I, uh . . ." The website. That's why I was here. "Yeah, almost done. Is that why you called?"

"No. A courier just delivered an envelope to the door for you."

"A courier? At eight o'clock on a Friday night?"

"It's nine."

Was it? "At nine o'clock at night?"

"I know. I thought that was weird too. I wouldn't have called but it seems official and important. It's from the agency."

"The agency?"

"Your old work?"

I sat up and turned sideways to let my feet hit the floor, hoping that would help me feel more grounded. "Open it."

"You want me to open it?" she asked.

"Will you?"

"I was hoping you'd say that."

Behind me, Oliver had sat up as well. I wanted him to put

a hand on my back or run a finger down my arm, anything to remind me of what had just happened between us. Anything to keep my brain from jolting back into the reality of my overwhelming life. He didn't. He swung his legs to the floor, stood, and disappeared into the bathroom.

On the phone, I heard the zipper-like rip of a cardboard envelope being opened.

"It looks like a contract or something." She flipped through pages, or at least that's what it sounded like she was doing. "Oh, here are some tabs."

"Like the *sign here* tabs? Rob wants me to sign something?"

"No, it looks like a copy of an old contract. Did you sign something when you started there?"

I thought back. A shiver went through me and I pulled the blanket up and around my shoulders. "Yeah, I think I did."

"Oh . . ." she said.

"What?"

"He's tabbed the parts that talk about how you aren't allowed to solicit his clients now that you've left."

"Solicit?"

"Reach out to, offer your agenting services to, you know, that thing we talked about doing."

I knew what *solicit* meant, it had just taken my mind a second to understand it in this context. "Does it mention anything about our shared clients?"

"Yes. They're included in the no-soliciting section."

"And the people he's rejected?" I asked.

"You're not allowed to use personal information about authors you've gained through working at his agency if you find yourself as his competitor."

"He knows I'm going to open my own agency?"

"Or work for another agent," she said.

"Oh, right. That's probably what he thinks I'm going to do."

"It's possible one of the editors you talked to this week spilled the beans about you becoming an agent."

"Possibly. So much for the head start I thought I had."

"How is he going to know?" she said. "He's not going to remember every author who ever reached out to him."

"Like I said before, the publishing world is very small. Things have a way of coming out."

"This doesn't say anything about any authors, past or present, reaching out to *you*. Just that you can't reach out to them. I guess you're going to have to put yourself out there and hope they come."

I pinched the bridge of my nose to stop my stinging eyes.

"Margot, this changes nothing. You can do this."

I nodded even though I knew she couldn't see me. "I can't believe he sent that to me. He's the one who screwed me over, not the other way around."

"We knew Rob was an asshole. He's very good at proving it."

"Yeah."

"Go finish your website. You're going to need that. I'll see you when you get home."

"Thanks, Sloane." We hung up the phone and I threw it onto the bed beside me like the bearer of bad news that it was. I pulled the blanket tighter around my shoulders. My mind spun. Maybe I'd have to pay for advertising. I couldn't afford that; I already didn't have enough savings to last me as long as I knew I'd need it for.

Oliver stepped out of the bathroom a few minutes later and our eyes found each other. The tension in my shoulders relaxed a notch.

"Everything okay?" he asked from where he stood ten feet away.

"Not really. Just Rob reminding me that anything I learned while working for him I need to expunge from my brain. He'd probably want me to get my memory wiped if it were possible."

"I'm sorry."

"I . . ." I loosened my hold on his blanket and it slid down my shoulders and back onto his bed. I stood and reached behind me, up under my shirt, trying to rehook my bra. "I should probably go read through the contract. Regroup." Bras were easier to unhook unseen than they were to hook, and I struggled. "Hey, help a friend out," I said.

He chuckled and closed the distance between us. "I got it."

His fingers fumbled on my bra strap, but eventually I felt it tighten into place. He pulled my shirt down and ran his hand down my back a few times. "What can I do for you?"

"You're doing it. Thanks for the website help."

"Of course."

I turned back toward him and gripped the sides of his T-shirt. "In case it wasn't clear." I nodded toward the bed. "I don't do that with my friends."

He let out a loud laugh. "Yeah, me neither, obviously."

"Are you ready to try the get-it-out-of-our-systems approach yet?"

The look of hurt that flashed through his eyes wiped the smile off my face. "I'm kidding," I said. "We got this. We have self-control. It was just a setback. A slipup. I can keep my hands to myself." I clasped them behind me and took a step back. "See? We're still getting to know each other."

He gave a whisper of a laugh. "I'm worried I'm making your life more complicated."

"You really do think too much."

"You have no idea."

"I should probably go. Can you . . . ?"

"I can finish up the website tonight and get it to you to-morrow."

"Thank you so much." I spun around, made short work of the hall, collected my things from the office, and headed for the front door.

He was there unlocking it for me when I arrived. "Good night."

"Good night." I stepped onto the lit porch and down the two steps toward my car.

"Margot?"

I looked over my shoulder.

He smiled that killer smile at me. "You owe me a coffee."

My heart stuttered in my chest and I smiled back. Despite what I'd told him, I wasn't actually sure I had one single ounce of self-control when it came to Oliver.

CHAPTER 24

My sister's name scrolled across my phone screen the following afternoon and my heart jumped to my throat. We hadn't talked since my drunken texts to her, despite my multiple attempts to do just that.

I shifted, moving the laptop I'd been holding for the last several hours to the coffee table. I'd been composing and re-composing social-media posts announcing my agency. Nothing sounded right. Oliver was on his way over to show me the finished website, but until I could direct people to that, I couldn't post them anyway.

"Hello," I answered, trying to infuse my voice with the proper amount of penitence.

"Hi," she said. I couldn't tell from that single word how she felt.

"Hi," I parroted. "How are you? I mean, how are you feeling? The baby okay? The boys?"

"We're all good." Okay, that response was clearer. She wasn't happy.

"I'm sorry for not being completely honest with you about my job and my promotion."

"Completely honest?" she said. "You lied, Maggie."

"I know. I was embarrassed. Everything you touch turns to gold and I feel like the opposite happens for me. What's the opposite of gold? Horseshit? I have a life full of horseshit right now."

She snorted out a laugh. "You don't."

"I really did start my own agency. And it might be nothing right now, but I think it can be something. I have a website and everything."

"You do? I'd love to see it."

"It's not quite ready, but it will be."

She sighed. "You're a teddy bear, not a shark."

"You don't think I can do this?"

"You can't start your own business on a whim. That's something you do after months of preparation."

"That ship has sailed, Audrey. I can't turn it around."

"You can always turn it around."

If she knew one of the reasons I couldn't, she'd be even more disappointed. "I'm not going to."

"Then you need to activate your fighter."

This was her way of saying no, she didn't think I could do this, which scared me. If my sister didn't think it would work, maybe it wouldn't. She knew business. "I'm trying."

"If you need any advice, help, I'm here."

Considering she'd been avoiding my calls for days, I didn't feel like that was true. But I wanted it to be. I needed it to be. "I watched your channel three times this week to see what was going on with you."

"My channel isn't my real life."

That was the first time she'd ever admitted her channel was highly curated. "I know. I just wanted to see you."

There was some mumbling in the background that sounded suspiciously like my mom.

"Would you like to come for dinner next Sunday?" Audrey asked. "We're barbecuing."

I swallowed hard, sure Mom had made her ask. But at the same time, I hadn't seen my family since the T-ball game several weeks ago and I missed them. "Yes, I would love to come. Can I bring something? A side dish?" My bank account was dwindling and my credit card was rising and the other half of my rent was due in a week. I shouldn't be offering to buy food for the barbecue, but I already felt like I'd let my sister down. I wanted her to know I could contribute.

"No, that's okay," Audrey said.

"Come on, Audrey. Let me bring something."

"I'll look over my list and send you a text with what you can bring."

"Sounds good."

"Okay, see you next Sunday at four. Bring your suit if you want to swim. The boys would love that."

"Then I will for sure. See you then." And because I couldn't contain my snark I added, "Tell Mom I say hi."

I could practically see the eye roll she probably gave our mom in that moment. "Maggie says hi."

"Hi!" Mom called from the background.

I tugged on a loose string on the arm of the couch. "Audrey, if you don't want me to come to the barbecue, if I'm too much chaos right now for you—"

"No," she interrupted. "I do. I want you to come."

There was a knock on my door. Oliver.

"Do you have company?" Audrey asked.

"Just a friend."

"You're starting a relationship in the middle of all this?"

"I said 'a friend.'"

"It was the way you said 'friend.'"

I had no idea how I had said it, but she obviously knew me better than anyone. That's why her not believing I could start my own business was hard to hear. "We're taking it slow."

"Not a good idea."

"I shouldn't take it slow?"

"You know what I mean. You shouldn't be starting anything new right now. You need to focus."

"Thanks, Audrey," I said, holding back a sigh. "I'll take that into account."

"Good," she said.

We hung up and I answered the door. Oliver stood there wearing a gray hoodie, jeans, and a pair of black Vans. He held his laptop under one arm. It was bright outside. I squinted up at him, my heart picking up speed.

"Hi." His eyes were soft and warm and looked like they were happy to see me. "You're annoyed. You were expecting me, right?"

"Yes, sorry, come in. This is a leftover annoyed face from the phone call I just finished." I took a step back and opened the door wider.

He walked inside, bringing his Oliver scent with him. I couldn't decide if his scent made him fifty percent more attractive or if that was giving it too much credit.

I shut and locked the door. I wanted to hug him, I needed a hug, but we'd just recommitted to starving ourselves of physical affection so I kept my hands to myself.

He held up his laptop. "Where do you want to do this? Here?" He pointed to the couch that I had obviously just abandoned. My butt print was still on the cushion and everything. Or maybe it was my laptop and empty coffee cup on the table that tipped him off. Or the contract Rob had sent the night before spread across the coffee table, the pages crinkled from my intense study. I hadn't found any new info. It was everything Sloane had claimed it to be the night before.

"Yes, have a seat," I said. "Thanks for bringing it to me. You didn't have to."

"I'm pretty close, remember?"

"Oh yes, did you need to borrow my toilet?"

He gave me his wide smile and perched himself on the edge of the couch. He placed his laptop next to mine while I gathered and stacked the contract pages, attempting to tidy up the space.

"The infamous contract?" he asked.

"When I was twenty-three, signing this thing, I was pretty naïve. I thought this was the first step into the future. I didn't realize it would later become something else holding me back."

"Is it predatory?" he asked in a voice that seemed to say, *Give me one reason to fight Rob and I'm there.*

"No, it's pretty standard. I understand why everything is in here. I just wish it wasn't."

"I'm sorry." He opened his computer and began typing.

"Can I get you anything? Water? Something stronger?"

"I'm good, thank you."

"Okay."

He had sat on the middle cushion of the couch, which made me smile because that meant I had to sit right next to him. And I did. As close as humanly possible without touching.

The muscle in his jaw jumped. He had a nice jaw. It had several days' worth of scruff on it, a look I was fond of. He pulled it off very well. It emphasized the sharp lines of his face even more.

"Can I get your Wi-Fi info?"

"What?" I asked. "I was distracted because you look really good today."

"Just today?" he asked, with a head tilt.

I shrugged. "This is the first time I've noticed."

He laughed. "The Wi-Fi."

"Right." I gestured toward the keyboard and he turned it to face me. I typed in the required password and then leaned back as the Wi-Fi thought hard about connecting.

His phone, which he had set on the coffee table, buzzed with an incoming call. Without meaning to, I looked at the screen. *Sophie.*

I swallowed as a tightness gripped my throat, but he ignored the call and his phone went still.

"You can get it," I said, when it buzzed to life again.

"Just let me make sure . . ." He cringed but stood and walked to the opposite side of the room while swiping to answer. "Hello."

His back was to me and he absentmindedly studied the bookcase full of knickknacks and random things Sloane and I had collected over the years as he listened to whatever the woman on the other end was saying. He picked up a Velma figurine and turned it toward me with a questioning eyebrow raise.

"It's a classy decoration," I said, and he smiled and put it back.

"Soph, it's fine. Mom doesn't hold it against you," he spoke into the phone. "She understands."

My wave of unwanted jealousy from before evaporated.

"Of course I understand. Don't worry about me." He let out the most affectionate low chuckle. "Yes, I will ditch her on her birthday next year to make you feel better." A pause. "You're welcome. I have to go . . . None of your business . . . No. Bye." He hung up the phone and came to sit back down.

"Everything okay?" I asked.

"My sister is feeling bad about missing a birthday dinner in a couple days."

"Does she live close?"

"Relatively. About seven hours north. She has a lot of guilt that I am burdened with Mom. It's not a burden, though, and my sister spent lots of time looking after my mom when I was in college."

"You're a good son," I said.

"I'm an average son."

"And you are apparently a terrible judge of character. Look at all these things I'm learning about you."

He shook his head with a smile and turned his attention back to his laptop.

My phone buzzed in my hand. "Speaking of sisters." I turned the phone to face him.

"Fruit tray?" he asked.

"She's having a barbecue next weekend and I've been granted the opportunity to bring the fruit tray." My voice was laced with sarcasm.

"I take it things aren't . . . better between you two yet?"

"Not really. I mean, I told her that I lied and what really happened and we talked it out but she's still irritated. It's going to take her a minute to get over it."

My phone was still facing him when his expression went slack.

"What?" I asked, turning the phone back to me to see if anything new had come through. It was only our already exchanged texts. The most recent one literally just said fruit salad. The previous texts that he would've been able to see were me apologizing and telling her I had been drunk and how I said stupid things when I was drunk.

Those probably reminded him of my drunken voicemail, of my chaotic nature.

"You ready to see your website?" he asked.

Maybe that's why his expression had changed—he was nervous. I tucked my hands under my thighs and focused on the screen. "Should I be scared? You have a very intense look on your face."

"I've been told I have RBF."

I rolled my eyes. "You have not. Your default is golden retriever."

"What does that mean?" he asked.

"It means you're adorable and ready to please."

"I am," he said in a scratchy voice that my body was fond of.

His finger dropped onto the return key and my brain was not ready for what popped onto the screen. I let out a sharp gasp. The website header was a backlit man, the shadows in front of him spelling out my agency name like we'd talked about. His features were too dark to make out any details, just like I knew they would be. But he looked amazing. His chest, despite the shadows, defined and muscular. The messy bed shone bright behind him, and images of being in that bed with him rushed into my mind along with the emotions attached to them.

"You hate it?" he asked.

"No . . . I . . ." I tried to slow down my racing heart, the throbbing between my legs, with two deep breaths and said airily, "You did all this after I left?"

"Yes. I had some energy I needed to burn off," he said, that sparkle returning to his eyes. "You didn't?"

"Wish you would've done this while I was still there." I nodded toward the shirtless pic.

He let out a throaty laugh. "Then you like it?"

"It's definitely worth a coffee, maybe two."

"I have an option with just the bed too," he said.

"No, I like half-naked men," I teased. "And so will the rest of the world."

"Right," he said, his voice tight.

"No, but really. It's great." I studied his face. His unreadable expression was back. "You didn't . . . I hope I didn't . . . Did you feel guilted into doing that? If so, just the bed is fine. I don't want you to . . ." *Feel pressured into putting yourself online* was how I almost finished that sentence, but instead I trailed off, letting him fill that in however he wanted.

"No, I didn't. The more I looked at the empty image with just the bed, the more I realized you were right. A person would make it more compelling. And after I took some practice shots, I knew you were also right about nobody being able to tell it is me."

"Yes, I like this trend of recognizing I'm right about things."

"And you're still happy with the rest of the site?" He clicked on a few tabs to show me they worked and where each one navigated to.

"So happy," I said.

"Here's that query form we talked about."

"Perfect," I said. "You are amazing."

Again, my phone buzzed on the coffee table, and we both turned toward the screen. I thought it would be another text from my sister deciding I needed more specific instructions than Fruit and Tray, but it wasn't. It was from Rob.

Did you get the contract? it read. At the top of my screen, Rob's name had a little fire emoji next to it. Shit. I'd forgotten to change that to devil horns. I growled.

"Margot." Oliver said my name like a sigh or a whisper. One of those would indicate frustration, the other adoration, and I couldn't decipher which one he intended. His hand was on the couch cushion by my leg and I shifted so that our skin touched, the back of his knuckles rough against the underside of my thigh. His fingers may as well have been made of hot coals the way heat poured down my calf and my cheeks instantly flushed.

The front door swung open and Sloane walked in with two plastic bags, trailed by Miles, who had two bags of his own.

"Oliver, I'm so glad you're here. I have enough Chinese food to feed a football team and not enough mouths to eat it." She nodded over her shoulder. "This is Miles, by the way."

"Hi, nice to meet you," Oliver said, his hand shifting away from my thigh.

"Why so much food?" I asked.

"The office bought it for lunch yesterday, and since I had to swing by the office today, the leftovers became mine." Sloane stopped short of the coffee table on her way toward the kitchen. "Holy shit! Is that your website? That looks hot. Who is . . . Wait, is that . . . ?" Sloane stepped closer, leaning over to get a better look.

"It's a random image from a stock photo site that I paid

for." I tried not to say the words too quickly or too defensively. I had promised Oliver I wouldn't tell Sloane, and considering how much work he had done for me, I was going to fulfill my end of the bargain.

"I thought you were being extra frugal."

"I really am."

"Well, it was worth it." She squinted at the screen. "You decided on *heart*, the word, not *Hart* your name?"

My eyes went back to the screen and sure enough, in my distraction over Oliver's naked torso, I hadn't noticed the shadow spelled H-E-A-R-T instead of H-A-R-T. "Oh, yeah, I meant my last name," I said to Oliver.

"Your last name?" he asked.

"Hart."

"Your last name is Hart?" he asked.

I smiled with the realization that he didn't know my last name, that I didn't know his. "It is. What's yours?"

"Gray," he said somewhat distractedly, because he was changing the spelling of *heart* on his computer.

Oliver Gray. That was a good name.

"Well, your website looks amazing," Sloane said. "You really leaned into your romance branding with this."

"You don't think it's too much?" I asked, suddenly second-guessing myself.

"Do *you* think it's too much?" Oliver asked me.

"It's perfect." Sloane said. "It should open the floodgates of romance authors looking for representation."

I rubbed the back of my neck and nodded.

Sloane gave the image another scrutinizing stare and then turned to face me. "Wait, does this mean it's official? Your website is out in the world and the requests are going to come pouring in?"

"All she has to do is push the publish button," Oliver said. He hovered the arrow over that button but then backed away, leaving the final action for me.

I looked around the room, where each set of eyes seemed to be frozen in anticipation. And then I pushed publish. I was officially an agent.

CHAPTER 25

"What day is it?" I asked Sloane as I dragged myself into the kitchen a few mornings later. She was pouring coffee, dressed for work, but Miles was sitting at the table. I had thought it was Monday, but Miles usually only stayed over on the weekends. Her work clothes said that wasn't the case this time, though. I hadn't worn work clothes in over a week and it felt weird. I kind of missed it.

She laughed but then looked at my face. "Oh, you're serious. It's Tuesday."

"Tuesday?" I looked at Miles. "It can't be."

"It is," he said.

"Since your internal calendar is obviously messed up," Sloane said, "I need to remind you that I'll be out of town starting Thursday for that film festival."

"That's this weekend already?"

"Yes."

I slid around the counter to where she'd been standing and pulled a mug off the mug tree.

"Where has Oliver been?" Miles asked.

"Yeah," Sloane agreed. "He seemed a bit standoffish on Saturday. Did something happen?"

I hesitated with Miles in the room.

"I'll tell him later anyway," she said.

"Fine, Friday night I told him that we should just have sex and get it out of our systems. I think it hurt his feelings." I'd been analyzing how he'd been on Saturday too, and the fact that we hadn't hung out since. That was the only logical conclusion I'd come to.

"You did not!" she all but screamed in my direction. "Why?"

"I don't know! Because we should."

She lowered her brow. "Are you still trying to pretend he's wrong for you?"

"I don't know what I'm doing, Sloane. My life is a mess and maybe now isn't a good time to start something," I said, thinking about what Audrey had advised. "I'm pretty sure Oliver agrees, anyway. The more he hangs out with me, the more he's learning I'm not right for him. I'm too chaotic, too complicated."

"Is that what he said?" she asked.

He *had* said he thought he was complicating my life even more. Which implied he thought it was complicated to begin with. And he'd read those drunken texts I'd sent to my sister.

"Didn't he learn your last name for the first time on Friday?" Miles said, before I could respond. "He probably googled you while sitting on the couch and definitely thinks you're complicated."

Sloane backhanded him across the chest. "Wrong answer."

"Oh," he said. "I mean, *you're* not complicated . . . but your sister's kind of out there, and for a guy who's all but invisible online that kind of notoriety might scare . . ."

Again, Sloane leveled him with a look.

"What I meant is, *life* is complicated and finding a person to navigate the rocky path with makes it feel much smoother," he said in a singsongy voice.

I took a sip of coffee that burned my tongue. I sucked in some air, then said, "Thanks for the wisdom, Miles. And I'll let my sister know you're a huge fan."

Sloane squeezed my arm. "Sorry to leave you in the middle of this crisis, but I have to get to work."

"It is Tuesday, after all," I said.

She kissed my cheek. "Have a good day, honey."

"Thanks, dear." She left the apartment with Miles. I listened as the lock clicked into place. I took my cup of coffee to the couch, then stared at my phone for a moment before googling my name.

The top hit was my sister's channel even though I'd never been on it. The next one was my Instagram page. I clicked on the link and scrolled my page, wondering what Oliver would've found had he decided to look me up after going home. I smiled as memories accompanied the pictures: going to the beach with my friends, my nephews opening Christmas presents, my mom blowing out candles on a cake. I kept going further and further into my history when an old picture of Rob came flitting across the screen. Just Rob, standing outside the agency, pointing at the sign. I clenched my teeth and hit the trash button, deleting it.

Great, I really wasn't making a guy who'd been cheated on twice feel safe. I breathed out a sigh. Whatever. He was the one who'd declared us friends. It wasn't my job to make him feel safe. "We're friends," I said, as if my brain needed it to be spoken out loud to believe it. Why did that word taste so bad in my mouth?

I swiped out of the app and over to my email, checking it once again, like I had been doing obsessively since I published my website on Saturday. Three days and it was still empty.

My other obsession was posting on social media. At first, I'd been super careful about composing the perfect pitch. But since so few people were seeing my posts (based on the likes and reposts), now I just wrote whatever came into my head.

Are you an author looking for a literary agent for your romance novel? Consider someone who is fighting it out in the current dating pool on a quest to find her true love. Me. That's me. #amwriting #litagent #amquerying

I added my website and pressed the publish button.

Doubt spread through every inch of my body. I had thought maybe the clients I shared with Rob would reach out since I wasn't allowed to reach out to them. But they hadn't. Maybe they didn't know I'd left. He certainly wouldn't tell them. If they happened to see my posts, they would know. But what if they didn't? What if nobody saw them? What if I never got a client? What if I never even got a single email? Kari's words—*Call me in several years when you've gotten your feet wet*—pounded through my head.

I had to get out of my head. Laundry. It needed to be done. The sweats I'd been wearing for the last several days could attest to that.

• • •

There was a note on the washer full of wet clothes that read: *Text me if the cycle is done and you need this.* It was followed by a phone number. Since it was the only washer not running at the moment in our apartment's laundry room, I texted the number.

Your clothes are done, I sent, then sat down to wait on one of the three chairs next to the folding table with my basket full of clothes. On my phone, I navigated to my inbox again. Empty.

I opened the book I had brought. It had never taken me so long to finish a book in my life and it wasn't Lord Leopold's fault. He was as rakish as they came. I read a few lines before my phone buzzed me away from the page. It was a GIF in our group chat from Cheryl. I hearted it and then started to put my phone away when I saw Oliver's name below Cheryl's. I clicked on his name and read through our last couple days of texts.

Sunday:

Me: Good morning.

Oliver: Where is the 'beautiful' that's supposed to follow that?

Me: Oh, oops, I must not have highlighted the whole message to paste.

Later:

Oliver: I'm beginning to think I should be offended by the golden retriever thing.

Me: I love golden retrievers.

Oliver: And here I thought you weren't a dog person.

Me: I said I liked some dogs!

Oliver: I think what you said is that some dogs like you.

Me: You're right. I did say that. I guess it's still true.

Oliver: Yes, I am offended.

Monday:

Me: When can I see you again?

Oliver: I have plans with my mom this evening for her birthday, but if you must see me, I have a website you can check out. It's called Hart Lit.

Me: Wait, is that you?! I thought it was some random guy in some random location.

Oliver: It is.

Me: Tell your mom happy birthday from me.

Oliver: Will do. Should I let her listen to your drunken voicemail as well?

Me: You're dead to me.

Our exchanges seemed normal. But he hadn't texted a *good morning* today. In fact, he hadn't initiated conversation at all over the last two days. That was a bad sign. A sense of panic welled up in me. I didn't want to be ghosted by Oliver. I didn't even want to be haunted by him. The thought scared me because I sensed that was exactly what he was doing.

There was no response from wet-clothes person.

I tossed Lord Leopold onto the folding table. Touching other people's clothes, clean or not, gave me the ick, but I grabbed the communal basket and set it on the floor in front of the washer. It was a man, I established very quickly as I pulled out wet T-shirts and athletic shorts and long socks. He wore boxer briefs. Colorful ones. I moved them over, using as little of my thumb and pointer finger as possible, pinching the very corner of the red material.

"Excuse me?" came a deep voice from behind me. I whirled around, underwear still in hand, to see a guy standing in the doorway. He was handsome. Dark hair and dark eyes. He wore a tank and swim trunks. He was even holding a book, like he'd been reading out by the pool while he was waiting for his laundry. "I was coming," he said.

"An *on my way* text is all it would've taken," I said, flinging his underwear into the basket.

"You gave me five minutes." He stepped forward, threw his book next to mine on the table, and joined me at the washer. Our books collided. He was reading Jane Austen.

My eyes went wide, but still I said, "I should've given you no minutes."

"I got this," he said when I reached into the washer for another article of clothing.

I raised my hands and took a step back, then picked up my basket, waiting for him to finish.

"I'm sorry," he breathed out.

"What?"

"I would be annoyed if someone left their clothes too."

His words defused the anger that had obviously been pouring off me. "Yeah . . . thanks. It's okay."

My phone chimed with an email notification. I balanced my basket on my hip and dug out my phone. The word *query*, bold and bright, seemed to shine at me from the subject line of my inbox. My cheeks felt numb and my chest felt like it was going to explode. My first potential client. "Oh my god."

"Is everything okay?" Laundry Man asked.

"What? Oh, yes. I just . . . Are you done?" I shoved my phone into my pocket and pointed to the washer.

"Yes," he said, moving to the dryer across the aisle.

I dumped my clothes into the washing machine as fast as possible, sloppily poured my detergent, and shut the lid. It slammed in my haste and I startled. "Sorry." I pushed the normal wash cycle button and rushed for the door, empty basket in hand.

"Hey," Laundry Man called from behind me. I turned. "Is this your book?"

"Oh, yes, thank you." I tried to grab it from him but he held on.

"What's your name?" he asked.

"What?" I asked.

"I'm Aaron."

I laughed a little. Wasn't that the name I had assigned to Oliver on our first date?

"Is that funny?" Aaron asked.

"Oh, no, it just reminded me of something. Hi, nice to meet you. I have to go."

"Can I text you sometime?"

I stopped cold.

"I mean," he said with a shy smile, "you were holding my underwear when we met. How can I not ask?"

"Oh," I said. He was right, that was a pretty epic meet-cute. But I found I didn't care. There was only one person I wanted to see right now, be with, tell my query news to. I wanted Oliver, and not just because he made me feel like I was full of molten lava every time we were together. But because he was funny and thoughtful and sweet. "No, I'm sorry. You're cute but I have a . . . a someone."

"Good luck to you and your someone," he said.

I made it back to my apartment in record time, then pulled out my phone, ready to call Oliver and profess my like to him. But when I tapped the screen, my email box was still open, my very first query waiting there. I'd almost forgotten.

I looked around the living room. Where did I want to be when I read it? This was the moment I'd picture for years. By my bookshelves? No, my room was a mess right now. On the balcony with the slight breeze blowing through my hair? *Not everything has to be a scene out of a book*—the voice in my head was Audrey's.

I sat on the couch and pulled up the email.

Dear Ms. Hart, it started. I smiled at those words.

I saw your website and knew you would be perfect for my adult romance.

"Thank you, shirtless Oliver," I whispered.

Imagine a world where there is only one man.

"Oof. I don't know if I want to."

He is only good for one thing. We all know what that is.

"His sperm?" I guessed.

But he falls in love and can't bring himself to be with anyone but her. He would give up the entire future population for his one true love.

"Are there are no sperm banks in this world? Or cups? Or turkey basters?"

How will humanity survive? Is love worth everything?

There were a couple more lines about how long the book was and what genre it fell into best and then a little about the author. I sighed and closed my email. It wasn't the worst query I'd ever read. That counted for something. And it was the first one ever specifically addressed to me. *That* was a milestone. My eyes fell on the mug I'd left on the coffee table that morning still half-full, crusty coffee around the rim. I should've read the email on the balcony.

I checked the time on my phone. Ten thirty A.M. Oliver's

gym time. That was the one good thing about having such a regimented schedule: I knew where to find him. I'd gotten my first query solely based off the website that wouldn't have existed without him. I owed the man a coffee. Was I fabricating an excuse to see him? Absolutely.

CHAPTER 26

"Membership number?" the woman behind the counter at the entrance said.

I held the coffee up. "Just here for a delivery." Maybe I should've waited in my car. That was my intention as I drove over here: to catch Oliver as he was leaving. But the motivation to surprise him had come over me as I parked the car.

"Someone ordered a coffee delivery to the gym?"

"Yep."

"Just leave it here and I'll call them up front. Who's it for?"

"I have to hand deliver it. That's what is in the instructions." I said all this while walking past her. I was surprised when she just shrugged and went back to flipping through papers on the desk.

The gym smelled like rubber and sweat and lemon-scented cleaning products as I wound my way through the cardio section, full of stair-steppers and treadmills and stationary bikes. It wasn't until I was almost to the free weights section that it occurred to me that Oliver might not want to see me. What if he had come to the opposite conclusion I had in the past few days—that he *didn't* like me? I stutter-stepped past a man at the squat rack, hesitating. But then I saw Oliver toward the back. He wore a T-shirt, shorts, and a black pair of running shoes. I was hoping for more exposed skin, like the man standing next to him at the squat rack in a sleeveless shirt and short shorts, but that wasn't Oliver, I was learning. My heart expanded in my chest and I finished my walk.

"I'm here to settle a debt," I said.

Oliver, a dumbbell in each hand, met my eyes in the mirror he stood in front of. A smile that filled me with hope lit up his face. "And you thought this was the perfect time for settling debts?" He took in my outfit: a pair of ripped jeans, a tank top, some flip-flops.

"I was hoping for more skin, but yes," I said.

"I'm showing my calves." He extended one out for me to get a better look.

"Beautiful," I said.

He reracked his dumbbells and turned to face me. "I'm pretty picky about my coffee."

"Based on the one time I saw you drink it, I think I know your order. But in case I'm wrong, I have a backup option in the car."

"You can tell someone's order just by looking at it."

"It's one of my superpowers."

He narrowed his eyes and reached for the iced coffee I held. He took a sip.

"Am I right?"

His eyebrows popped up in surprise. "Yes."

"Really?"

"No."

I laughed. "I have one more chance. When you're done here, though. Keep working out." I sat on the nearest bench as if I was ready for the show.

"I can be done."

"No, no, finish. I really didn't mean to make you stop. I was just too excited."

"To bring me coffee?"

"No, I got my first query today." I assumed he remembered what the word *query* meant from helping me with the website.

"Someone wants you to be their agent?"

I nodded, feeling a little choked up all of a sudden.

He took two big steps forward and used his hand that wasn't holding the coffee he didn't want to pull me up off the bench and into a tight one-armed hug. "Congratulations," he said against my temple.

He was slightly sweaty and warm, which sent a shot of energy straight through me, leaving me buzzing. "It probably won't result in anything," I said, clinging to his shoulders. How could I miss someone so much that I'd only seen in person a handful of times? "It takes a hundred queries to get a few promising ones."

"It's a step worth celebrating."

I nodded. That's why I was here. He was the first person I wanted to tell. "I was so scared nobody was going to email me."

"I had no doubts," he said. Someone dropping a weight bar behind him rang out.

My cheeks felt warm and my heart fluttery. "I got a query, Oliver."

"You did."

I used his shoulders to push away from him, look him in the eyes, and yell, "I got a query!"

He smiled big. "You did," he responded in an inside voice.

"I'm going to get you your real coffee from my car." I took the one from his hand and dropped it in a trash can to our right. "Prepare to be impressed."

"I would've drank that," he said.

"The designer of my perfect website deserves his real coffee order."

I headed for the exit. Out of the corner of my eye I saw him pick up a duffel bag and towel near the weight rack and jog after me.

"Thank you," I said to the front desk lady.

"Did you get a good tip?" she asked.

"The best," I said, thinking about that warm, sweaty hug.

"Have a good day, Oliver," she said as I pushed open the door.

"You too," he responded.

I slowed my walk so he could catch up and steered us toward my car. We passed his on the way and he deposited his duffel bag in the trunk.

"Welcome to my car," I said when we arrived. "I know you've met her before, but you didn't get a proper introduction due to the whole, you know . . ."

"Crying thing?" he asked.

I smiled. "Exactly. Anyway, this is Persephone." I opened the passenger door for him.

"Persephone?"

"Yes, I've always been dramatic. She's been with me for

eleven of her thirteen years of life and, despite her namesake's ties to the underworld, she's never done me dirty."

"You got her when you were sixteen?"

"I did."

He pointed to the door I was still holding open. "Are you wanting me to sit in the car?"

"Yes. You must sit and relax with your coffee for a few minutes. You and your muscles have earned it."

I shut the door after he climbed in and walked around to the other side. Once sitting down, I set my phone on the center console and gathered the drink from the cup holder, presenting it to him like a prize. "Since you wouldn't let me pay you for the website, I have to pretend like this is more valuable than it is."

"It's priceless," he said.

I waited eagerly while he took his first sip. He tested it like a glass of wine on a vineyard tour. "Did you hear me order at the coffee shop?"

"I didn't. I'm just that good."

When he didn't seem to buy that explanation, I said, "I've been someone's assistant for four years. I've seen a lot of drinks. Plus, I saw a couple of the letters they wrote on your cup." I admitted.

He laughed. "You pay attention." His eyes drifted to the gym. "Really pay attention."

"You told me your schedule. And you're a schedule guy. Like my sister. Remember? I knew you'd be here."

"Right, like your sister. Predictable," he muttered. "Where's yours?"

"My schedule? You know I don't have one of those. Organized chaos."

"No, where's your coffee?"

"If I got one for myself yours wouldn't seem so special."

He chuckled.

I swallowed, not sure how to tell him what I wanted to tell him. *I like you* seemed too flippant. I didn't want him to think I was just telling him because I wanted to sleep with him. Because even though I really really wanted that, I wanted other things more—his calming presence, his contagious laugh, his cheesy jokes . . . him.

The timer on my phone screen caught his attention. Fourteen minutes and thirty-four, thirty-three, thirty-two . . . "Am I on the clock?"

"Sorry, I have clothes in the dryer as we speak." I had moved them over right before I came, wishing I hadn't discovered my feelings for Oliver *after* I'd started the washing machine. "Fourteen more minutes before I become the annoying person who leaves clothes in the communal laundry."

"I only have fourteen more minutes with you?"

You have all the time you want, I almost said. "You better make them good," is what I actually said.

His eyes darted to my lips and my stomach fluttered. But instead of doing anything, he took another drink of his iced coffee. "Tell me about the query."

"Last-man-on-Earth-in-a-sea-of-women type of story. I read the first five pages of the manuscript that were included with the email. Not a compelling start, and since I'm not in love with the premise to begin with, I'll pass."

"So what do you do, then? Tell her no, thanks?"

"Basically. That's the hardest part of the job. But just because her story wasn't for me, doesn't mean someone else won't love it."

"Is this how you soften rejection at the end of bad dates as well? Tell them someone else will love their less-than-lovable qualities?"

I laughed, then put on my best end-of-date voice. "Just because you're not for me doesn't mean someone else's standards aren't lower."

"Maybe someone else will have no feelings or self-esteem and love you so very much," he added to my pretend conversation.

"No, but really. Everyone has different tastes. In books *and* men."

"Speaking of, is your taste that book you had me read? Cash."

"Who's Cash?"

"The love interest in the book I borrowed."

"Oh, I have no idea. I remember liking the book, but I don't remember what Cash is like. I like all different kinds of book heroes." I tried to remember the specifics when suddenly it occurred to me that Cash was a bad boy. He was the *cuss at random strangers and animals but who was secretly hurting inside* type of guy. "No. Some heroes are fun to read about but in reality they'd be dicks. Cash would make a terrible boyfriend."

"So you're telling me I shouldn't develop pyromania?" he asked. "On the side."

"No . . ." My heart pounded against my ribs, trying to beat out of my chest. "You're just right."

"We are very different."

"You and Cash? I know."

"No, you and me."

My heart seemed to fall to my feet. Was he trying to break things off with me just when I'd discovered my feelings for him? "Is this about Rob?" I blurted. "Are you worried there's still something between us? I promise I am completely over him. That stupid fire emoji next to his name proves how little I pull his number up on my phone. I forgot it was there. And I deleted that picture from my Insta."

He nodded slowly. "That's good."

"I don't want you to worry about him."

"I don't," he said.

"Then what? Is it my sister?"

His brows shot down as if confused.

"I know it seems like she's a big deal, but she keeps us out of her small corner of fame. She's never put me on her channel. Never even asked to. It's very much a separate world from us. You would never be put on the internet. I know you hate that thought."

His eyes went to the countdown on my phone. Four minutes. Why had I started that stupid countdown? I would leave my clothes in the dryer forever for this man.

"I like you," I said. "I know I haven't done a good job of showing it, but I do."

He picked up my hand, brought my fingers to his lips, and rested them there for several moments. His lips were soft and his breath was warm. "My mom thinks you're pretty, by the way. I showed her some pictures when I took her to dinner yesterday."

"You were talking about me?" I asked, hope returning to my soul.

"Yes."

I smiled. "And she said, *Stop thinking so much and just be with the girl already*?"

He let out an amused breath. "Yes, actually, but there's something I need to—"

My phone's alarm went off, cutting his sentence short. I turned it off and we stared at each other for a moment. I could see some sort of resignation in his expression and he opened his mouth to speak again.

"I gave you time," I blurted. "Will you just wait?"

"What?"

"Whatever you are going to say, will you just wait? Give *me* time. I grow on people too." His trust issues were creating some kind of wall, I was sure of it. We just needed to spend a little more time together and he'd see that. I wasn't willing to give up yet. Not when my pulse was racing and my head was spinning and my heart was bursting just being in his presence, feeling what I felt.

"Time . . ."

I nodded.

"Okay," he said softly. "We'll take some time." He leaned over and pressed the softest kiss onto my cheek. "Thanks for the coffee, Margot." He climbed out of the car.

I reached for my door handle to go after him. To say what, I wasn't sure, but at least to give him a goodbye hug. But my phone rang, stopping me. The words maybe Kari Cross shone on my screen. She had *never* called me on my cell. I didn't even have her as a contact. Whatever powers that operated my phone were guessing that it was her. We'd only talked via email or on the office phone.

"Hello?" I answered.

"Hi, Margot."

"I'm sorry I don't have notes for you yet," I said.

"No, that's not what this is about. And I'm sorry to call you on your cell."

"It's okay." How had she even gotten my cell? Had Rob given it to her?

"You're right," Kari said.

"About what?" I asked.

"My setting is terrible, nonexistent, and I don't think it's gotten any better in my latest iteration."

"Completely fixable," I said.

"With a trip to my inspired location," she said.

"Exactly. Nothing a weekend in Paso Robles wouldn't solve."

"I couldn't agree more. That's why I was hoping you would go for me."

"I'm sorry, what? *Go* for you?"

"If you could go and take detailed notes and pictures, maybe even video for me, that would be so helpful. The location is only four hours from you."

"Kari." I fiddled with my car keys hanging from the ignition.

"I'll pay you. I know you're starting your career right now and left your old one . . . unexpectedly. I'm sure you could use the money. I'll pay for your hotel, your food, and your time."

I should've said no, especially considering the contract Rob had sent over, but I wasn't propositioning her. She was asking for research, not representation, anyway, so the words "How much?" came out of my mouth. I had my savings, but that wasn't going to last forever. I needed to supplement it soon if I hoped to survive in this industry. Even if I got a client tomorrow and sold their book the next day, I knew how long contracts took. I was at least a month, probably three, away from *any* money. And realistically, that timetable was very delusional.

"Five hundred," she said.

Was I about to go from being Rob's personal assistant to Kari's? I wanted to say no, but how could I? I was desperate, with zero prospects on the horizon. "Okay." There was no other answer.

"Great! Thank you so much! You're a lifesaver. If this book ever gets published, you'll be at the top of the acknowledgments."

For all the work I was putting in, I deserved the dedication page. "Hart is my last name," I said, even though I knew she was half kidding. But just in case she'd been serious, maybe my name in the back of one of her books could get me a Google search or two.

"I'll send over the details. I already booked you a hotel."

"Already . . . You . . . When do you want me to do this?"

"This weekend."

Of course she did. But why not? I had literally forgotten what day of the week it was because there was nothing on my schedule. Four hours away wasn't bad, I could even make it back on Sunday for my sister's barbecue. "Yes, send me the details."

We hung up the phone and I peered out my side window, but Oliver's car was gone.

CHAPTER 27

I turned my key in the ignition for the fifth time, and like the four other times before it, my car let out a choking sound that faded into nothingness. My bags for the weekend in Paso were in the trunk and I was ready to go. Of course my car would choose now to die on me. After I'd just boasted to Oliver that she had never let me down.

I picked up my phone and dialed my dad's number.

"Hello, love," was how he answered.

"Hi, Dad. I'm going to let you listen to a sound and you are going to try to guess what it means."

"Ooh, I love this game," he said. "Okay, ready."

I held my phone away from my ear, put him on speaker, and turned the key again.

"Um . . ." he said as though seriously pondering. "The beginning of a song? A dying cat?"

"It's my car. What do you think it means?"

"Did you mistake me for your dad who is a mechanic?"

"No, but I thought I'd have a better chance with you than Mom."

"Because I'm a man?" he asked.

"Because you drive an older car that I assume has broken down more."

"True," he said. "But I have no clue."

I groaned. "How would you like to let me borrow a car this weekend to drive four hours away?"

"When would you need it?"

"Now? And I'd need you to drive here and drop it off."

"Oh, hon, you know I'd do anything for you."

"If the word *but* comes next in that sentence then I don't know that," I teased.

He laughed. "I'm sorry. Your mom is running errands all day in our only reliable car."

"No, it's okay, I understand. I'll see you Sunday."

"Good luck."

I could rent a car, but that would render the moneymaking aspect of this weekend pointless. I dialed another number.

"Hi," he answered after a few rings, a smile in his voice. "How are you?"

"Meh. Do you know anything about cars?" I hadn't seen Oliver since Tuesday. We'd exchanged texts every day and I felt like we'd fallen right back into the friendship we'd had for the past several weeks, like I hadn't confessed my like for him three days ago. I tried not to think about how sad that made me feel.

"Because I'm a man?"

I snorted out some air. "You are the second person to say that to me today."

"I was your second call?"

"My dad was my first. Sloane would've been my second but she's out of town at a film festival." Her car parked at the airport forty-five minutes away, useless to me. "You're my third choice."

"Ouch," he responded.

"Listen closely." I turned the ignition.

"Battery?" he said. It was obviously a guess. "Starter? I don't know, Margot. I'm pretty useless in the car knowledge department."

"You don't have an extra car that I can borrow for the weekend lying around, do you?"

"Only one that comes with me attached to it."

I paused, staring at the logo in the middle of the steering wheel, assessing his sentence. "Are you offering to take me?"

"Where exactly?"

"I'm doing a research trip to Paso Robles for an author."

"Oh . . . I . . ."

His hesitation spoke volumes. We were obviously in two completely different places. I wasn't going to beg someone to like me back. My eyes stung and I blinked several times, trying not to be hurt over this. "Never mind. You don't have to take me, Oliver."

"Can I get back to you? If I can move one thing on my schedule, I will."

My heart thudded twice and I wanted to say *Yes, please*, but I heard myself say, "No, I can't let you do that," instead.

"How else am I going to get my coffee fix?"

"This favor is worth more than a coffee," I said.

"Two coffees?" he asked.

"This is worth a weekend of favors. I will provide as many as you like," I said, a smirk coming onto my face.

"You're terrible," he said.

"I don't know where your mind went. I meant that I'd buy you food all weekend."

He laughed. "I'll call you back."

"Okay . . . thank you," I said, realizing he really was my only hope to make this happen. And his willingness to do it made me think that maybe we were closer to the same place than I thought. Maybe time really was what he needed.

. . .

I threw my small suitcase in his open trunk, shut it, then joined him in the car with my backpack. His car was pretty—a Lexus, with leather seats and fancy gadgets and screens.

"This is a new car," I said, running my hand over the tan dash. "Not the one I have a history with."

"You had a history with my car?" he teased.

"Yes, we were good together. So. Good. He held me up when I needed support. Cradled my ass perfectly."

He laughed. "Hopefully you and this car will get along just as well."

"We can test that out right now." I patted the console as if assessing its capabilities.

He nodded toward the screen. "How about we start with an address. See if it can handle that much."

I gave him the address and he entered it in as I buckled my seat belt.

"I packed snacks." He pointed to a bag on the floorboard behind his seat. "If you're a road-trip-snacks type of woman."

"Is there any other type of woman?" I lifted my backpack. "I also brought snacks. Should we see if our snacking tastes match up?"

He pulled out onto the road as the robotic voice of his navigation system prompted him to turn right at the end of the street. "Yes, reveal your snacks."

I pulled out a bag of kettle-cooked salt-and-vinegar potato chips. "First must-have."

"Not surprised by your choice in flavor."

"What's that supposed to mean?"

"Very bold, is all."

"I like bold." I pulled out the next offering.

"Licorice?" he asked.

"Red Vines, specifically."

"Staple," he said.

"And finally, so much chocolate." I pulled out a bag of Reese's mini cups, some milk chocolate Dove Promises, and some Rolos.

"Are we going to be celebrating cavities by the end of the weekend?"

"I have excellent teeth-brushing habits. What did you bring?"

He blindly reached behind him, feeling around for his snack bag.

"I'll get it. You concentrate on driving."

"I can do both at the same time."

I slapped his hand away and picked up the bag, then reached in to reveal his first offering. A bag of veggie straws. "What in the healthy-living hell is this?"

"They are healthy *and* delicious." His other options were similar: raw almonds, banana chips, and coconut granola clusters.

"This is how you keep your body looking like it does, isn't it? My website thanks you."

He chuckled. "How do you explain how yours looks so good?"

My cheeks warmed with the compliment. "You haven't seen me half naked, and until you do, you might want to keep those compliments to yourself."

"I've *felt* a lot of you and I stand by my compliment," he said in a low voice.

My eyebrows popped up. Oliver had obviously decided to put all his worries about us away for the weekend or maybe he worked something out in his head over the last couple days, took his mom's advice, because flirty Oliver was back. This thought made my chest expand. "Does your car have a name?"

"The car," he said, straight-faced.

"Very creative," I returned. "I'll think of something better by the end of the trip."

"Do you road-trip a lot?" he asked.

"Not much. You?"

"I've done my fair share. Growing up, my parents made it a mission to take us to as many national parks as possible."

"That's cool. I've only been to a few. What are your top three favorite?"

"Yosemite, Zion, and Glacier," he said like he'd answered that question a hundred times. Maybe it was a first-date go-to.

"I've never been to any of those."

"You've never been to Yosemite? You live in California!"

"I've been to Joshua Tree."

He laughed. "Are you claiming that's the same thing?"

"No, I'm claiming I've been to at least one national park in California so you don't think I'm uncultured."

"Are you trying to impress me?" he asked.

"Only if it's working," I said.

At one point I had thought Oliver was easy to read, but I had been fooling myself, because I had no idea what he was thinking.

My phone buzzed in my backpack with an email notification. I reached for it to make sure it wasn't Kari with some last-minute instructions.

It wasn't Kari.

"Another query," I said.

"Number two?"

"This actually makes five."

"Five? That's great!"

"Yes," I said. "It is pretty great."

"Any promising candidates?"

"So far, no." I held up my phone. "But maybe it's this one. I should read it. Do you want to hear it?"

"Yes," Oliver said. "Desperately."

Those words made me want to kiss him all over again. I turned my attention back to my phone. "Okay, get ready to be blown away by a love story."

CHAPTER 28

"That was . . . really good," he said.

My eyes hadn't left my phone and they were still there as I scrolled back through the first five pages of the manuscript that Marissa, the author, had included in her email. "It was *very* good, Oliver."

"Keep reading."

"That's all there is. It's part of my submission requirements: just the first five pages."

"You'll ask for more?"

"Immediately." I pushed the reply button on my email and typed: Such a strong start! Will you send me the rest as soon as you can? Thank you so much.—Margot "Let's hope she's as obsessive at checking her email as I am."

. . .

I had been glued to my screen for most of the drive, reading the three queries that had come in right after Marissa's. It was like the universe was pouring out good vibes. Each query came with the first five pages of the manuscript included. I'd read them all out loud to Oliver and we discussed the strengths and weaknesses of each. It was nice to have a sounding board. And he was good at the job too. Out of the three additional choices, there was one that was promising, so I had sent her a request for the full manuscript. By the time we arrived at our hotel, I was buzzing with positive energy.

As I got out of the car, shouldered my backpack, and retrieved my suitcase from the trunk, I assessed our surroundings. It definitely had small-town vibes. It was both picturesque, with its blue skies and yellow hills, and unremarkable at the same time. That would be my job this weekend, to figure out what made this place unique, what could make the setting pop on the page and not just be every other generic small town.

Because my brain had been engaged the entire drive here and because before today Oliver wasn't a part of this weekend, it took until now, heading into the hotel, to think about the sleeping arrangements for the weekend.

I must've hesitated as we walked to the counter just enough, because Oliver said, "I'll get my own room."

"What? No. Why? Kari Cross is paying. We can handle a room together, can't we? I'll keep my hands to myself," I said. *If you want me to,* I added in my head.

"I'll get my own," he insisted.

I held back my frustrated sigh. So much for thinking he'd figured out how he felt. "I'll pay you back."

"No, you won't," he said.

I was waiting for the woman behind the counter to tell us there weren't any rooms left and we would, in fact, have to share one. But the universe wasn't in the habit of granting my storybook fantasies, because she handed us two keys.

I pocketed mine. "Are you from around here, Bree?" I asked, reading her name tag. "Or know this area well?"

"Yes, born and raised," she said.

"Is there anywhere around here where the internet is bad? Like famously bad? Somewhere off the beaten path where people might go to hide out, make out, or bury a body?"

She just stared at me, her expression going slack.

"It's for research," Oliver added. "For a book. She's not planning to bury a body."

I smiled. "I mean, I was, but now you've found me out."

"She's kidding," Oliver said. I wondered if I was making him uncomfortable or if he was just feeling sorry for the wide-eyed Bree.

"Yes, actually," she said. "Lots of teens hang out at the abandoned silos just north of here because it's a cell phone dead zone back in the hills. Their parents can't track them." She pulled a paper map out of a plastic holder on the counter and pointed to where I assumed these silos existed.

"Perfect. One more question, on the opposite end. What do locals do for fun?"

"Tourists are big on vineyard tours. But if you want to hang out with locals—"

"Which we do," I assured her.

"Then I would say Boots and Spurs." Her finger moved on the map to the center of town. "They have line dancing there tomorrow night. It gets pretty rowdy in the best way," she said.

"We can't wait to see what that means," I said. "We're there."

"She is there," Oliver said. "I'm just the Uber driver."

"It's true, he is. But when I asked him to come inside with me, he said yes. Don't report him to corporate, okay?" I said.

He gave me a side-eye but didn't tell her I was kidding this time.

"I won't," she said. "We respect our patrons' privacy."

"As any good hotel would." I patted my pocket where the key was and grabbed the handle of my suitcase. "Thanks again."

We walked away and were silent all the way to the elevator. When I pushed the button, Oliver said, "You're the worst."

I laughed. "Sorry, sometimes I just say whatever comes into my head. My sister says I lead with my emotions instead of my logic. Something I obviously need to work on if I want to be a shark agent and not a teddy-bear one. Her words, again."

"I thought it was funny," he said. "And I like teddy bears." That last sentence he'd said under his breath, almost like he was talking to himself.

Winged creatures took flight in my stomach as I stepped inside the elevator. He pushed the button for the third floor, the highest floor of this hotel.

"Do you have a best friend, Oliver?"

"I do."

"What's he like?"

"He moved up to Seattle for work. Got married a couple years ago. Has a baby on the way."

"Is that why you asked me if I'd ever been to Seattle?"

"I don't know why I asked you that. Probably. I was nervous."

"Do you visit Seattle a lot to see him?"

"Maybe twice a year."

I leaned back against the railing next to him. He mimicked my position, our shoulders bumping. "You really won't line dance with me tomorrow? For research?"

"I'm not big on making a fool of myself."

"I'm *so* big on you making a fool of yourself," I said, smiling his way. "No, but really, everyone will be doing it, so nobody will be watching you."

"Except you," he said.

"I'll be recording so that I can blackmail you into deleting that voicemail of me you have."

His throaty laugh was my favorite.

"You didn't seem nervous, by the way," I said. "On our second first date."

"You make me nervous," he said softly.

Was that a good thing?

The elevator dinged and the doors opened.

"What was with the burying-bodies question?" He put a hand on my lower back as if I didn't know how to leave the elevator on my own. I didn't mind the direction.

The wheels on my suitcase echoed through the empty hall as we walked. "I told you about this book, right? How the AI controls the town?"

"Oh, right. Yes, you did."

"There's this point where the main characters, Ana and Alan, need to talk without being listened to or detected, and right now that scene feels like it exists in white space. No real setting. I'm hoping to find some options while we're here."

"I see," he said. "Abandoned silos could work."

"They could."

We may not have been sharing a room, but we were neighbors. We each used our key at the same time, the green lights on our respective door handles flashing together.

"Back here in thirty minutes?" I asked, indicating the hall. "And we can check this place out." It was only three o'clock, plenty of day left to explore the even smaller surrounding towns and find the silos.

He nodded and disappeared into his room. I flung my suitcase onto the bed, then turned in a circle. A bathroom, desk, a mini fridge, a microwave, a king-sized bed, a slider out to a balcony, and on the wall that separated my room from Oliver's . . . a door. I walked over to it and opened it to reveal another door. I knocked.

A minute later, he opened it with a smile.

"Hi," I said. "We have adjoining rooms. Just thought you should know."

He laughed and I shut and locked my door.

"You're a goof!" he called out through it.

"I know!" I called back.

I placed my palm on his closed door as if my energy could somehow convince him that he needed to drop the last of his reservations, the ones that kept him from jumping on the opportunity to share a room with me. *No, it wouldn't be weird*, he could've said. *Why would it be? I want to ravage you all night anyway.*

I sighed and went to my suitcase on the bed, unzipping it and flopping it open. I dug around in my toiletries bag until I accepted the fact that I had forgotten my toothpaste. Audrey had a packing list she consulted before trips. I was sure she'd never forgotten her toothpaste.

I marched back over to the adjoining door, unlocked it, and swung it open, then let out a yelp when Oliver was standing in the frame, his door already opened.

"Sorry," he said, "I didn't mean to scare you. I was just going to ask if you have the Wi-Fi password on your key sleeve." He held his up. "It's not on mine."

"Maybe?" I walked to the dresser where I'd deposited my key. "It's Paso7."

"Thanks." Then, as if remembering I had opened the door before he'd knocked, he said, "Did you need something?"

"I forgot toothpaste. Do you have some or should I ask the front desk?"

"I have some. Do you need it now?"

I nodded.

He disappeared into his room and came back with a full-sized tube of Colgate. "Didn't you brag about being excellent at dental hygiene recently?"

"Shhh," I teased, taking the toothpaste. "I'll bring it right back."

I left my side of the door open and he did the same with his as I carried the toothpaste to my bathroom. This was going to be a hard weekend if one of us still had his walls up and the other wanted to strip down naked and splay herself across his bed to see how well he could control his hands then. Oh how I hoped he couldn't control them at all.

"Stop it, Margot," I mumbled. "He's doing you a favor. And it's not the first one."

"You talking to yourself?" he called.

How had he heard? "Yes," I said.

He poked his head into my room. I peered out of the bathroom, a toothbrush hanging from my mouth.

"What are you telling yourself?" he asked.

"That I hope this place has good food," I said.

"Me too," he agreed.

I smiled, then picked up his toothpaste and handed it back to him. "Thanks," I said around the toothbrush still in my mouth. "I'll be ready in twenty."

He shut the door between us. I went back into the bathroom, spit out the toothpaste, and rinsed out my mouth. If I didn't wash my hair, twenty minutes was plenty of time for a cold shower.

CHAPTER 29

"Is that it?" Oliver asked. We'd been driving on back roads, winding through grass-covered hills, past vineyards, and farms. My phone didn't have directions to the abandoned silos, but there were several social media posts I'd found that gave vague clues. On the journey so far, I'd taken lots of videos and pictures for Kari that she would love.

"I think so," I said. "Pull over up there on that dirt turnout."

He did just that and turned off the car. There were cows grazing in a field across the street, but other than that there were no signs of life. I approached the shoulder-high steel-mesh fence that was keeping us from the silos, which were a good hundred feet away. Every twenty feet or so along the fence was a thick round wooden post. I assessed the scalability of one and found it lacking. Running horizontally along the top of the fence was a long, thin wire.

"Do you think it's electric?"

"You're not climbing over this." He pointed to the no-trespassing sign zip-tied to a section of fencing.

"Of course I am. Bree said the silos were abandoned. That probably means no power, right? How else do the rebel teens get in there?"

"Maybe there's a back way or cut fencing somewhere."

I wiggled my eyebrows at him, then stuck the toe of my shoe into one of the squares of the metal fencing. It didn't fit well but it was good enough. But first I had to see if this thing was going to electrocute me.

I reached up only to be pulled back by my waist and wrapped up from behind in a bear hug by Oliver. "Are you serious right now?" he said by my ear, his arms pinning mine to my sides.

"So protective. My parents would give you a gold star." I leaned against him. "It was just going to be a fast tap. The cows touch it, right? It can't be that bad."

"People have died from being electrocuted."

"From a cattle fence? I doubt it. And even so, people have died everywhere," I said. "Even during sex. We can't live life in fear."

"Some risks are worth taking," he responded. "Some aren't."

"Which one of those examples is worth it? The fence? Or sex?"

"Funny," he said. "At least find a stick or something."

"For which one of those examples?"

His laugh vibrated against my back and I closed my eyes, soaking it in.

He held me for a few moments longer, perhaps weighing whether I was going to go straight to the wire again, like a child who'd been told no but couldn't help herself. Or maybe he wanted to feel me against him for as long as possible. I wasn't complaining; his arms felt good around me. *He* felt good.

Finally, he let go.

The ground surrounding us was just gravel, dirt, yellowing tall grass, and wildflowers. Not a tree or stick in sight. While he continued to search, I had another idea. I removed the thin hoodie I was wearing, moved to one of the posts, then flung my hoodie over the top wire so it draped down on either side of the fence. By the time Oliver looked over with a protest, I was already scaling it, my hoodie acting as a buffer for any current that might've existed.

With the help of the post, I jumped down on the other side. "You coming?" I asked him.

He pressed a button on his key fob, causing the alarm on his car to give a single honk, tucked the fob into his pocket, and followed me over.

The grass we walked through now was thigh high and several foxtails clung to my socks as we traveled through it. We reached the bottom of the first silo and I looked up. It was much taller than it seemed from the road. There was a rusty ladder on the side that led all the way to an opening at the peaked roof.

"Don't even think about it," he said.

I got out my phone and started recording for Kari. "It's just a little rusty," I teased.

He pointed to a door at the bottom.

"If this thing is full of grain, will opening that door result in us being buried?" I asked.

"I'll take my chances with the door over the ladder," he said, apparently knowing I was going to try one or the other.

"We should give Bree the MVP award. This makes a pretty cool backdrop for secret meetings." I turned a three-sixty, zooming in on the cows and hills across the way and a caved-in barn next to us. I ended my spin back on Oliver, where I zoomed in on his ass.

"So cool," he said, studying the door, oblivious to my gaze.

I turned the camera to my socks and the foxtails burrowing through the material, scratching my skin. I reached down and plucked them out, then held one up for the camera. "Include one of these, Kari," I said.

A grunting sound had me swinging my camera back to Oliver, who was tugging on the door of the silo. It finally gave way with a loud creak. No grain poured out of the opening. I followed him inside. The smell was stale, and aside from a single beam of light shining down like a heavenly manifestation from the hole directly above us, it was dark.

I walked over to a pile of grain on the far side that was taller than me. "How does this get in here? From that hole?"

"No clue," he said. "But I don't think that's fresh. It's been here awhile."

I turned so my back faced the pile, held my hands out to my sides, then did a trust fall backward. "Oof," I said as I landed. "Not as soft as I thought it was going to be."

"I wish I'd gotten that on video."

A tickling sensation on my arm prompted me to scratch it. That's when I saw a small weevil crawling across my skin. I shrieked, stood up, and began brushing myself off while spinning in a circle and chanting, "Bugs, bugs, bugs." I flipped my head over and shook out my hair. "Are there any more on me?"

"Stand still and let me look." Oliver turned on his phone's flashlight.

I went very still.

He inspected my back, then circled around to my front, where his eyes took in every inch of me. He smoothed my hair as he searched there, then brushed a strand off my face and met my eyes. "You're clear."

His hand hovered near my face, his flashlight still on me like it was highlighting every thought in my head.

"Oliver . . ."

A gust of wind burst into the silo, disturbing the grain as the air followed the path of least resistance out the top. It was followed by the loud slamming of the door. I jumped with the noise and Oliver let out a nervous laugh.

"Maybe Kari can claim the silo is haunted and that's what interferes with the signal." His hands retreated back to their space.

"It could be a thriller/romance/horror/ghost story."

He walked over to the door and turned the handle. "She's already bending genres. Might as well add one more." He pushed on the door but it remained closed.

I laughed.

He pushed again, with his shoulder this time. "It's stuck." He rammed his shoulder into it. Nothing.

"Are you kidding?" I asked, walking over to him. "Tell me you're kidding."

"I'm not." He stepped aside to let me try.

I definitely didn't think I was stronger than him, but this felt like a prank to me, so I tried. It didn't budge.

"Good news," Oliver said, looking at his phone.

"What?" I asked.

"You can tell Kari that inside a grain silo would be the perfect place for no cell service."

I held up my phone. No bars. Then I laughed. It was a disbelieving laugh or a laugh that found this all very ironic.

"Speaking of books," I said. "This is a well-loved trope in romances."

"Getting stuck in a silo?"

"Getting stuck in general. It can be anywhere. A rooftop, an elevator, a library."

"And then what happens?"

"Then the characters make out, which seems to either inspire them to figure out how to get out or sends some sort of signal into the universe to let some peripheral character in the book know they are trapped."

"Are you suggesting we make out to bring order back to our world?"

I smiled. "Absolutely."

His eyes collided with mine and his expression got serious. "It's not, I uh . . . we . . ."

"What were you going to tell me in the car the other day? I stopped you, not wanting to hear it. But I need to know. Why don't you like me back? It seemed like you did at one point or at least wanted to try. Am I too messy? Do you need me to be perfect before giving us a chance? Because I'll never be perfect. I'm not my sister. If you want someone like that—"

"I don't," he interrupted. "At all. But it's complicated."

"How? What is it? My past? My boss?"

"It's *my* past," he shot back.

"Your exes really screwed up your ability to trust, didn't they?" I asked.

"My exes are definitely screwing me over here." His eyes looked sad.

I wondered if there was anything I could say to convince a guy who had been cheated on twice before that it wouldn't happen again. That I was a safe bet. "The past is in the past, Oliver. You can't let it dictate your future."

"Do you really believe that?"

I nodded.

"So what . . ." He looked around the dark circular space where we stood. "You want me to take you right here, right now, in this bug-infested silo?" He stalked toward me, a new intensity in his eyes.

My heart pounded heavy in my chest. I waited with bated breath for him to collide with me. I wanted him so badly. I was more sure about that than I was about almost anything in my life right now.

But then he stopped, his mind taking over, doubt clouding his face. "I can't . . . We can't."

I crossed my arms in front of me, suddenly feeling vulnerable and embarrassed. Because right now, I was leading with my emotions, like I always did, and he was leading with his logic, like he always seemed to. "I don't need to be somebody else's mistake. I was that for two years."

"You're not a mistake," he said.

"Just a bad decision?"

He finished his walk toward me. But instead of pulling me against him, he brushed past me to the stale grain and began climbing the pile, slipping and losing purchase with every step. Eventually, he was at the top.

"What are you doing?" I asked.

"Seeing if there is a signal up here."

"Of course you are," I muttered under my breath.

"There is," he said after several minutes. "We'll be unstuck soon."

And it didn't even require a makeout, I thought bitterly.

CHAPTER 30

"I feel like there are still bugs on me," I said, rubbing my hands up and down my arms as I sat in the passenger seat. It was dark outside. The sun had set while we were trapped. Oliver had called the nonemergency police line and in less than an hour a handful of firemen had pried open the door and freed us. We got a serious lecture about trespassing. And had I been less irritated, I might've noticed that two of the fire-fighters were attractive and seemingly single, and that being rescued from a silo would make an amazing meet-cute. Fine, I noticed. But I didn't care. I wished I did because that would mean I wasn't hung up, once again, on someone who was apparently completely wrong for me.

"There aren't any bugs," Oliver assured me. He'd already checked twice before we'd even gotten in the car.

"I know, but it *feels* like it." I raked my fingers through my hair. "Did you hate every minute of that? The trespassing, the being stuck inside, the lecture from people in authority?"

"It wasn't my favorite." He took the turn toward our hotel. "Food first or shower?"

"We don't have to do everything together," I said.

"I figured since we only have one car . . ."

"I can get something delivered. I don't want to keep you from doing whatever you might want to do here." Yes, I was pouting. It was more than pouting; my heart hurt and I hated that I'd given him enough of it to affect me this much.

"I'm not as free-spirited as you. I'm careful. I like to calculate risks and rewards of things and sometimes that bites me in the ass."

"There aren't enough potential rewards to justify the many risks with me?"

"What?" he said, confused. Then his eyes went wide. "No. That's not what I was talking about. I was literally just talking about trespassing."

"Well, I'm talking about us. Stop being so careful and take some damn risks." And I was back to being mad at him as he pulled into the parking lot of the hotel. We went inside and rode the elevator to the third floor in silence.

We reached our doors and he said, "I'll probably head down to the bar for a couple drinks. Text me if you need the car or anything." He was obviously mad at me too. Mad that I had dragged him out into the middle of nowhere and was now demanding that he explain why he didn't like me the way I liked him.

The light on my lock lit up green. "Yep," I said as the door shut behind me.

I walked straight to the bathroom, turned on the shower, stripped down, then stepped under the practically scalding stream of water. I scrubbed my skin with the tiny bar of hotel-provided soap, washed my hair with shampoo that smelled more like chemicals than the cucumber-and-aloe scent it was claiming to have, and stayed in the steamy shower until my skin was red and blotchy. I dried off with a scratchy towel, then pulled on a tank top and a pair of cheeky underwear.

I found the delivery apps on my phone and discovered that at this hour there were no drivers available to take my order in this small town. It didn't matter. I wasn't all that hungry anyway. I pulled out my toothbrush only to remember I'd forgotten toothpaste.

I shot Oliver a text. You downstairs already? Can I borrow your toothpaste again?

While I waited for his answer, I opened my side of the adjoining door, then tested the handle for his door. It was unlocked. His room was dark, the only light coming from the bathroom. He wouldn't care if I just grabbed some toothpaste and went on my way.

I looked at my phone again, but he hadn't responded. The image that came into my mind was him at the bar chatting it up with some girl from San Francisco or New York. Someone who hadn't slept with her boss or just lost her job, someone who'd known what she wanted to do with her life the second she'd entered college, probably before then. Someone who didn't take him over fences and into old rusty silos. "She sounds boring," I mumbled to myself, but I knew she wasn't. She was probably like my sister. Cool and confident and uber-successful. Despite what he claimed, it was obvious that those were the kind of people who didn't make Oliver hesitate, or weigh options, the kind who didn't make him nervous, I was sure.

Those were the images that were circling my mind as I

took my toothbrush and stepped into his room. A room that after less than eight hours already smelled exactly like him. I headed for the bathroom. I could see the toothpaste sitting there on his counter, through the open door. My hand was unscrewing the cap when the sound of water hitting tile and glass . . . and most likely skin . . . rang out behind me. A yelp escaped my lips and my eyes darted to the mirror, where a misty reflection of the shower shone in front of me. My hand, toothpaste still in its grip, slapped the lights, plunging us into darkness.

Oliver let out a short, strangled shout.

"I thought you were downstairs!" I yelled. "I was just borrowing toothpaste!" I held up the tube that he couldn't see. With the motion, something small and plastic hit my foot, then bounced on the floor a couple times. I assumed it was the cap of the toothpaste. I felt around with my foot for a second, shuffling several steps one way and then the other, but couldn't find it.

A laugh rang out. "You didn't hear the shower?"

"I really didn't!" My mind had been too preoccupied to think about what sounds meant.

"Margot, I can't see," he said.

"Exactly!" I responded. "Neither can I."

More water sounds rang out, like he was rinsing off shampoo or soap or something. "Are you really not going to turn the light back on?" he asked, a smile in his voice.

"No. I mean, yes, I will. I'm trying to figure out how to get out of here in a way that neither of us will get an eyeful." I also didn't want to run face-first into a wall or have him slip in the shower, but without lights, the odds of one or both of those things happening were very high.

"Are you not dressed?" he asked.

"I am semidressed." The cold counter against my backside reminded me how little my chosen underwear covered. And the thought of him standing there naked ten feet away made me feel every inch of my thin tank top against my sensitive parts.

He chuckled again and then there was silence. He'd turned off the shower. I heard the glass shower door slide open. "Just getting a towel," he said. His hand slapped the wall several times followed by the sound of cloth sliding off the metal bar.

"Don't slip," I said.

"A light would help," he teased.

"I'm sorry," I said. "If you close your eyes. I'll turn the light back on and leave."

"And if I don't close my eyes?" he said, that smile still in his voice.

"Oliver," I sighed out. "Don't . . ."

"Don't what?" he asked.

"If you don't like me back, you have to stop saying things like that. You're sending me mixed messages."

My statement was followed by silence, and I wished the lights were on so I could see the expression on his face. But they weren't, and I was literally left in the dark, wondering what he was thinking.

He put me out of my misery by saying, "I *do* like you, Margot. A lot."

My eyes stung in confusion. "But?"

"But I don't know if I'm right for you," he said.

"You are. So right. I think what's really stopping you is that you don't know if *I'm* right for you."

Another stretch of silence passed where he didn't deny my

statement. His voice finally cut through the darkness, deep and scratchy. "I need to tell you something about my past relationship."

"I honestly don't care about your past relationship. I meant what I said in the silo. We need to leave our pasts in the past. We can't let the people who hurt us still have such a strong hold on us now."

"No matter who they were?"

"Even if we were engaged to them or if they were our bosses," I said, covering both of us with the statement. "I think we have to live in the moment. Do what feels right now because what if nothing feels this right again?"

"*You* feel right," he said. "You always have. From night one."

My eyes were slowly adjusting to the dark and I saw the glowing white shape of the towel wrapped around him move until he stood in front of me.

The air was hot and muggy. I wanted to reach out and wrap myself around him, but once again I felt like I was talking him into liking me. I wanted him to want me, to not be able to control himself when we were both in various stages of undress. Not to have to be talked into feelings.

I realized I still held my toothbrush in one hand and his toothpaste in the other. "I'm sorry for cornering you. I came here for toothpaste," I said softly. "That's all." I squeezed a bead, another spot of white in the darkness, onto my toothbrush, placed the capless tube back on the counter, then rushed for the door that I could now barely make out.

Oliver caught me by the hand before I got far, pulled me back into the bathroom, and backed me up against the counter, like a man who had suddenly discovered what he wanted and was prepared to get it. He reached over to the wall and the soft light that surrounded the mirror flickered on, lighting him up in a glowy haze.

"What are you doing?" I asked, meeting his eyes, but my voice lacked conviction because whatever he was doing, my body liked it. A lot. "If you don't want this . . ."

His eyes traveled from my head all the way down my barely clothed body and he stepped even closer, the steam in the air floating between us, dampening my skin. "I do want this. More than you know." His body was still dripping, and as much as I wanted to stand there and pretend he was having no effect on me, I couldn't. I dropped my toothbrush to the side, listening as it clattered onto the counter. My hands glided along his shoulders, then his defined pecs, seemingly of their own accord, needing to feel the slickness of his skin beneath my touch. His actions were slow, calculated, as if his brain had to be involved in every tiny movement, from his hand trailing along my waist, to his lips brushing along my cheek.

"Stop thinking so much. Stop being careful," I said through gritted teeth.

My words flipped a switch in him. His thumbs dug into my hips as he pulled me flush against him, his erection pressing into my stomach. I moaned my approval. He hooked his thumbs into the waistband of my underwear and dragged them down until they fell in a puddle around my ankles. I stepped out of them just in time for him to grab me by the ass and lift me onto the counter. He stepped between my knees, our chests coming together, his still damp, my tank top now stuck to my skin with moisture. His lips collided with mine, wet and salty. Desperate and messy.

My hands used his shoulders to pull myself forward on the counter, to feel his rough towel rub against my bare, aching parts. I slid my hands down his back and just as I came to the top of his towel, my intention to remove it, he reached behind him and caught my hands in his.

"Please don't stop," I all but begged.

He shook his head, trapped my hands on the countertop, and lowered himself to his knees. He draped my legs over his shoulders and I sucked in an air of surprise as his tongue explored my folds, teasing me in just the right places before applying pressure. Every nerve ending sang with his exploration. I whimpered, one hand grabbing hold of his hair, the other hand grabbing the faucet to steady myself as his tongue found a pattern that brought me to the brink of release. But he stopped short, my groan of disappointment eliciting one last thrust of his tongue before he kissed each of my inner thighs and stood. He loosened his towel and let it fall. It caught on the length of him before joining my underwear on the ground.

I took in every solid inch. Before I could even ask if he had a condom, he was freeing one from his toiletries bag. I leaned back and braced myself on the counter, one of my hands landing on the tube of toothpaste, which sent a stream of white paste through the air and onto the ground beside him. He smiled down at the mess. "A little premature there, Margot."

I laughed. My palm also had a smear of white across the center. Just as I lifted my hand to my mouth, he brought it to his. His warm tongue licked across my palm as his eyes met mine. Then he scooped me off the counter and carried me into the bedroom, where he set me on the edge of his bed. He lifted my arms above my head and freed me of my tank top.

His eyes devoured me. "Gorgeous," he whispered. I moved

back to the pillows and he crawled across the bed toward me. Watching him set my skin on fire.

My knees fell open, ready for him. He trailed kisses up my body, pausing at my breasts. My nipples pebbled as he drew one into his mouth. He used one hand to support himself as his other brushed along sensitive areas of my skin—the bend in my arm, my lower abdomen, my inner thigh. His mouth and tongue continued to tease my nipple.

I arched against him. "Please."

"Please what?" he asked in a husky voice, his mouth moving to my neck, then my ear.

"Take me."

"Take you?" He softly bit my earlobe, his hand cupping my breast, his thumb teasing every nerve ending at its peak.

I flipped him onto his back and climbed on top. "Or I can take you, if you'd rather."

A smile spread across his face and he rolled us back to our original position. "I'll do the taking tonight." He produced the condom out of thin air, it seemed, and ripped the package open with his teeth. The action, seeing Oliver uninhibited, turned me on more than it should've.

His mouth came back to mine and I dug my fingers into his hair.

He wrapped my leg around his waist and, without another moment's hesitation, thrust inside of me.

I let out an embarrassing half gasp, half scream, and he paused.

"Am I hurting you?"

I shook my head. "No, no, keep, don't think, yes, please."

A throaty chuckle escaped him and he thrust into me once more, then settled into a slow, steady rhythm. Our bodies worked perfectly together, as though in sync, anticipating each other's moves and adjusting to them. Why had we waited so long to do this? Why had I walked away that first day when all he'd wanted to do was take his time? I'd denied myself the feel of this man for three years.

When he lost control with a ragged moan, I reached my high. Then he collapsed onto me and I held his head against my chest as our breathing slowed and our heartbeats filled the silence in the room.

CHAPTER 31

I lay in bed, more than halfway through the book Marissa had sent me at approximately three thirty A.M. The time stamp didn't surprise me. Many writers were nocturnal creatures. I'd started it at five thirty A.M. when I'd woken up to pee, untangled myself from Oliver's arms, and checked my email as I sat on the toilet. It was now eight thirty. That's how good the book was. So good it was making me giddy, unable to go back to sleep. I hoped I wasn't being influenced by my after-sex high and that it really was that good.

Oliver stirred beside me, rolling over, snaking his arm around my waist and nuzzling his face into my neck. I couldn't get over how good it felt to have him there—the weight of him against me, his warmth.

"You're awake?" he mumbled.

"Reading."

"Guess we should've gotten just one room after all."

"It's not too late," I said.

He groaned as he stretched. "You make a good point. What time is it?"

The room was still dark, the blackout curtains drawn over the windows. It could've just as easily been four A.M. as noon. "It's eight thirty."

His fingers lazily traced lines across my bare stomach as he let out a happy sigh. All my parts tingled to life.

"How long have you been up?" he asked in a voice deep from sleep.

"Long enough to know that as long as Marissa doesn't screw up the ending of this book, I'm going to offer her representation."

He propped himself on his elbow. "That's huge, Margot. Should we celebrate with some morning sex?"

I laughed and stretched my arm out to deposit my phone onto the nightstand.

"I was kidding," he said, pulling my arm back. "You keep reading. I'll get us some breakfast."

"And then sex?" I asked.

He chuckled. "Is it the book or me?"

I laughed. "The book is sexy, but it's you."

"Is this what Kari had in mind when she paid you for this weekend?"

"Kari would love this. She is the queen of romance."

He smiled and hovered his upper body over where I still lay, sheet up to my chin. "Is this romantic?" He kissed my neck, hitting a ticklish spot.

My shoulders shot up and I laughed. This time, I really did abandon my phone on the nightstand. "Yes, so romantic." I draped my arms around his neck.

He kissed along my jaw to my cheek and then the very

corner of my mouth before he lowered his weight onto me. I could feel all of him through the thin layer of sheet, but even so, that layer felt like a barrier.

"I'm getting breakfast first," he said as his mouth moved to my neck.

"Okay," I said, working the sheet out from between us, freeing my breasts first and then my stomach. His chest against mine created a friction that radiated through me and vibrated between my legs. As if he sensed the energy existing there, he freed me from the rest of the sheet, and his finger pressed against my opening. He felt sleep-warm and perfect against me and I wanted him closer.

"Yes," I said, when he didn't go any farther.

He slid his finger inside, and as if realizing just how ready I'd been for him, he added another, finding the spot he'd mapped out three years ago.

I bucked against him, unable to control my reaction to the sheer pleasure he unearthed in me. "If you don't stop, I'm going to go faster than I want," I muttered against his ear.

"Nothing would make me happier," he said, curving his fingers slightly.

I let out a moan of ecstasy, pushing myself against his hand. He continued working that spot inside for several more minutes. I tried to make it last, but when he drew my nipple into his mouth, it only took two swipes of his tongue before I could no longer hold back. I cried out his name as waves of pleasure coursed through my body. He continued the actions that got me there until the tremors died down. Then he rolled onto his side and pulled me against him, tucking me into the bend of his neck, our breathing labored.

My hand moved down his side, and even though I could

feel how much he wanted it, before I could return the favor, he said, "Breakfast." He kissed my cheek and sprung out of bed.

"I hope you're putting some clothes on first," I said as I watched his completely bare backside head for the bathroom.

"I'll think about it."

"You have a nice ass!" I called as he shut the bathroom door.

"Squats. Lots of squats!" came his muffled reply.

I let out a satisfied hum and continued to read.

He was right. I was here for Kari and videos. We needed to get out and see more of the town today even though all I wanted to do was stay in bed all day and be ravaged.

Oliver poked his head out of the bathroom. "There's toothpaste all over the floor and counter. Any idea what happened in here last night?"

"I'll never be able to look at toothpaste again without getting wet. That's what happened."

"That could be a problem," he said. "A lifelong problem."

"You don't sound sorry."

"Should I be?"

"No."

He gave a throaty laugh and dug through his suitcase, pulling on underwear, a tee, and some athletic shorts. "Any requests for breakfast? I haven't eaten that meal with you yet."

"I'm not a big breakfast person. But I could go for some coffee and some form of carb. I've been burning some calories."

"You went to the hotel gym?"

"No, I meant—"

He looked over his shoulder at me with his teasing smile.

"Right, sarcasm. I should've picked up on that."

"I'll see you in a few. I want to hear all about that book

when I get back." He started to leave, then turned around and gave me a quick peck before he left me. I counted to ten before I called Sloane.

"Did Rob get a hold of you?" is how she answered.

That name wiped the smile right off my face. "Rob? No. And how could you possibly know he's trying to get a hold of me when you're out of town?"

"He called me."

"He called *you?*" I was so confused. I pulled my phone away from my ear and saw two missed calls from yesterday. They must've come in when I didn't have service in the silo. I hadn't noticed the missed-call notification. Who else had he called in search of me? "What does he want?"

"I don't know. I told him to piss off."

"You did?"

"Yes, I did."

"Just ignore him. You know how he is."

"Yes, I know exactly how he is. I'm glad you finally see it too. Hey, I can't talk. I'm literally on my way into a short film showing but I love you and whatever you are going to tell me I really want to hear later."

"It will keep," I said. I hung up kind of relieved I didn't actually tell her about the book I was reading or the amazing sex I'd had. I got to keep it for myself a little longer, and that made it feel all the more special.

I settled back into the book, and after thirty minutes or so of reading, the progress bar at the bottom of my screen said I was seventy-five percent done.

You love this book, just make an offer.

The thought came to me in my own voice. It was time to

start trusting that voice, even if she did lead with her emotions. If the last twenty-five percent of the book fell apart, we could make it better.

I got out of bed and pulled on one of the hotel robes. I didn't need to make my first offer in the buff, although that could've been a funny memory to pull up in the future. I brushed my teeth because that seemed important too. Oliver must've cleaned up the mess we'd made the night before because there was no longer toothpaste on the floor or countertops. Then I opened the curtains and sliding glass door and stepped onto the balcony.

The phone rang once, twice, three times. My entire body stilled as I listened, my breath, my movements, my heart even, it seemed.

"Hello," came the tentative voice of Marissa through the phone.

"Hi, Marissa. It's Margot Hart."

"Hi. Hi!" she said. "How are you, Ms. Hart?"

"I'm great. I'm almost done with your book and I couldn't help myself, I needed to call. It's brilliant."

"You like it?" she asked.

"I love it. I can think of several editors who would love it too."

"You can?" she asked.

"Absolutely. I'd love to represent you."

"I . . . That's . . . That's awesome." Her words came out haltingly, but I could tell it was from excitement, not hesitation.

"I'd take you out to about six to eight editors to start and see what their feedback was. If we needed a second round, we'd go out to six or eight more." I loathed Rob with all my heart, but he had given me a good script to work with over the years. I felt comfortable talking to authors and editors. "What do you think about that plan?"

"It sounds great. Can I have some time to think and let the other agents who have my manuscript know I have an offer?"

This wasn't an out-of-the-ordinary request. It was pretty standard, actually. "Of course. How much time do you need?"

"A week? Is that okay?"

"Yes. I'll keep my fingers crossed. I love this book and would be honored to work with you." Arms wrapped around me from behind and I jumped, nearly letting out a yelp. I settled back against Oliver's chest.

"Thank you, Ms. Hart. I really appreciate your interest," Marissa said. "I'm excited."

"Me too. I look forward to hearing from you."

We disconnected the call.

"You scared me," I said, looking out at our view, which was mainly a parking lot. But in the distance was a vineyard, uniform rows of vines lining the side of a hill, the sun blasting them with light.

"Sorry, I thought you heard me come in."

I turned in his hold and stretched up to wrap my arms around his neck.

"Was that Kari?" he asked, referring to my phone call.

"No, that was Marissa, the author of the book I'm reading. I offered her representation."

He pulled back from me, a look of surprise on his face. "Why don't you seem more excited about this?"

I smiled up at him. "I am. She just hasn't accepted yet. I will save my excitement for when she does."

He lifted me into a hug. "I will spend my excitement now."

"I could get you even more excited," I said in his ear. "It's your turn."

He lowered me back to my feet. "Don't you want breakfast first?"

I undid the tie on my robe, letting it fall open. "Does it look like I want breakfast first?"

He took hold of the open sides of the robe and pulled me forward and into the room by them. "God, you're beautiful."

"You are too," I said. "And you have entirely too many clothes on that beautiful body."

"Yeah?" he said, slipping his hand into my robe and around my waist. He trailed kisses along my jaw and down my neck.

"Yes." I stepped back, detaching him from me, and took hold of the bottom of his shirt, working it up his body. "I hear you're rideable. I would like to see if this is true."

He helped me finish pulling his shirt over his head and then flung it onto the chair beside us. "Only for a carrot."

I laughed, then let my hand trail beneath the waistband of his shorts, where I grabbed hold of him. "Is this the figurative carrot she was referring to?"

A spasm went through him, causing him to jerk in my grip. "Considering *she* promised it to *me*, I doubt it."

"Well, *I* could be motivated by this promise."

He let out a growling laugh that made my cheeks go warm. He tugged me even closer by the sides of my robe, then peeled it off of me. I relieved him of his shorts, then pushed him back onto the bed, where I climbed on top of him. My hair draped down like a curtain around us.

"Thank you for coming with me this weekend," I said.

"It's been a real hardship," he teased, pulling me down to his lips.

"Do you ever wish we hadn't given up so easily three years ago?" I asked. "When we first went out."

"We were both in a different place. It might not have worked out. It's better here . . . now." His hand cupped my cheek, his eyes assuring me that this was the time. And as his hands moved down my body, touching me, coaxing me, caressing me, I agreed.

CHAPTER 32

"Are you upset that I also wanted to be tourists today?" Oliver asked as we stood at a pub table, a large oak tree stretched out above us. A wide array of cheeses was in the center of the table and a selection of wine had just been poured.

"Of course not," I said. I wore a sundress and sandals, which felt good because even in the shade it was hot for early May. "This is fun." I swirled the deep red wine in my glass and took a sip. It was fruity and rich. "What are you like when you're drunk?" I asked. I'd never seen Oliver drunk and I wasn't sure a wine tour, where we were only taking sips at every vineyard we stopped at, was going to get him anything more than slightly tipsy, but I was curious.

"Quiet, I guess. I've only been drunk twice before," he said.

"Twice?" I asked in shock.

He chuckled. "I'm careful, remember?"

"Not anymore, not with me," I teased, thinking about that morning in bed.

His jaw tightened, his brow dipped, and he said, "No, self-ishly, not with you."

I leaned in close to him, my breast pressing against his arm. "Should we find a place to be selfish now?"

He gave a breathy laugh, his jaw finally loosening, and took a sip of wine.

. . .

"I thought you said you were a quiet drunk," I said. The bus, which had taken us to five vineyards that day, had dropped us off at the downtown city park two hours ago. The park was surrounded by shops and restaurants and bars.

The wine tour turned out to be perfect for research. I got lots of videos for Kari of scenery and vineyard owners and people and wine. It was lovely. I tried to keep my drinking to a minimum because this really was a working weekend for me. So I was only slightly buzzed. But Oliver had tried every wine they offered, oftentimes drinking an entire glass, and now, downtown, we were following up our day of wine with food and beer and several Jell-O shots for Oliver that I'd poached off a group of college kids in the midst of a bar crawl.

Oliver was drunk. Even though he kept insisting he wasn't.

"I'm not drunk," he said again. "I'm just expressing valid thoughts."

"Very valid," I said, taking hold of his hand because he kept slowing down to peer in store windows. We were heading to Boots and Spurs, the last stop of the night. "I want to hear all your thoughts. It's nice that you want to take care of me." That was the last thing he'd said.

"But I know you don't need to be taken care of. You can take care of yourself. I'm a feminist, you know."

I held back a laugh. "Yes, you keep telling me that."

"Because I am. My mom did the same exact job as my dad, probably did it better, in fact, and made less money. It was maddening to see."

I squeezed his hand. "I'm glad you're still a golden retriever even when you're drunk."

"I'm not drunk."

"Where is your dad now, by the way?"

"No idea. It was an ugly divorce. Hard for all of us to live through."

"I'm sorry," I said, pulling his hand in front of me and running my other one up his arm.

"It had been bad for a long time before that. Lots of pain, lots of tears." He paused. "Probably another reason I'm still single."

"Are you? Still single?" I teased. "Good to know. I might know someone who is interested."

"Oh," he said, as if the reality of his relationship status just dawned on him.

"Do I have to officially ask you to be my boyfriend? Would you like me to ask in note form with multiple-choice answers you can circle?"

He squeezed my hand. "I'm supposed to ask."

"I thought you were a feminist," I whispered.

He was quiet for a moment, then said, "I don't want to see you hurt. Remember that day you were crying?"

I let out a single laugh. "Yes, I remember it well."

"Me too. I hated it. I wanted to punch Rob in the face. I think I could take him. Do you think I could take him?"

"I think you could take him."

He pulled me against his side and his expression went dark. "You're good for me. I don't know if I'm good for you."

"You make me feel safe because of who you are, and it's been awhile since I felt that way." Even though I teased him for his careful, thoughtful personality, it's what helped me feel secure with him. After being with someone who wasn't careful at all, I needed that.

"I like you," he said. "A lot."

"I like you a lot too."

"Are we going to that bar with all the people?" He pointed ahead to a building that was packed. People were standing around tables outside and a steady stream was flowing inside. The smell of barbecue filled the air, along with loud music pouring out into the streets from the open doors.

"That's the place."

"That's a lot of people," he said. "You like people more than I do."

"Is that why you work from home? Because you don't like people?"

"I work from home because it saves me overhead and helps me make more money. You work from home now too."

"I guess I do."

"You need a space in your apartment that is different from the space you live in. It will help you get in the right mindset for work."

"My apartment is too small for that."

"A corner of your bedroom would work. I could help you design something."

"Are you trying to take care of me again? Is that why you helped me make my website and drove me here this weekend?"

"Yes!" he said loudly.

I wrapped my arms around his waist as we walked. Turns out I didn't mind being taken care of. "You are so drunk."

"I'm just a little buzzed," he said.

We showed our IDs to the bouncer at the doors to the bar. The music was even louder inside.

A man on the stage with a microphone was calling out steps as a large group of people in the center of the room followed along, stomping and turning to the beat. I immediately steered us to the bar, where we had to wait behind a dozen people before we could order drinks. I just got a sparkling water, but Oliver leaned onto the bar littered with peanut shells and said, "A beer, please. Whatever you recommend."

With our drinks in hand, we wound through the crowd until we found the empty corner of a tall table off to the side of the dance floor. We watched the dancing while we drank.

"You want to do that, don't you?" he said after a while.

"Dance?" I asked.

"Yes," he said.

"I do. But only if you do it with me."

He downed the rest of his drink in two big gulps and said, "Let's do it."

"Seriously?"

"Seriously."

"You need to get drunk more often."

"I'm not drunk." He said it, and yet on the dance floor, he couldn't keep his hands off me. Not that I wanted him to. He stood behind me, holding on to my hips as I moved with the instructions from the announcer. Oliver moved with me, usually a step behind, but laughing and trying. Several times his hands grazed the sides of my breasts or rested on my ass.

I was perfectly sober and couldn't keep my hands off him either. I clung to his bicep for several steps or grabbed hold of one of the belt loops on the back of his jeans or held his hand. And I laughed too, and got half the steps wrong. He ordered more drinks and we danced until a fifteen-minute break was announced. Then we stumbled out of the bar. The night air felt cool on my hot, damp skin.

The hotel was a short Uber ride away. As I climbed into the car after Oliver, he pulled me to the middle seat, his arm immediately going around my shoulders after I buckled in. I held on to his hand with both of mine.

He kissed me on the temple. "I had fun," he whispered.

I smiled up at him. "Did you have the time of your life?"

"And I owe it all to you?" he asked.

I smiled. "I knew that movie was on my deal-breaker list for a reason."

He placed a kiss on my lips. Soft music played from the Uber driver's car stereo, but she didn't try to talk to us other than confirming our destination.

"Did you get video for Kari at the bar?" he asked, seeming to remember again why we were here. His breath smelled like peanuts and whiskey.

"I did. While we were dancing."

"I didn't notice."

"You were too distracted by my boobs."

"I was."

The Uber driver met my eyes in the rearview mirror with a smile in hers.

I kept Oliver's arm around me as we walked into the hotel because he was drunker than I realized, uncertain on his feet.

"You okay?" I asked inside the elevator, holding some of his weight.

"You're right, I'm drunk. Tomorrow is going to suck." He put his forehead on my shoulder.

I hugged him around the middle. "You're going to hate me for letting you drink so much."

"I would never. You're funny and free and smart."

"What about beautiful?"

"Very beautiful," he said. The elevator doors opened on our floor and I helped him down the hall. We'd canceled the second night of his room that morning and moved all his stuff over to mine. I led him there now.

I tapped the keycard on the door and opened it. He walked straight to the bed, collapsing there, while I turned on the entryway light.

"I'm getting you some water," I said. "And potato chips from the lobby store. I'll be right back."

"Don't be long. I want you to take me. *Please* take me."

I laughed and headed back downstairs for the hangover-prevention supplies. Well, they wouldn't prevent it, but they would help.

I bought a bag of Lay's, a large water, and a small bottle of aspirin in the lobby store.

Back at the room, I opened the door to heavy breathing. Oliver was out. He'd gotten his shoes off and his pants halfway off before he'd given up and lain back on the bed. I set my supplies on the nightstand and pried his pants the rest of the way off his legs.

He startled awake and sat up.

"Shh," I said as he looked around the room. "It's okay. I

want you to eat a handful of these, take three of these, and drink half this water."

He was halfway asleep still but he obeyed. "I'm sorry," he said.

"You don't have to be sorry," I said, pulling the comforter on the bed back and helping him beneath it.

"I just realized something. The past can't be left behind because it's still your present."

"You're my present? Is that what you're saying? You're adorable." I kissed his cheek.

"You can have me now," he said. "I'm yours."

"You're drunk, babe," I said. "I'll take you tomorrow. Promise."

"You like to take care of me too," he mumbled.

"I do," I said, a warm feeling spreading across my chest. I really did.

I kissed him, his lips salty from the potato chips, and then pulled the sheet up over his shoulders. His breathing went heavy again, and as I stood there staring at him, I realized something that scared me more than anything ever had—I was falling in love with this man.

CHAPTER 33

"You really have to leave?" I reached over him, feeling along the side of his seat for the button. "You sure you can't come in and meet everyone?"

"I have so much work to catch up on. What are you doing?" he asked as the driver's seat moved slowly backward.

We'd woken up that morning in the hotel room tangled up in each other, warm and happy and rested. "Thanks for taking care of me last night," he'd said, his memory surprisingly intact for someone who had been so drunk.

"How's your head?" I'd asked.

"Not bad, actually. Just a little stabby."

I'd kissed him and he'd held me close.

"Oliver?" I'd asked as we lay there in each other's arms.

"Yes?"

"Yesterday you said you'd only been drunk twice before."

"Yes."

"Was it the two times you found out you were being . . ." I didn't want to finish the sentence, bring down the mood. But it hadn't occurred to me until that moment that being cheated on might've been the motivating factor for him drinking in the past.

"Yes," he'd said, his muscles tight.

"I'm sorry. Maybe that's why you said you were a quiet drunk. Because I hate to break it to you, but you're not a quiet drunk."

He gave me his throaty chuckle, holding me there against his chest. "It's nice to have a better association with the whole thing."

"It's kind of annoying that you remember last night so well. I want a drunken voicemail of you."

He laughed again.

"I don't want this weekend to end, but I have to get home for a barbecue at my sister's today. You think you can drop me off there on your way home?"

"At your sister's," he'd said. "You're bringing the fruit tray."

"Exactly."

He took two breaths before he finally said, "Sure, I can take you there."

Now we were here, in front of my sister's house, ten minutes before the four-o'clock start time for her barbecue. "I'm making out with you," I said. "That's what I'm doing. I have ten minutes."

His seat finally stopped its slow progress backward and I climbed onto his lap, straddling him. He smiled, both his hands grabbing hold of my ass.

"I'm on the clock again?" he asked.

"Yes, this time will you make better use of it?"

He laughed. "Did you call me *babe* last night, by the way?"

"I did," I said, smoothing my hand down one side of his hair and then the other. "It felt right."

He pulled me down for a kiss. One weekend with him and his mouth already felt like home on mine. His lips were soft and firm all at once, his tongue traveling along my bottom lip before exploring my mouth. I wiggled on his lap as I felt the evidence of his arousal against me. His fingers gripped my hips and he moaned.

I tried to adjust my legs when my back hit the steering wheel, causing a loud honk to ring out.

He startled and lifted me off his lap and back into my own seat in a surprisingly fluid motion. My back bumped the passenger-side door, not hard, but it made a sound. My feet were now in his lap.

"I'm so sorry," he said. "Are you okay?"

"I'm fine. It didn't hurt," I assured him. "You're so jumpy." I nudged him with my foot.

He looked over my shoulder out the window and toward the house as if my whole family would come pouring out at the sound of the horn.

"They're probably in the backyard," I said. "And with kids screaming and the music playing, they won't have heard it." Extra cars lined the street and I'd realized right when I'd seen them that this wasn't just a family party. "Are you scared of my parents catching us? We're not teenagers."

"Then we probably shouldn't be making out in a car," he said.

"But cars are kind of our thing."

"They shouldn't be," he said stiffly.

My mouth snapped shut in surprise. "Right. Okay. That's my cue." I pulled my feet off his lap.

"I'm sorry, Margot, I'm a little stressed."

"It's okay," I said. "The weekend is over. Back to reality, I guess." A heaviness settled on my chest with the thought that maybe Oliver had just thought of this as a weekend fling. An in-the-moment thing. *Like Rob always did*, came the unwanted thought.

"No, come here." He put a hand on either side of my face and brought me in for a slow kiss. "I didn't mean to be short with you. My head is hurting and I'm worrying about . . . things at work and . . ."

"I could've helped you talk it out on the drive."

He smiled. "You're right. You could've." His eyes darted to the house over my shoulder before they were back on me. "I'm also worried about things here."

"Things here? With us?"

He nodded out the window. "Things with you and your sister."

"You're sweet. We'll get over it. We've fought before. I think we're to the smoothing-it-over portion."

He drew in a long breath.

"Wait, is this why you don't want to come in and eat before you leave? Because me and my sister are fighting?"

His hands were still on my cheeks and he brought my mouth to his, letting our lips meet.

"I want to meet your family," he said between kisses. "But today isn't the right time. I want to give you and your sister space to talk. Work things out."

He was right. I hadn't seen Audrey since I'd made a mess of sharing my agency news. And even though I really did feel like we were in the smoothing-it-over portion of making up, bringing an unexpected guest wouldn't help. Audrey didn't like the unexpected. Plus, Oliver and I were brand-new. We didn't need to involve families yet. We needed to figure out how to navigate what we were first.

"We always make up. It's what sisters do," I said. "But you're right. We should save meeting families for later."

He gave a slow nod. "Call me later? Tell me how it all went?"

"Yes, I will." I reached for the door handle.

"Margot."

I looked over at him. He leaned closer and pulled me in for a passionate kiss that left me aching all over again. Even after he backed away, I kept my eyes closed, a smile on my face.

"You're everything," he said.

Finally, I blinked my eyes open. "I miss you already."

"Same," he said.

I stepped out of the car and it wasn't until he was driving away and I was walking up the pathway, dragging my suitcase in one hand and my purse and backpack in the other, that I remembered the stupid fruit tray. How could I have forgotten? "Because you're irresponsible," I muttered.

I pulled up a delivery app on my phone and found the closest grocery store. Between having to buy the already cut tray of fruit, having to order a few more items to meet the minimum requirement, and adding a tip, I spent way too much for someone who was watching her money.

I knocked on the door and waited. The process of ordering the fruit had made me go from on time to ten minutes late. I tried the door handle. It was locked. Like I'd told Oliver, they were probably all in the backyard. I left my suitcase on the porch and headed for the side gate when my phone started buzzing in my pocket.

I pulled it out, thinking it might be Oliver. Maybe he'd changed his mind about wanting to stay. It wasn't Oliver. It was Rob. I hadn't answered his phone calls all weekend and I didn't want to now, but something came over me.

"Rob," I answered. "Stop calling me."

"You got a copy of the contract," was how he responded.

"Is that what this harassment is about? Yes, I got it."

"Then why the hell do you think you can poach Kari Cross from me?"

I was stunned silent. He caught me off guard and I stuttered out a defensive "I-I, that's not what I'm trying to do. I have to go. I'm at my sister's." I hung up the phone, my hands shaking. Shit. It probably did look a lot like I was trying to steal her, with her calling me on my cell and sending me on research trips. Was that why he sent me a copy of the contract? I sighed out a frustrated breath of air. I'd deal with him later. Tell him that she'd only hired me in an assistant capacity. I'd done nothing wrong.

I climbed up on the stone border of the flower bed and reached over the gate to unlatch and open it. I could hear the boys splashing in the pool as I made my way around the house. My mind was still spinning with the phone call.

I plastered a smile on my face because the only thing worse than being late to a party was being late *and* pissy.

My sister's yard was just as gorgeous as her house. A big pool surrounded by stamped concrete and a built-in bar and barbecue under a large gazebo took up half the yard. Lush green grass framed the pool, and flowers and trees lined the cedar fence. Her yard had been featured in some home-and-garden magazine last year, the cover of which was framed in her house.

Mom saw me first from where she was sitting in a lounge chair under a patio umbrella. She held a frozen drink and waved. "Margot!"

"Hi, everyone."

Like the cars out front indicated, there were more people in and around the pool than just my family—several couples I didn't recognize. Obviously, some friends had been invited, their kids playing alongside the twins, pool noodles flying.

My sister glanced over from where she was arranging food on a wooden table. Her eyes took me in and I knew exactly what she was looking for. "It's coming," I said when I was within talking range.

"What's coming?" she asked just as I noticed a gorgeous tray of fruit already on the table.

I pointed at it. "I was bringing the fruit."

"It was getting late so I just whipped something together. No big deal."

It was too late to cancel my order. I knew that much. It had already been claimed by someone named Denise and had an estimated delivery time and everything. "I was bringing it," I said.

"Should I put this away?" she asked in a perfectly innocent voice.

Mom had joined us now and she kissed my cheek. "You look like you got some sun this weekend."

It was probably just frustration that had turned my cheeks pink, but Oliver and I had been outside more than I typically was, so I could've been a little burned. "Hi, Mom." I gave her a hug. Then, realizing I was just frustrated about the fruit because I was trying to save money, I gave my sister a hug too. "Sorry I'm late."

"It's okay," she said. "Glad you made it."

I went and greeted my dad and Chase, who were by the grill.

"Are you going to swim with us, Aunt Margot?" Samuel yelled from the pool.

Most of the other adults wore swimsuits even though none of them was actually in the pool.

"Yes," I said.

"Yay!" he cheered.

"I left my suitcase on the porch," I said to my dad. "I'll go change and be right back."

"Okay, sweetie," he said.

I stepped into the house. The AC was on, and compared to the warmth outside it was freezing. Goose bumps instantly formed down my body. I walked through the oversized kitchen adorned with every upgrade available, through the neutral-colored living room with pops of burnt orange, and opened the front door. My suitcase looked small on the wide porch. I wheeled it inside and changed into my swimsuit in the guest bathroom.

I'd forgotten to pack a cover-up, so I just pulled my T-shirt over the top of it and deposited my suitcase back by the front door.

The delivery app showed me my subpar fruit tray was en route. There was also a notification informing me of another missed call from Rob. I ignored that one, but did not ignore the little red number one on my email. Thinking it might be another query, I opened it as I walked toward the back door.

It was from Marissa and my heart stuttered. This was too early. She said she wanted a week. I stopped on the middle of a fluffy beige area rug. Maybe it was good news. Maybe all the agents had gotten back to her fast and she was accepting my offer. That would be the boost I needed right now.

I opened the email.

> *Dear Ms. Hart,*
> *Thank you so much for your interest in Over the*
> *Moon. It means the world to me that you were the first*
> *to believe in it. I reached out to the agents that still*
> *had my manuscript and informed them of a pending*
> *offer. I heard back from my dream agent at Mesner &*
> *Lloyd Lit. I accepted her offer this morning. Thanks*
> *again and good luck with your agency!*
> *—Marissa*

CHAPTER 34

My heart dropped as I closed the rejection email and exited my inbox. I'd been on the other side of this exchange for years. Authors reaching out to Rob with offers on the table to motivate him to read their books faster. It just hadn't occurred to me until this moment that I was the negotiation piece now, not the goal.

I pulled up my texts and scrolled back to the one Rebecca had sent congratulating me about talking to Rob. My only reply to her at the time had been that I quit. She had been so kind to me and seemingly supportive and she was the only person I could think of at the moment to ask this question to. Or at least the only person whose cell phone number I had.

Rebecca, how long did it take you to start earning money as an agent?

I was lucky to have a roommate to share expenses with, but my ever-dwindling bank account needed to know when it was going to start receiving life support.

I got my first commission check at six months. Following her text, Rebecca had sent a celebrate emoji, like this was a good piece of information she just shared.

My heart dropped to the floor.

Or did you mean a livable wage? was the follow-up text.

I did not want to know that right now. I was already reeling from the first answer. No, you answered the question. Thank you!

I stared at her name on my phone. I was so tempted to follow up my question with: *FYI, Rob and I were sleeping together for two years off and on.* At this point, I didn't even want to do it to get him in trouble, but more to save her if she was on the verge of ruining her life with him. The problem was that I still wasn't sure if I'd imagined something between them. If it was all in my head or not. The more I thought about it, the more likely the scenario that I'd just imagined it became.

Behind me, someone knocked on the front door, and I jumped. I opened it to see the delivery driver standing with my tray of fruit. "You Margot?" she asked.

"Yes, thank you." I took the tray from her but she continued to stand there, waiting.

"I tipped you on the app. I don't have any cash."

"Cheap," she muttered as she walked away.

I shut and locked the door, then nearly tripped over my suitcase as I headed to the kitchen.

The fruit tray was sad. Small, watery pieces of fruit filled cheap plastic compartments. I couldn't take this outside. Not with my sister's offering already there, beautiful and fresh. I stuck the tray in her overly wide fridge and went back outside.

"Are you swimming with us, Aunt Margot?" Sammy called from the pool.

I nodded.

"Everyone, this is my sister," Audrey announced as I joined them.

"Hi, nice to meet you all," I said, making my way to the steps in the shallow end of the pool. My mom sat on a lounge chair nearby and I took off my shirt and threw it toward her. She caught it.

"Tell me about your weekend," she said as Jack handed me a pool noodle and then used the one he was holding to hit my new weapon. I engaged, wading to my waist in the water.

To my mom, I said, "I did some research work for an author up near the Central Coast."

"That sounds fun."

"Yeah, it was."

Now Sammy was hugging me from behind, trying to drag me under the water. "Get your hair wet," he yelled.

I pried his little arms off me and flung him away while he laughed. This was our game.

"Dad said your car was out of commission?" Mom was saying.

"Yeah, a battery or something. I haven't been home yet to get it checked out."

A pool noodle hit me on the side of the head and I grabbed hold of it and tugged, pulling Sammy with it. I spun in a circle while he hung on squealing.

Another noodle hit me from the other side and soon I was surrounded by kids pummeling me with their not-so-soft weapons.

"Food!" my sister called, and all the kids in the pool went running, leaving me, now shoulder deep, alone.

I paddled over to the side, closer to my mom, and rested

my arms on the warm cement and my chin on my arms. "I just got rejected," I said with a sigh, the disappointment catching up with me.

"By who? He obviously doesn't deserve you."

"No, not by a man, by a potential client."

"Oh, honey, I'm sorry."

I swallowed. This was hard for me, but after Rebecca's text, I knew I had to ask. "Do you think I could borrow some money? Just until I pick up a few clients."

"You don't have any money?" Mom asked.

"I have some savings but not nearly enough, I'm learning. I've just started my business and I think it will be amazing once I get my feet under me, but right now, I'm struggling."

"You've always been a dreamer, that beautiful head of yours up in the clouds. Have you jumped into this prematurely? Before you had a proper plan?" she asked with a smile, like her words weren't hurtful. "Maybe you could get your old job back. I bet Robert would rehire you. Sloane says you're amazing at your job."

"He won't hire me back, Mom."

"Why not? Did you leave on bad terms?"

"Sort of. But, Mom, that's not what I want anyway. This business is going to give me so much more freedom and success in the future."

"Big dreams," she reiterated.

One of Audrey's friends, plate full of food, sat on the lounge chair next to my mom's. "Margot, did you say?"

"Yes, hi. Sorry, I didn't catch everyone's names." Swallowing down the hurt of the conversation with my mom and trying to be cordial was harder than I anticipated. My throat sounded scratchy and raw. I slowly kicked my feet, letting the water flow between my toes and legs.

"I'm Felicity. I went to UCLA with your sister. We all did, in fact." She pointed to the other two women in the food line with their husbands.

"Oh, is this, like, a college reunion party?" I asked.

"I guess you could call it that, but we get together quite a bit."

My sister had friends. Good friends that she got together with regularly. She really did tick off all the boxes on her optimal living checklist. "That's nice that you've stayed in touch."

"Did you go to UCLA too? You look so familiar," she said.

"No, I didn't. But I am Audrey's sister. Some people say we look alike."

She pulled a face. "Really? I wouldn't even have thought you were related if she didn't say."

"Yeah, some people say that too," I said.

She laughed, picked up a perfectly squared piece of watermelon, and stuck it in her mouth. "Maybe I've just seen you on her channel before."

"No, I haven't been on that."

"Huh. It will come to me. Oh! Did you work with Gray at the Lancaster? I feel like we were there all the time when he and Audrey were together."

"No," Audrey chimed in. She'd obviously been following the conversation from a distance. She joined us now. "She never went to the Lancaster. But you met Gray, right, Maggie?"

"I don't think so. I remember you talking about him."

"That's because we were friends for a while before we got together. All of us were."

"How is Ollie these days, anyway?" the other UCLA woman asked. She sat on the edge of the pool and put her feet in. "Has anyone seen him at all in the last eight years?"

"I saw him about five years ago," Felicity said. "He's still as nice as ever and such a cutie."

"Ollie?" I asked. It's like my body knew what was coming before she said it. My skin felt cold and prickly.

"Gray was his last name," Audrey said. "Oliver was his first. Oliver Gray."

"Oliver Gray," I repeated, because I needed her to say it again.

"Yes," Audrey said. "Do you know him or something?" She asked that question like it was a rhetorical one. Like the last thing I could say was yes.

Maybe now was not the time, but her reaction prompted me to say, "I matched with him on a dating app."

Her mouth fell open, but before she could say anything else, a booming voice rang out from the side of the house. "Margot! Are you back here?" And then Rob rounded the corner of the house and scanned the group of people.

I wanted to melt off the edge of the pool and disappear under the water.

"Is that Mr. Bishop?" Dad asked from behind me.

"Did you invite him?" Audrey asked.

"No," was all I could manage to say.

"You look pale," Felicity said. "And who's Mr. Bishop?"

"Her boss," Audrey said.

"You mean Hot Boss," Felicity said, wiggling her eyebrows.

"It's her ex-boss," Mom added unhelpfully.

This couldn't happen, whatever was about to happen, in my sister's backyard in front of my sister's friends and their kids, with my family watching on. That thought propelled me up and out of the water and onto shaky legs. I walked as fast as I could without running, straight toward him. He was walking my way as well, but instead of stopping in front of him, I passed and continued straight out the side gate, praying he'd follow.

He did.

I used the walk to summon up all the anger I could, so by the time he joined me I was fuming. "What the actual hell?" Water dripped down my body and legs and onto the grass around my bare feet.

"You've been ignoring me, dodging my calls all weekend, and then hung up on me today."

"This is completely inappropriate and you know it." I crossed my arms over my chest, suddenly very aware that I was standing there in a two-piece soaking wet.

"Kind of like stealing someone's client. I can sue you and I'm seriously considering it." I had no idea why he was convinced he was losing Kari, but it had nothing to do with me. Maybe she was taking her business somewhere else because he didn't support her latest book.

My teeth started chattering from the cold or shock or embarrassment. "Rob, *she* approached me, hired me for research. And you won't sue me. Because if you do, I will tell everyone that we had a sexual relationship for years and you will lose a lot more than just one client."

There was a gasp to my left and I looked over to see my sister standing there holding a towel. "Maybe take this more than ten feet from the back fence, Maggie?" She tossed the towel in my direction and left.

I was quiet for several deep breaths, tears burning hot

behind my eyes. I didn't want to let them out because I didn't want Rob to think they had anything to do with him. I picked up the towel and wrapped it tightly around me. "Leave," I was finally able to say.

He didn't leave, just nodded to where my sister had disappeared. "Is she going to go public with this?" He knew my sister had a popular channel. He knew a lot about my family. I wished I'd told him nothing over the years because then he wouldn't be standing here now, overstepping huge boundaries. I shouldn't have been surprised. He was really good at stepping over boundaries.

"Leave," I repeated.

Again, he stayed where he was.

"She said leave." That was Oliver's voice, and both Rob and I turned toward it.

He was standing on the sidewalk, his car, I could now see, parked across the street. In his hand he held a fruit tray, a nice one. He must've realized I'd forgotten it at the same time I had.

Rob let out a grunt. "This isn't some lover's quarrel, so no need to come up here in a jealous rage. You can have her. This is strictly business."

Oliver took three large steps forward and Rob squared off with him, as if daring him to do his best. Oliver's free fist was clenched tight and his eyes were full of rage.

"Don't!" I screamed, stepping in between them. "Don't."

Oliver stopped, his hand going limp at his side.

"Leave," I said to Rob again. "Now."

He let out a huff, but headed to his car. "This isn't over," he said.

"It is," Oliver replied.

To that, Rob didn't respond. He got in his car and drove away.

The tears that had been burning behind my eyes ran hot down my cheeks. Oliver took a step toward me but I took a step back, clutching the top of my towel tightly.

"You dated my sister? She was the one who cheated on you in college?" I pointed toward the backyard even though she was no longer standing there.

I wanted him to deny it. To say, *Who's your sister again?* And realize in real time the horror of our shared past. But the look on his face let me know that he already knew this fact.

"You can leave too," I said, my blood running cold.

He didn't move. "Can I explain?"

"Now!" I screamed.

He held out the fruit and I took another step back. He hung his head, turned, and walked to his car. If it weren't for the fact that I didn't have a car here, I would've left too. Fled the scene. Not had to face my family. Had they all heard me? What was my life?

My sister was waiting in the side yard, out of view of the rest of the party, which meant she heard not only my interaction with Rob but also with Oliver.

"I didn't know," I said. What else was there to say? I felt empty. Defeated.

"Are you . . . are you *dating* him?"

I wasn't sure if she was talking about Rob or Oliver, but the answer for both was a most definitive "No."

"How could you not know it was him? You saw pictures! I posted him online." She was talking about Oliver, then.

"For what, like, six months? Eight or nine years ago?" I said, remembering that Oliver had said he hadn't been with his college girlfriend long but how it still hurt when she was unfaithful. The lies and secrets were the most hurtful, he had said. How could he have said that all while lying to me? The lump in my throat grew even bigger. "I was eighteen or nineteen. You weren't living at home. I didn't pay attention to who you were dating."

"Not surprising," she said.

"You're right. I'm a horrible person."

She sighed. "You're not a horrible person, but your boss, Maggie? My ex? You're on a path of self-destruction."

"Not just a path, Audrey. I've completed the goal. Run face-first into it." With those words I walked past her to see if there were other relationships in the backyard I could blow up. Apparently, I was on a roll.

"I don't want you dating him," she called to my back.

I lifted my hand in the air, turned, and said, "Don't worry. If you've had him, I don't want him." I knew that was mean, hurtful, even. But she hadn't thought about my feelings once in anything she'd said. It was time to stand up for myself.

"You *always* want what I have."

I took two steps closer to her. "What?" I may have been jealous of my sister at times, but I didn't want what she had. I looked around, looked her up and down, then said, "There is nothing about this life I want."

"What is happening over here?" Mom asked, joining us. "What happened with your boss?"

"He left," I said. If she was asking, maybe she hadn't heard my shouting match in the front yard.

"She was sleeping with him," Audrey spit out. "That's why he won't hire her back."

I sucked in some air and shot my sister a look. Obviously, my comments had hurt her and she was lashing out.

"Margot, is that true?" Mom asked.

"It's not her business, and I love you, Mom, but it's not yours either." I'd never said anything like that to my mom before, and it made my shoulders tighten with tension that spread all the way up my neck.

"If you're going to ask me for money to fund your life, I think it is my business to know why you're in this situation."

"You asked Mom for money?" Audrey said. "Nice."

"A loan. I asked for a loan. But I'm fine. It would've been helpful, but I can live without it."

Audrey, her arms crossed over her chest in a defensive manner, said, "I might've been able to help, but there's nothing in my life that you want. Except my ex-boyfriend, apparently."

"When did you become such a judgmental bitch?" I asked.

Mom gasped.

"I'm going," I said. Halfway to the back door, I remembered again that I didn't have a car. I pulled up a ride app on my phone only to see that it would be more than a hundred dollars for the hour-long drive home. My parents lived two miles away. Inside, I grabbed my overpriced fruit tray and my suitcase and started down the sidewalk for the twenty-minute walk to my childhood home.

CHAPTER 35

For several hours, I'd been sitting in the dark in my old room (that was now a workout room turned craft room turned office) crying. My parents didn't know I was here. They'd gotten home about an hour ago. I could hear them downstairs shuffling around. I was sure they assumed I'd gone back to my house.

They lived exclusively on the first floor. It had everything they needed—all the main living areas plus the primary bedroom and the laundry room. Upstairs just had two bedrooms and a loft area where Audrey and I used to watch movies and play games with our friends.

I hugged a pillow to my chest, my tears finally drying up. I wasn't sure how to fix all the ways my life had gone wrong today. I wasn't apologizing to my sister this time. She couldn't sling hate every time she got mad. I couldn't forgive Oliver. He knew the past and still slept with me. I deserved to know too, so I could make an informed decision. Maybe I would've chosen him if he had given me the opportunity.

I thought about him with my sister, about the fact that if he had ever loved her, he could not possibly be compatible with me.

No, I wouldn't have chosen him. And that went double now.

As for my career, there was nothing left to do there. I couldn't change the fact that for the next few months I was going to get used over and over again to help authors get the agent they really wanted.

Sloane was still out of town and hadn't answered my you around to chat text. I figured she wouldn't. Tonight was the big awards show at the festival and I hoped she was living it up in that fancy dress she had bought.

I felt fifteen and helpless all over again, everything out of my control.

"You're not fifteen, Margot, and you're not helpless," I muttered, frustrated with myself. I sat up and went to my backpack, where I freed my laptop. There was one thing I had control over right now: my work with Kari.

I started by reading the last set of pages she had sent me a couple days ago. I shouldn't have. Somewhere in the midst of being in love with her book, I'd forgotten it wasn't a romance. It was a thriller/romance with a horror ending. And the horror part was taking over.

The main character, Ana, had decided after her near-death experience at the end of the last chapter that had she listened to the AI, she wouldn't be in this mess. The AI only wanted what was best for her, or so she thought. But what Kari was expertly letting the reader see was that the AI was, in fact, getting bored and testing psychological theories on unsuspecting humans. And Alan had no idea that Ana was listening to the AI again. He thought they were going to let love conquer all and screw the recommendations of something that had never experienced that all-consuming emotion before.

"Love is for losers, Alan," I whispered to my computer as I scrolled to the next page. "And Ana is going to screw you over. Just like every human in every relationship in every era of time has."

Maybe I wasn't in the right mindset to read this book. Or maybe I was in the perfect mindset. I typed out some notes that I hoped didn't sound too bitter and sent them off to Kari, adding the words I'll have your videos for you by tomorrow at the end of the email.

I opened the package of watery fruit, popped a grape into my mouth, then AirDropped the videos to my computer so I could edit them.

By the time I was done, I was crying again. I wasn't anticipating how much Oliver would be in the videos and how much seeing him would stir every emotion in my body.

As if he knew I was thinking about him, my phone buzzed on the bed next to me. You have no idea how sorry I am. Nothing I say can possibly justify why I didn't tell you, but if you will give me a chance, I would like to try to explain. If you'd rather just ghost me, I deserve it.

I threw my phone back onto the bed with a growl. "Ghost. I pick the ghost."

I closed my computer. I'd put the finishing touches on the videos and send them to Kari in the morning. All I wanted to do now was sleep.

. . .

My head felt like it weighed a hundred pounds as I tried to lift it off my pillow the next morning. And it was throbbing. My eyes felt puffy and raw. It took me a moment to realize it was the buzzing of my phone that had woken me.

"Hello," I answered, my voice scratchy.

"Margot! I thought you were murdered by someone from one of those dating apps." It was Sloane. "Your car is here. Where are you?"

"At my parents' house."

"You sound terrible."

"You woke me up." My phone said it was barely seven A.M.

"I was worried."

"You home?"

"Yes, got in late last night. I tried calling but you didn't answer."

"I've had a weekend. I'll tell you everything later. How was yours? Any of your clients win any awards?"

"Yes, actually. It was pretty amazing."

"That's awesome."

"I'm glad you're alive. I'll see you after work."

I nodded but then, realizing she couldn't see me, said, "Okay."

The phone went silent. I sat up and rubbed my eyes, then listened intently for any movement from my parents downstairs. There was nothing. I padded to the bathroom, where I washed my face and brushed my teeth. I was still wearing my clothes from the day before, so I changed into a fresh outfit from my suitcase, then rezipped all my belongings inside.

My mom was sitting at the kitchen table drinking a cup of coffee when I went downstairs. She let out a short scream when she saw me, her hand flying to her chest. "You scared me. I didn't know you were here."

"Sorry. I crashed upstairs last night. You and Dad are going to end up on the news as the couple who had a person living on their second floor for years if you don't start doing a security sweep at night."

"Very funny."

"It wouldn't be that funny, actually." I gave her a small smile. "I had no way of getting home. My car is out of commission." I pulled a mug out of the cupboard and filled it with coffee from the pot.

"That's right. How did you get to Audrey's yesterday?"

"Her ex-boyfriend dropped me off." Apparently, I was feeling snarky this morning.

"What?" Mom asked, confused.

I sat across from her at the table. "Where is Dad?"

"He started walking in the mornings. Something about sunlight and vitamin D."

"You don't go with him?"

"Honey, your dad and I spend a lot of time together. When I have an opportunity to be alone, I take it."

"Understandable." I took another sip of coffee, then held the warm cup between both hands. "Do you think you could give me a ride home sometime this morning?"

"This morning, I—uh, well, I think I have something," she said in a terrible attempt to pretend she was busy. I knew what was coming next before she even said it. "But let me call Audrey and see if she can take you home." She reached for her phone.

"Mom," I said in a low voice. "I do not want to see Audrey today."

"Margot, I think it's important that the two of you talk."

"And we will. Not today. Please."

She sighed. "You don't think you have an apology to make?"

My eyes stung with the suggestion. "I don't. Not this time. She said some horrible things to me."

"You called her a bitch."

"And I stand by that." Maybe I led with my emotions, like Audrey had always accused me of, but I decided if the alternative was no emotions, like she seemed to lead with, I'd stick to my way. It's who I was and I was done thinking she was better than me for it.

Mom held up her hands. "Fine. I'm staying out of this one. Not taking sides." For once, I wanted her to pick a side. I wanted her to tell me that Audrey had been horrible to me yesterday and everyone knew it. But apparently she thought we were equally horrible.

"Thank you." I brushed a crumb off the table. "So are you really busy or was that a lie?"

"It wasn't a lie. Just a motherly fabrication to help my children."

"Okay, motherly fabricator, I'm ready to go home whenever you're ready to take me."

"Give me an hour."

CHAPTER 36

The fiddle-leaf fig tree in the corner of my bedroom had dropped all but one of its leaves in my absence. My plant app would probably tell me it was just as depressed as I was if I used it for a diagnosis. Instead of confirming what I already knew, I poured the rest of my water bottle into its pot and attempted to give it a pep talk. "You'll be fine. You didn't need all those leaves anyway. One looks good on you."

The last leaf dropped to the floor dramatically, like it knew I'd been lying.

"Nice."

I gave my bed a side-eye. It was never going to see any action, was it?

My chest felt tight and empty at the same time. Like someone had hollowed it out, leaving me sore in the process.

I freed my phone from my pocket and stared at the screen, void of any notifications. Tears stung my eyes and I gritted my teeth and quickly swiped to the app store, then began the

process of redownloading the dating apps. I felt like Ana from
Kari Cross's book, ready to turn my life over to the AI.

. . .

"What are you doing?" Sloane asked when she came home from
work several hours later. I was sitting on the couch, a glass of wine
next to me, my phone in my hand.

"I'm trying to find someone to sleep with who is a somewhat
decent human being."

"Somewhat?"

"Not married, doesn't think women are second-class cit-
izens, doesn't have a list of demands."

"And you're struggling in this goal?" she asked, eyes going
wide.

"You'd be surprised."

"Why are you trying to sleep with someone?"

"Because! Because men are stupid and only good for one thing.
And I've embraced the power of the apps to bring me that one
thing." I was really hoping that sleeping with someone else
would get the taste of Oliver out of my mouth. Help me forget
this heartache faster. Because I didn't like feeling like this.

She hung her keys on the hook in the kitchen and sat by me
on the couch. "You want to talk about it?"

"I found out Oliver is Audrey's ex yesterday and then I
called her a bitch."

"Wow. I . . . I didn't see any of that coming and I read movie
scripts for a living."

"Oh, and Rob showed up at Audrey's house ranting about
me stealing Kari from him and now everyone knows I was
sleeping with him."

"I'm confused."

"By which part?"

She toed off her shoes and pulled her feet up onto the couch with her. "By all of it. Oliver dated Audrey?"

"For about six months in college, I guess."

"And he didn't feel the need to tell you this?"

"Maybe that's why he's hesitated to date me for three years."

"You think he's known this *whole* time?"

"I don't know." I analyzed that thought. Maybe he really didn't know until . . . "That day he showed me the website over here," I said. "He'd spelled my last name wrong, remember? *That's* why he got all weird that day." So, the week before the trip.

Sloane gave a short laugh. "I bet your sister freaked out. Thought you did all this on purpose."

"She did."

Sloane put on her best Audrey voice and said, "I had him eight years ago for a minuscule amount of time, nobody else can have him, especially not my sister."

"Just thinking of the fact that Audrey dated him first is a total turnoff for me, Sloane. I don't want him."

She sighed. "She's married with almost three kids, Margot. Guarantee she doesn't remember what color his eyes are, let alone how his dick feels inside her."

"You're the worst."

My phone buzzed and I looked at the most recent message from some guy named Phillip. Want to send me dinner?

I turned my phone toward Sloane. "This is what I'm working with."

"What does that mean? He wants you to bring him dinner?"

"No, he doesn't want me. Just the food."

"Ugh. You're right, men are gross. Maybe you need to get off the apps and go back to trying to find your perfect meet-cute in real life."

I sighed and slid my phone onto the coffee table. "Maybe I'll move to a deserted island and swear off men forever. Oliver knew who I was and decided to sleep with me anyway, Sloane."

"You slept with him?" she all but yelled.

"Yes."

"And?"

"And what? It was incredible and then I found out he's a liar. You're telling me you'd be okay if that happened to you?"

"Probably not. How did he defend himself?"

"I haven't really let him. He didn't deny knowing, though. That's all I needed to hear."

"You're probably right."

Her words, even though they were affirming my decision, made my chest tighten. Maybe I was hoping she would have some magical argument that would make everything better. Her giving up made me know there wasn't one.

"Why does Rob think you're trying to steal Kari?"

"Kari must've called him to get my cell number when she was asking me about the research trip. I don't know why else he would think that."

"You do more for her than Rob ever did and he knows it. That's why he's scared."

"He threatened to sue me." I nodded toward the contract that was still in a neat stack on the corner of the coffee table.

"He did?"

"So I told him if he did that, I would tell everyone we'd been sleeping together."

"You were on fire this weekend. I wish I could've been there to see his face."

I laughed a little. "It looked like his head was going to explode."

"I bet it did."

I sucked in some air and my eyes went blurry with tears. "I miss him, Sloane."

"You better not be talking about Rob."

I shook my head no.

She pulled me into a hug. "I know."

"When he talked about being cheated on in college, I could tell he was still torn up about it. He had strong feelings for Audrey."

"I'm sorry," she said. "Do you want to watch revenge movies and eat ice cream?"

I nodded. "I'm so lucky to have you. I love you."

"No need to get all sappy. Let's get angry instead."

. . .

My second author rejection came a couple days later. Her name was Lauren and she wrote a stunning book about families and their many complexities. There was also a love story that I adored. But once again, Lauren got a better offer.

Maybe it was the fresh rejection or the two hundred bucks I'd spent on a new battery for my car, or maybe it was that I hadn't heard from Oliver since his apology text giving me permission to ghost him. Whatever the case, I wasn't in the right mindset when Cheryl called Wednesday morning. I had just popped a piece of bread in the toaster and was en route to retrieve the butter from the fridge when my phone vibrated with her name.

"Hello," I answered.

"Margot, hi. How are you?"

"I'm okay. How are you?"

"I'm good. A little nauseous these days, but for a good cause."

"For sure." Thinking about her pregnancy reminded me that my sister hadn't tried to contact me either.

"So," Cheryl said. "I know you're not looking for a job, what with starting your own agency and everything, but if you need something to fill the gap, my company is hiring."

"Oh." The word came out as shock. Maybe even offense. "No. I mean, I have a job. I'm trying. I don't need . . ." I paused as my pride settled and the thought of Rebecca's text took over, about how long it might be before I started making any money, let alone a livable wage. I hadn't heard back from Kari about the videos I'd sent her either and she still hadn't paid me. Maybe Rob had threatened her as well. Maybe she was going to ghost me as well. And maybe I was going to fail miserably at this whole agenting thing. I was used to having backup plans. It seemed like I always needed them. "Yes, actually, I could use a temporary job."

"Great! I'll send you the info and put in a good word for you. They're interviewing tomorrow."

"I'll be there."

CHAPTER 37

"What qualities will you bring to this job that other candidates might not?" the man who couldn't have been more than twenty-four asked me.

Tomorrow had come, and here I was, all dressed up, makeup on, talking to the assistant of a movie producer asking me what qualities I could bring to taking coffee orders and stocking dressing rooms with snacks. For some reason, when Cheryl told me her company was hiring, I had pictured something more administrative. She was a casting director. I thought she wanted me to give input there. But I realized that was a ridiculous notion. That wasn't a job someone walked into with no experience. I'd also thought this interview was a formality, but as I took in the overly serious expression of Mr. Jeans and T-Shirt, I knew that it wasn't.

"I'm really good at blending in," I said to the twenty-four-(twenty-three?)-year-old. "Making myself unseen in the most helpful ways." That probably wasn't the answer he wanted. He wanted to hear that I was a hard worker or a team player or had a photographic memory or something. But my answer felt more true right now.

The impressed downward turn of his lips made me think that being invisible was probably something he hadn't considered a strength before now.

We were sitting on high stools in the corner of a warehouse, set pieces and lights being moved around us by a dozen or so people in orange shirts. A golf cart zipped by outside. My heel slipped off the bottom rung of the stool where it had been resting, causing me to jolt forward before regaining my balance.

"Well, Margot, the job is yours if you want it."

"I got the job?" I asked, somewhat surprised. My answer to the last question wasn't any better than my answers to the dozen before that had been. Maybe this really was just a formality.

"Yes," he said, standing. "Report here tomorrow at seven A.M. sharp." He took in my pencil skirt and button-down blouse. "You can wear something more comfortable."

"You don't think this is comfortable?" I asked.

He finally cracked a smile. "You'll want sneakers. Trust me, you'll be walking a lot."

"Okay, I'll see you tomorrow . . . I guess," I said.

"Great," he said.

Yes, great, I thought with a sigh as I walked away. This was just temporary, I reminded myself. Just until I could get some clients, sell some books. Just temporary.

I drove home trying to think of this as a good thing. I'd have some money coming in. The pay wasn't terrible. It would take some stress off. It would keep me busy. Help me not be in my head all day or incessantly checking emails.

I had all but talked myself into how amazing this was

going to be when I pulled into my designated spot back home and walked the path to my door. I stopped in the middle of the sidewalk, twenty feet from my destination. A figure sat on my front porch.

She stood when she saw me. "Hi."

"Audrey."

"Can we talk?" She pointed over her shoulder at the apartment.

"Okay." I finished my walk and unlocked the door, her floral scent hitting me in the face as I did.

She followed me inside.

I threw my keys on the kitchen counter, then stood facing her, my arms crossed, waiting.

She took in my living room, her eyes landing on each of the poor decorating decisions Sloane and I had made over the years. A mishmash of clutter, really. She sunk to the couch. "We've never fought like this before."

"That's because I always apologize," I said. "I'm not apologizing this time."

"You want *me* to apologize? You called me a bitch."

"A judgmental bitch," I amended. "You really didn't come here to apologize?"

"I came here to talk."

I sighed, bracing myself on the back of the love seat. "I'm not in the mood, Audrey. I just took a job as an assistant to an assistant, so you can gloat and leave now."

"You took a job? I thought you were starting your own agency."

"Didn't you assume I'd fail at that?" I said.

"Maggie, you're not being fair."

"You made a fruit tray, Audrey. You didn't even give me

a chance to follow through. You didn't even trust me with fruit." Maybe it wasn't the right example, since I did not, in fact, follow through with the fruit. But that was beside the point. The point was that she didn't believe in me, not even with the most minuscule things, like a stupid fruit tray.

"I trust you," she insisted. "Don't give up. Don't take an assistant job."

"Wasn't it you who said I live in a dream world? Encouraged me to go to Santa Barbara instead of UCLA, told me to give up screenwriting. Said it was impractical? I'm just being realistic, Audrey."

"I was trying to help," she said.

"Were you?"

She blew a breath out her nose. "Fine. Whatever. Do what you want."

"Thank you. I will."

She grunted and crossed her arms. "And Oliver?"

His name made me flinch, then settled in the pit of my stomach and seemed to harden there into a painful knot. "What about him?"

"It's just, my viewers have researched me. Found pictures I posted online years ago. They know I've dated him. How will that look if they find out you're dating him now? It will be weird."

"I don't care about your viewers."

"It's my life, Maggie. My livelihood. I care."

I sighed. "I already told you I'm not dating him anymore. So you can stop worrying. There is no evidence of our time together anywhere on the internet." That thought made me sad. Made it seem like it had all been something I'd conjured up in my imagination. I stepped out of my heels and used my foot to slide them next to the couch. "Wait, is that why you came here? To make sure I wasn't dating him?"

"I came here to try to make things right."

"Okay, well, things don't always happen just because you want them to. I need some time."

"I don't understand why you're so mad at me," she said.

"I think that's the main problem," I returned.

She stood. "Maggie, you don't have to get a job. I'll let you borrow some money. Help you develop a plan for your business."

"Absolutely not."

"But you were going to let Mom loan you money?"

"Mom wouldn't hold it over my head. Tell me exactly how I need to spend it."

"I run a successful business."

"You know nothing about publishing and yet you still think you would do a better job than me. You don't believe in me. Only in yourself. That's why I'm mad, Audrey. That."

· · ·

"*I* don't believe in me," I said.

"What?" Sloane asked.

We were sitting at the dinner table, a plateful of street tacos between us. We'd both just gotten home from work. Mr. Twenty-Three (twenty-two?) was right, sneakers were a must. I'd been on my feet all day and I was tired. I hadn't even had a second to feel sorry for myself. Okay, fine, I had a few seconds for that.

"I don't believe in myself," I said again. "I believed in everything my sister ever did with all my heart, knew she would succeed. But when it came to me, I second-guessed, let myself be talked out of everything, just assumed I would fail. I have always gotten in my own way."

"Your sister isn't innocent in all this."

"I know," I said, squeezing a lime over the cabbage and meat on my taco. "But it's not her life. It's mine. She is not the arbiter of success. I do not have to do things the way she did them in order for them to work. I don't always have to defer to her."

"Amen," Sloane said.

"I'm going to post in more writer forums and travel to writing conferences. Get myself in front of writers."

Sloane's eyebrows popped up. "Yes, you should."

"I know, I should save my money."

"I wasn't thinking that at all."

I laughed. "Yes, you were."

"Yes, I was," she said around a bite of taco.

"I'm going to borrow money from my parents so I'm not so strapped. Because I believe I'm going to be successful and I didn't do a good job of making them believe that. I'll make a PowerPoint or something. They'll eat that up."

She squeezed my arm. "Tell me you're going to quit your new job."

"Ha! Yes, I am. Because I'm going to put more time into my business."

"Because you are going to succeed," she said.

"Because I am going to succeed," I repeated.

CHAPTER 38

I endlessly swiped as I lay in my dark room. Rejection after rejection. I knew which face I was waiting for. He had come up time and again whenever I'd redownloaded the apps for the last three years. He would come up now and it would be a sign that I was supposed to message him, forgive him. After all, he'd only known a week before I had. And he had tried to tell me in the car and in the silo and now that I thought about it, when he was drunk too. I hadn't let him. I needed to get over myself. Our meet-cute was these damn dating apps. They'd thrown us together in the beginning and they'd throw us together again now.

Only he wasn't coming up. It felt like my finger had crossed my screen more than a hundred times. The screen was smudged at this point and it was harder to swipe away each denial, my palms clammy. Maybe this was the actual sign.

I exed out of the app and set my alarm for eight o'clock the next morning. I had work to do. Now wasn't the time to get sidetracked with the drama my life had turned into.

. . .

"Okay, I'll do it," Kari said.

The living room was dark. Sloane had paused *Promising Young Woman* when my phone rang and we both saw Kari Cross's name on the screen. It had been another long day full of quitting a job I'd only worked one day at. Apologizing profusely to Cheryl about how I hoped this wouldn't reflect poorly on her (she understood and said it wouldn't). Presenting a PowerPoint to my parents, who were both delighted to hand over the asked-for sum with assurances about how proud of me they were. I was sure my mom felt guilty about how the showdown in Audrey's backyard had gone, but I wasn't going to question the change of heart.

It was now nine P.M. Not too late, but too late for Kari Cross to be calling me. It was eleven P.M. her time.

"You'll do what?" I asked Kari, confused. "Is this about the videos I sent? Did they come through okay?"

"They were amazing. Everything I needed and more. You went above and beyond."

"Thank you. I had fun."

"I could tell. I need to pay you. Will you send me your e-pay info?"

"Of course. Thank you."

"But that's not why I called. These videos along with the latest notes you sent and how genuinely invested you are in my career is why I'd like you to be my agent."

I stood up and the popcorn bowl that was in my lap crashed to the floor, hitting the coffee table on the way down and spewing popcorn all over the carpet.

"What was that?" Kari asked. "Are you okay?"

"I have a contract" was all I managed to get out. "Rob will sue me."

She laughed for what felt like a full minute. "Margot, Rob can't sue you. I came to you. And besides, Rob will get a percentage of the royalties on all my books he sold forever. Don't worry about Rob. Do you not want me as a client? You don't think you can sell my AI book?"

"I will sell the hell out of your AI book," I said, even though I actually wasn't sure I could. I loved it, though, and I could think of two editors off the top of my head who would love it too. "I might need to add a robot to my website."

"In the messy bed behind Oliver," Sloane whispered.

My eyes went wide. That little punk knew it was Oliver all along. Forgetting I was mad at Oliver for one moment, I mouthed, *Don't you dare tell him.*

She zipped her lips with a smile.

"What do you think?" Kari said. "Will you draw up a contract and get to work? I'm going to have this book done by the end of the week."

"Absolutely. Thank you." I excitedly ran in place, crunching popcorn under my toes, but not caring. "I look forward to working with you."

"We've been working together for years, Margot. This will be fun." The phone went dead.

Sloane jumped up and crushed me into a hug. "Your first client is Kari freakin' Cross!"

"I can't believe it!" My high slowly teetered on the edge of a cliff as I thought about how complicated this was. "Kari must've said something to Rob. That's why he was convinced. He's going to kill me."

"Thank goodness you slept with him. He'll slink away quietly. He knows what he has to lose."

I shook my head but smiled. "You're right."

"Of course I'm right. He has zero ethics and this is his own fault."

"True."

"How does Kari's book end, anyway? As terribly as you imagined?"

"Yes. It's definitely horror. Ana kills Alan per the AI's instructions, but she's very happy, just like the AI told her she would be. And there is no punishment since the town has vowed to live by the AI's rules. It's super creepy, and honestly, I kind of loved it."

Sloane gave an ironic laugh. "I'm sorry Oliver broke you."

"He didn't. God, he'd be so excited about Kari becoming my first client." My mood immediately dropped. I picked up the empty popcorn bowl and started scooping handfuls from the carpet back into it.

"You should tell him. He did take a weekend out of his life to help you with the videos."

"He got plenty of payment for that," I muttered.

"You're really not going to forgive him?"

I plopped the popcorn bowl on the table and sat on the floor. "Even if I wanted to hear him out, Sloane, it's complicated. Audrey and I may be fighting but I don't want to hurt her."

"Why would this hurt her so bad? I'm having a hard time understanding."

"Because . . ." I tried to think of reasons to fill in after that word but was coming up blank. "I guess because he was hers at some point in the past."

Her eyebrows popped up as if to say *exactly*.

"For six months," I said. "Eight years ago."

"That was a tiny amount of time in the grand scheme of things."

"And yet she still thinks she has some sort of claim on him."

"But . . ." she said, seeming to know there was more.

"But I've known Oliver for over three years. She can't hold him hostage over a six-*month* relationship. He's *mine* to call dibs on, not hers."

"Damn straight he is."

"I guess I need to talk to her. Tell her how I feel. And then give Oliver the chance to explain himself."

"How *do* you feel?" she asked.

I picked up a stray kernel of popcorn from beneath the coffee table and turned it slowly in my fingers before depositing it into the bowl. Then I met her expectant stare. "I love him."

She smiled and let out a small squeal.

"But love doesn't always conquer all," I said.

She rolled her eyes. "You can no longer rep romance."

"In romance books, everything works out. In real life, I'm not so sure."

. . .

"How many editors have you heard back from?" Sloane asked several days later. I had met her at her office so we could go to lunch together. Apparently, these were things I did now that I was in charge of my own schedule: lunched at restaurants near Sloane's work.

"They've only had it for one day," I said. The first two days after Kari had announced she wanted to be my client had been spent creating and signing contracts and putting together a list. Kari had lots of opinions about both.

"I know it's only been one day, but this is Kari Cross we're talking about. Nobody has said *anything*?" She looked nervous, like she thought Rob had called all the editors at every publishing house and instructed them not to touch me with a ten-foot pole. Okay, that was *my* nightmare. I was projecting.

"I've had one response. It was something like, *Kari Cross is writing what now?*"

She cringed.

"I know." I picked up a crystal paperweight with a video camera etched into the side and raised my eyebrows at her.

"Like I said, I have nothing in this office I would save in a fire."

I set it back down and she grabbed her purse off the chair. "You ready?"

"Yes, I'm so hungry."

"Are you worried at all?" she asked.

"About selling Kari's book?"

She nodded.

"No, you know how slow publishing can move."

"Almost as slow as Hollywood," she responded.

"Exactly. It's going to happen. Like you said, this is Kari Cross."

She waved to a coworker near the front as we headed outside. "And what about that other thing we talked about? What are you going to do about that?"

"What other thing?"

"That tiny revelation you had about being in love?"

I wanted to talk to Oliver. I was hoping with everything in me that what he had to say would be enough for me to get over the hurt that still lingered over the lies he told. And maybe that thought was why I was stalling. As much as I missed him, I worried that it wouldn't be enough. That no matter what he said, I wouldn't be able to trust him again. And that thought broke my heart all over again. "I don't know."

. . .

The rest of the week I counted in messages. Every day something new from someone new.

Audrey: Maggie, I'm sorry. I realized I never said that. But I am. And I am a judgmental bitch. Please answer my calls.

> Margot,
> I adore Kari Cross and if she writes another romance, please send it my way. But horror is not my specialty or interest. I'm going to pass . . .

Rob: I'm consulting a lawyer. It's not too late to make this right.

> Hey Margot,
> We'd love for you to come to our romance con. Please see attached itinerary and let us know if the proposed panels work for you.

> Margot,
> I like to keep my horror acquisitions pure. I don't think I can get behind something so convoluted. Thanks for thinking of me . . .

Kari: Rob's an ass, he has no ground to stand on. Please don't worry about any threats he might make. Just focus on selling my book.

> *Ms. Hart,*
> *Attached is the full manuscript of my rom-com you re-*
> *quested. I hope you love it and look forward to hearing*
> *from you soon . . .*

Oliver: Margot, I know you aren't speaking to me, but when you get clients, if you want me to add them to your website, let me know. I didn't teach you how to change things. I should've taught you how to change things. I should've done so many things. I'm sorry . . . Also, I miss you.

> *Margot,*
> *We love Kari Cross, we don't love this idea . . .*

"Shit," I said as I read the most recent rejection in my in-box. "I can't fail." I was home alone, talking to nobody, yet still felt the need to say it out loud.

I had actually gotten dressed that morning, in a pair of slacks and a blouse. Work clothes. Because even though my apartment was too small to have a dedicated office space, Oliver had been right, I needed something to mark my work hours from the rest of my day. Otherwise it all blended together in a big continuous stream of time.

Speaking of Oliver, I'd read the text he sent that morning at least a dozen times. Soaking in each sentence, analyzing every word choice, second-guessing every meaning. *When you get clients*, he'd said. When. He believed in me. And yet I didn't respond. At this point, I wasn't even sure what I was waiting for. Maybe I was waiting for my brain to turn off and my feelings to take over. Something I wasn't used to. And the fact that it wasn't happening worried me more than anything.

CHAPTER 39

I sat up in my bed with a gasp. I had been scrolling the apps again. Rejection after rejection. Face after face. It had become my habit before drifting off to sleep every night. My new mind-numbing ritual. A ritual that tonight I was jolted out of with the face I'd been waiting for. Oliver's.

It didn't surprise me that as I stared at him, took in his kind eyes, great hair, and heart-melting smile that tears came to my eyes. I missed him so much. This was the sign I was waiting for. The jump start to my emotions. Did I force the sign? Maybe. But still, the universe provided.

I bit my lip nervously, thinking about what my first message to him should be. *Fancy meeting you here? So we meet again? We have to stop meeting like this?* They all seemed too basic or too flippant. I needed to be sincere. Something like: *I miss you. I'm ready to hear you out.*

It would be a full-circle moment. We met on the apps, we remet on the apps over and over, and now we'd make up on the apps. Our meet-cute.

I smiled and swiped right.

Nothing happened. No *matched* message appeared on my screen. Maybe I'd come across his profile first and now just had to wait for his acceptance. Or maybe he swiped left, rejected me.

It hadn't occurred to me until that moment that he could've decided it was too weird to date the sister of an ex. That all he wanted to explain was why he'd lied about it, because he was a nice guy and couldn't live with himself if he didn't, and then he'd go on his way. The fact that he was still on the apps at all was messing with my head. Had he never gotten off? How many women was he chatting with?

Maybe this was the real sign from the universe. And it was telling me to let him go.

. . .

Two people were in line in front of me at the coffee shop Monday when my phone rang. Sloane and Cheryl were supposed to meet me here on an early lunch break, so I pulled out my phone, thinking they were going to tell me why they were running late. The name on my screen stopped me cold.

"Hello, this is Margot," I answered, doing the best I could to sound professional in the middle of a coffee shop.

"Hi, Margot, it's James Rosen." Only one of the very best editors of horror around.

"Hi, James. How are you?"

"I'm good. Good."

"Next," the barista at the register said, obviously not for the first time.

Somehow the two people that were in line in front of me had already ordered without me realizing. I lifted my hand in an apology and stepped to the side, plugging my left ear so I could hear better. "Do you have good news for me?"

"This book, Margot, is amazing."

My chest expanded, close to bursting. "I knew you'd love it."

"I wasn't going to read it, but your passion for the project convinced me." He cleared his throat. "Now, who is my competition, and which boxing gloves do I need to pull out to acquire this?"

I tried not to react. As far as he was concerned, this was what I had expected. I was confident and calm. "I can let you know in the next day or two." Now it was my turn to use some leverage. Not for a different editor—he was the right one for this book—but to drum up more interest, which would result in a higher advance from him. "Put together your best offer."

"Will do," he said.

"Oh, and James. She wants to keep all the elements of all the different genres. You're open to that?"

"I am very open to that."

"Great. I'll speak with you soon."

I tapped the red button on my screen, disconnecting the call, and then silently screamed, spinning a circle and doing a little dance while I did.

"Excuse me, Miss?"

The voice had my head whipping in the direction of its owner, the blood draining from my face.

"I think they mixed up our drinks," Oliver said, a softness in his eyes. He held up an iced chai for me.

I looked at my hands, which held only a cell phone.

"You were supposed to get a drink," he said. "You didn't get a drink."

"I got a phone call," I said.

"Shit," he said.

I stared at the drink he held out for several long beats. It was like both my brain and my emotions had ceased functioning.

He slowly lowered his hand. "I'm sorry. This was a stupid idea that seemed more romantic in my head . . . I'll go."

"No," I said, and he stopped his retreat.

I took in our surroundings. I'd worked my way over to the side of the café when on the phone and that's where we stood, out of the way, by a bookcase that didn't hold a single book. There were plants and packages of coffee for sale and even candles. But no books.

He held out the drink again, and this time I took it, our hands brushing in the exchange.

"You didn't swipe right on me," I said, cupping the tea in my hands, like it was the only thing grounding me right now.

"What?"

"That was days ago. Which means you must've swiped left. I swiped right. And you swiped left. We weren't a match," I said, my throat tight from the memory, from the disappointment I felt.

"No," he said. "I'm not swiping. I didn't swipe at all."

"You're not swiping?" I asked, a little confused.

"I would've deleted the apps, but that's where our messages are. I reread them a lot. I know it's unhealthy and obsessive but I do it because . . . because I miss you, Margot. So much."

I nodded but couldn't say the words back no matter how much I felt them.

"I didn't know you were her sister," he said. "I mean, at first, I had no idea. Not three years ago in the car, not all these years of messaging, not the majority of our time together. Not until I saw her first name on your phone and then learned your last name. And even then I wasn't sure because her sister's name was Maggie. So I had to go home and google her and you."

"And then you knew," I said.

He nodded.

"*Before* you slept with me."

He closed his eyes and took a deep breath, then opened them again. "I'm sorry."

"Why didn't you tell me?"

"I was going to. I was processing. But you two were fighting and I wanted you to make up with her, I didn't want to be another source of tension, and I'd talked myself out of being with you once I found out. But you showed up at the gym. I tried to tell you then but you stopped me. Then you asked me for a ride to Paso Robles. And I didn't want to stay away from you. I thought maybe we really could just be friends. I wanted you in my life. Then in the silo you said that thing about the past being in the past and it's been eight years and I thought since we'd already . . ." He sighed, his shoulders dropping, as if saying everything out loud revealed just how much he had screwed up. "I have no excuse. I'm a coward. I should've told you."

"You should've."

He swallowed hard, a look of concentration taking over his face.

"I can see you thinking," I said.

"It's who I am."

"I know," I said. "And I'm impulsive sometimes . . . a lot of the time. I'm nothing like my sister."

"I know," he said.

"So what conclusions have you drawn?'

"Conclusions?" he asked.

"All the thinking you've been doing the last couple weeks. Have you concluded anything?"

"Aside from the fact that I'm stupid?"

"Yes, aside from that."

He laughed a little, maybe realizing my sarcasm had come out, maybe taking that as a good sign. "I've concluded that you're good for me. You get me out of my head and you challenge me and you make me happy. That you are smart and funny and interesting and sexy as hell. You're everything. And I . . ." He paused and took a breath, then met my eyes with wonder in his. "You swiped right on me?"

I nodded and held up the drink in my hands. "You wanted to give me a meet-cute."

"I love you, Margot."

My heart beat hard against my ribs, taking my breath away.

"Aren't you going to say it back?" came another voice.

I looked to my right to see Sloane and Cheryl standing there, arm in arm.

"That was a really good speech," Sloane said. "You forgive him, right?"

"Sloane, we're kind of in the middle of a private conversation here."

"In the middle of a coffee shop? This isn't exactly private conversation territory."

"You're right," I said. "It's not. We're leaving."

"What?" Sloane protested. "I'm invested now. I need to see the kiss."

"This isn't some movie set," I said.

She groaned. "Fine, get out of here."

Oliver held out his hand for me and I took it. He held on tight as we walked and a fuzzy warmth spread up my arms.

Outside, the trees around the coffee shop were being trimmed by a man in a large hat and an orange vest. The smell of freshly cut grass hung in the air. I took a sip of my tea and the liquid trailed a cool path down my throat.

Oliver turned toward me with a questioning head tilt. "Where are we going?"

"My place is closer." Which reminded me. "Why are you here?" This wasn't the closest coffee shop to his house.

He ran a slow thumb over my palm as he continued to hold my hand. "This is where I go for coffee now."

"Really?" I said. "The one closest to my house?"

"Yes," he answered. "I wanted to see you, if only for a minute."

"And what if I want to see you for more than a minute?" I asked.

"Do you?" he asked. "*Can* you forgive me?"

We stopped next to his car, which was parked along the curb, and he opened the passenger door for me.

"My car is in the parking lot," I said. "Meet me at my house?"

"Can I drive you? Please."

I smiled. "Are you worried I'm going to change my mind?"

"I'm not even sure which side of the aisle your mind is on yet," he said.

I thought the swiping right and the hand-holding and the inviting him to my house made things pretty clear, but maybe he sensed the lingering bits of hesitancy I still possessed about my sister and how this would make her feel. And yet as I stood here, staring at him, I knew that when all was said and done, this was my choice to make, not hers, and I chose Oliver. I chose me.

I took a step closer to him, the car door he held open

between us. I grabbed hold of the top of the doorframe and pushed myself up on my toes. "Does this make things clearer?" I asked, inches from his mouth.

He smirked. "A little."

I let our lips touch for a brief moment. "And that?"

"That helps," he said.

"Take me home," I said. "And we can show each other exactly where we stand." I stepped into his car, tucked my drink into the holder in the middle console, and clicked my seat belt into place.

On the drive, he never let go of my hand, even though at times it made driving difficult.

"Did you sell a book?" he asked. "In the coffee shop."

With Oliver showing up when he did, my brain hadn't processed that yet. "Almost," I said. "He'll have to convince an acquisitions board, but I think there's a good chance. It's the AI book."

"Wait. Kari Cross?" he said. "You're Kari's agent?"

I nodded, a goofy smile taking over my face. "Yes, I am."

"She's lucky to have you. What about Rob?"

"Rob is working on letting her go." I still got one text a day from him, full of threats. "He hasn't read one of her books in four years."

Oliver blew a huff of air out his nose. "Do you wish I would've punched him? I really wish I would've punched him."

"No," I said. "I don't. He would've pressed charges."

"I hadn't thought of that."

"*You* hadn't thought of that?"

Oliver parked in my marked spot at the apartment. "I'm proud of you."

"I am too."

He turned off the engine and faced me.

I leaned toward him, ready to feel his mouth on mine.

He stopped me with, "We could just talk, Margot. If there's more you need to say."

"I love you, Oliver. That's all I need to say right now."

He kissed me, our lips coming together like they'd been denied their means of existence for the last couple weeks. His mouth was warm and he tasted like cinnamon.

"I missed you," I said between kisses.

"I was lost without you."

"I do love cars," I said. "But can we go inside?"

"Let's go inside."

We managed to make it into the house with several points of our bodies touching the whole way. As soon as the door was shut behind us, he was peeling off my shirt. I was un-buttoning his pants and we were leaving a trail of clothes as we worked our way down the hall. In my room, he wrapped a strong arm around my waist and carried me the rest of the way to my bed.

"It's not made," I said against his lips.

"I didn't notice," he said back, lowering me to the bed and climbing on after me.

"Is this weird for you?" I asked.

"Your unmade bed? I'll survive."

I laughed. "No. That I'm Audrey's sister."

Those words had him collapsing to my side and propping himself up on his elbow. "You need to talk more."

"I guess I do."

He picked up my hand and brought it to his lips, resting his mouth against my knuckles while he thought for a moment.

"Maybe it should be weird for me, but I hadn't thought about your sister in years . . . no offense."

"You don't watch her daily videos online?"

"I didn't even know she did that until you said something."

At some point in our shedding of clothes and our bumping of walls on the way into the room, one of us had hit a switch, and the ceiling fan turned a lazy circle above us. I watched it rotate several times. "My whole life I've been compared to her and come up short. She's always been better than me, older, prettier, smarter, more successful."

He started to object but I held up my finger.

"She excels at everything. She even had two babies at once! And honestly, it was fine because we had such different interests that I could tell myself that I didn't want the things she had anyway. But when I found out she had you first, loved you first, I didn't think I could get past it."

"And now?" he asked, tucking a lock of hair behind my ear.

"Now I realize that I can't live my life constantly trying to impress my sister, trying to live up to the bar she set. And she doesn't get to run my life along with her own, no matter how successful she's turned out to be."

"This is a very good realization." His finger traced a slow line along the lace edging of my bra, the only piece of clothing left on either of our bodies, sending a shiver through me. "Also, you are the smartest, prettiest, funniest woman I've ever known."

His finger continued its line to the strap of my bra, where it slid beneath it and coaxed it off my shoulder. All the nerve endings in my body sang with pleasure. "Is talking about my sister turning you off?"

He laughed. "It normally would, but you lying here in just

your bra is having a counteractive effect on the words coming out of your mouth."

"Good." My eyes roamed down his strong arms, then I ran a hand along the smattering of hair across his toned chest. "I missed you. I missed this."

He took me by the hip and turned me flush with his body. "Me too."

"I can tell," I said, pressing myself even tighter against him.

"Margot?" He undid the hooks at the back of my bra and I maneuvered it off my body and tossed it to the floor.

"Yes?" I asked.

"Are we going to be okay? Is this okay?"

I nodded. My chest was warm against his.

"Because I want you." His hands explored me with the words, sliding along the sides of my breasts to my waist, pausing at the sensitive spot just below my hip bone and gripping me there.

"Well then take me," I said.

In a fluid motion, he rolled me to my back, his body resting on top of me. The weight of him sent a thrill through me that settled and throbbed between my legs. His mouth, soft and urgent, explored every inch of me. And as I held on to him, I knew I'd made the right choice. That we really would be okay. More than okay. Perfect.

CHAPTER 40

"I don't want to do this," Oliver said. We sat in the car in front of my parents' house the following weekend. We were here for a family dinner, my sister already inside. Neutral ground, I had thought. But maybe he'd been here before. Maybe this wasn't as neutral as I'd planned.

I took his hand in mine and smiled. "Too bad. This is your penance."

"This feels like revenge, not penance."

"Oliver, she's going to be part of our lives forever. If you can't accept that, then . . ." I wasn't sure how to finish that sentence. I wasn't trying to give an ultimatum, but this was my family and he was my boyfriend and I needed them to get along. I needed it so badly.

"No, I can. Look at me," he said, and I turned away from studying the front porch out the side window to looking at his soft brown eyes. "I can. I'm just whining. The first meeting will be awkward. It will be better after this."

"Promise?" I asked, because now *I* was wondering if this

was a good idea. Maybe it was too soon. Maybe I should've waited until I'd been able to talk to my sister face-to-face. We'd only had a phone conversation where I'd informed her that I actually *was* going to date Oliver, in fact already was, because she had no claim on him.

I couldn't see her face, so I wasn't sure if she really meant it when she said, "You're right and I'm happy for you."

"They do know I'm coming, right?" Oliver asked now from where we both still firmly sat in our seats, no attempt to open our respective doors at all.

"Yes, they do. I'm not *that* cruel."

"Bill and . . . ?"

"Jennifer," I said, providing my parents' names. "And Audrey is married to Chase and their kids are Jack and Samuel."

"Okay, got it."

"How are you when meeting families?" I asked him.

"Under normal circumstances, I am a dream."

I snorted. "I bet parents love you."

"I've only met one set."

"So you *haven't* been here before," I said.

His eyes went wide. "No, I haven't. You thought I'd been here before?"

"I wasn't sure. And what about Chase? Did you ever meet him . . . back in college?"

He gave a breathy chuckle, seeming to know what I was implying. "No. I was just told about him in a very straightforward manner by your sister."

"That sounds about right," I said, grabbing hold of his forearm that was resting on the center console.

He placed his hand over mine. "I feel the need to reiterate that I am over all that. You know I'm over that, yes?"

"Yes," I said.

"How are *you* when meeting parents?" he asked, curious. "I imagine they love you."

"Are we stalling?" I asked.

"We are absolutely stalling," he said.

"Should we leave?" I asked. "We could get out of here and go get some tacos and then have shower sex. We haven't had that yet."

He laughed. "You make a very compelling case, but no, we're not going to leave. We're here. We can do this." He opened his door first. I was still sitting inside when he walked around the car and opened my door. "It will get easier after this," he promised again.

I stepped out and we linked hands. "I haven't met parents in a while," I said, answering his previous question as we walked. "But I wasn't great. In the most recent instance, I had no filter and ended up insulting their much beloved cat. It was definitely the beginning of the end."

"My mom and sister would love you."

"And your dad? I know he left a long time ago and you don't see him, but do you *talk* to him at all?"

"Not once."

"We'll unpack that later," I said.

"Before or after shower sex?" he asked.

"It seems I'm good at bringing up family members during sex. We could try that."

He groaned. "Please, no."

As we reached the porch, I squeezed his hand and turned to face him. "Thank you," I said.

"For what?" he asked.

"For doing this. For being you. For loving me."

"Easiest thing in the world."

I reached for the door handle while knocking at the same time. "Hello!" I called, stepping inside. "We're here."

"Back here, honey!" Dad called out.

"Last chance for shower sex," I said to Oliver under my breath.

"Are you saying it's now or never? Because that changes my answer."

I smiled and took his hand in mine again, leading him through the formal front room and into the great room at the back of the house. My nephews reacted first, barreling toward me and wrapping my legs in a hug.

"I thought you said other people's kids didn't like you," Oliver said quietly.

"These aren't other people's kids," I said, ruffling their hair as they screamed my name. "These are family."

"Boys," I said squatting down. "This is Oliver."

"Liver?" Sammy asked, curling his lip.

"She said Oliver," Jack said.

"Oh! Hi!" Sammy laughed and then they both ran out the back door, where I assumed their parents were.

"Welcome!" Mom said from the kitchen, where she stood next to my dad. Together they were chopping up veggies for a salad.

"Mom, Dad, this is Oliver."

"I forgot the wine in the car," Oliver said. "I brought you wine." He took a step back.

I looked over at him. His face was on the pale side. He was more nervous than I thought. "It's okay, we'll get it in a bit," I said.

"That was thoughtful," Mom said. "Thank you."

"I'm sorry," he said. "It's nice to meet you. Thank you for having me."

"Of course," Mom said. "We're glad to finally meet you . . . I mean, through Margot, not through . . ." Okay, my mom was nervous too.

The back door opened and Audrey breezed in. Chase must've been out at the grill. "Hello!" she said, light and airy. "Oliver! So great to see you. You look exactly the same." She gave me a hug and then extended a hand to Oliver.

He took it in a single shake, then let go.

"Okay," I said. "Now that we've all gotten the awkward part out of the way, can we all be normal now?"

Dad laughed. "Can I get you a beer, Oliver?"

"Yes, please." He followed my dad to the fridge.

"Was *I* awkward?" Audrey asked. "I didn't feel awkward."

"You put on your YouTube voice," I said.

"You did," Mom agreed with a giggle.

"You were no better," I said to Mom.

"I'm sorry! He's so handsome, I couldn't help it."

"He's still in the room," Dad said. "At least wait until I take him outside."

Oliver gave me a *save me* look and I just mouthed *penance*.

It didn't take long for everyone to settle into normalcy. We ate outside on the patio with bistro lights strung overhead and soft music piped through the outdoor speakers. Chase was telling a story about a property he showed where a rat fell from a ceiling panel directly onto the client's head.

"How do you recover from that?" Oliver asked. The color had returned to his cheeks and he was sitting back in his chair, relaxed. He'd even rested his hand on my knee or my back or my arm throughout dinner.

"You don't," Chase said with a laugh. "You lead them back outside, wish them well, then immediately call an exterminator."

Audrey stood and picked up her empty plate, then raised her eyebrows at me, asking if I was done. Instead of handing it to her, I stood as well, helping her clear. When Oliver moved to do the same, I placed a hand on his shoulder. "Give me a sec to talk to her," I said near his ear.

He nodded and settled back into his chair.

Audrey and I carried four plates each into the kitchen and began scraping the leftover food into the garbage. She was uncharacteristically quiet.

"How are you feeling? About tonight and all this?" I asked.

"I didn't think that mattered." She set her latest scraped plate on the counter.

I sighed. "Audrey. Of course, it matters. Don't you understand? My whole life, everything I've done was to try to make you proud of me. I looked up to you so much. Everything you said held more weight in my life than anything anyone else said. Including myself. I never had to really think things through or analyze what exactly I wanted because I had you for that. And then my life imploded and I had to figure some things out. And I did. I wasn't trying to hurt you in the process, I was just trying to find me."

She met my eyes, and hers were shining with held-back emotion, all the dirty plates now on the counter waiting to be loaded into the dishwasher. "And did you?"

"I think so. I'm still working on it. And even though what I found might not have been the way you would've done my life or the things you would've picked for me, I hope you can be happy for me."

"You really do think I'm a bitch, don't you?" she said, a tear escaping from her eye and trailing down her cheek.

I couldn't remember the last time I'd seen my sister cry. "No! I don't. I really don't."

"Of course I'm happy for you, Margot," she said.

"I'm Margot now?"

"I don't know. What do you want me to call you? Maggie was your childhood name."

"I'm good with Maggie. Just from you, though."

She stepped forward and brought me into a hug. "I'm sorry. I was only ever trying to help. I didn't mean to make you unsure of yourself."

"I know," I said, hugging her back.

"I'm not as confident as you think I am," she said. "Half the time I'm faking it."

"Aren't we all," I said. "It's good to know you're human."

She pulled back and looked at me. "You have such an easygoing, fun nature. Quick to laugh, quick to make friends. I was always jealous of that."

"You were?"

She nodded and pulled gently on the end of my hair hanging over my shoulder. "I'm so proud of you. Always have been."

Great, now she was going to make me cry. Not hard to do, but still.

"Everything okay in here?" Mom asked, coming in the back door.

"We're good," I said, then looked at Audrey.

"So good," Audrey said. "Is everyone ready for dessert?"

"Yes, I'll help," Mom said, then to me, "You should go rescue your boyfriend."

"Does he need rescuing?" I asked, my eyes darting to the window.

"Dad is asking him to explain coding in detail."

I laughed, gave Audrey's hand one last squeeze, and then rejoined Oliver outside. They must've moved past the coding talk, because Chase and Dad were discussing the last T-ball game while the boys ran circles on the grass.

I sat on Oliver's lap, wrapped my arms around his neck, and pressed my cheek against his.

His arms immediately went around my waist. "Everything okay?"

"Yes, I'm glad we came," I said.

"Me too," he said. "I like your family."

"I like you," I said.

His laugh vibrated from his chest to mine as he held me tight.

ONE YEAR LATER

New York was not LA. It was hot and muggy and crowded and vibrant and exciting and interesting. It was full of people always in a hurry because there were so many places to go. And buildings that rose so high into the sky they touched the clouds. It was loud with honking horns and ringing bike bells and shouting cab drivers and construction workers and also music and laughter and conversation. And there were trees. More trees than I was expecting. Some with little iron gates around them in the middle of a sea of concrete. There were vines that climbed up brick walls and potted flowers that sat on porches and hung in window boxes. Food carts dotted corners and people played guitars with boxes full of change in front of them.

It didn't surprise me that this was the heart of publishing.

"This place is so full," I said, Oliver's hand in mine as we headed for the Ritz-Carlton.

"Full of what?" he asked.

"Of everything," I said.

"You want to move here?"

"I want to visit here. Way more often. But no, LA is home."

He squeezed my hand. "You excited for this?"

Kari's AI book came out on Tuesday to rave reviews, and right now at the ballroom in the Ritz, we were having a book launch. Lots of important people from the industry would be there and we would celebrate Kari and her success. She took a risk. She stepped outside her genre and it was paying off in a big way.

"I am. I have some editors I want to talk to about Lacey's book." I had clients now. Lots of them. Even some of my old clients had found me and joined me for their current projects. And I'd sold more than just Kari's book. In fact, I'd been featured in *Publishers Weekly* as a Rising Star. I was still paying back my parents' loan and barely managing my bills, but I was on my way.

"Don't work too hard. This is a party too," he said. "A celebration."

"I like celebrations."

"I know you do."

At the front doors to the hotel was a larger-than-life cutout of Kari's book cover. I passed Oliver my phone and he took a selfie of us standing in front of it. Then he turned the phone toward me, showing me the screen. "Your sister is calling."

I nodded for him to answer the FaceTime call. The image that came on the screen was my sleeping niece. "Adeline wanted to wish you luck tonight," Audrey said. Her daughter was seven months old now and the sweetest baby ever.

"Aw, I miss her," I responded, taking over holding the phone.

"Hi, Audrey," Oliver said. Yes, it had been weird at first, anytime the two of them interacted. And perhaps I hadn't fully anticipated the feelings of jealousy I'd have at the beginning.

But then those feelings faded away, because aside from the few stories they shared from the past, they really were like strangers getting to know each other. It was obvious I knew more about Oliver than Audrey ever had.

"I know you're busy," Audrey said. "I just wanted to say congratulations. Tell Kari hi from me and that I adore her book."

"No advice for me tonight? It's my first big party."

"You should be giving me advice, little sis. You're killing it."

"Love you."

"Love you too."

We hung up and Oliver and I finished our walk inside to the ballroom already full of people dressed up and enjoying themselves.

On a big table just past the doors were stacks and stacks of Kari's book. She'd signed them earlier to give away to the guests tonight.

Kari met me in the middle of the ballroom and brought me into a hug. "Don't be alarmed, but Rob is here."

"You invited Rob?" I asked.

Rob. He did not go quietly. We fought and threatened each other weekly for three months after I signed Kari. But he didn't sue me. And I didn't expose him. Then one day, he just stopped. I didn't ask him why, not wanting to reopen dialogue. The romantic in me told me it was because he fell madly in love and his anger disappeared. Sloane had said, "Let's hope it's not with his twenty-four-year-old assistant."

"I did not invite him," Kari said now. "But you know how publishing is . . ."

"Small," I said.

"Exactly. You can play nice?" This she directed at Oliver.

"I don't know who Rob is," he said.

She laughed. "Good answer."

A woman approached from my right and I immediately recognized her as Doris Mesner from my dream agency. "You must be Margot," she said, extending her hand.

"I am. It's so nice to meet you, Doris."

"What do I have to do to get you over to my agency?"

"Move to Los Angeles?" I smiled.

"Let's talk later." To Kari, she said, "Congratulations. Your book is phenomenal."

"Thank you."

"We're going to grab drinks," I said to Kari. "Would you like anything?"

"No, but I need to talk to you later too. I have an idea for something outside the box."

"More outside the box than this?" I nodded toward her table of books.

She smiled.

"I'm sure it's amazing."

As we headed toward the bar Oliver said, "You like people more than I do."

"As long as you like me, I'm okay with that."

"Not even a question," he said.

My phone buzzed and I pulled it out of the pocket of my dress, hooking my arm in Oliver's so I could read and walk at the same time. Sloane had sent a text that was accompanied by fireworks shooting across my screen. The fireworks are supposed to represent yours and Kari's success, not whatever you and Oliver have been doing in your fancy hotel.

Thanks for the clarification, I typed back.

Congrats! Oh, and you left your notebook on the coffee table and I may have read a few lines on the page. Are you writing a screenplay?!

I had started writing again, just for fun. It was amazing how much I wanted to, now that I was listening to my own instincts. And maybe it would be more than fun one day. Don't read my stuff, nosy!

I won't have access to your stuff anymore if you would talk to Oliver about the whole moving in thing. I want to sign a lease with Miles next month.

Glad to know you can so easily replace me. And asking someone to move into their house is a delicate matter. It takes time.

More fireworks exploded on my screen. Those represent me and Miles.

Ew. I gotta go. I'm in the middle of a party.

Love you!

We stopped at the back of a decent-sized line for the bar.

Oliver pulled out his phone, read something on the screen, and looked at me. "You want to move in with me?" he asked.

My mouth fell open. "Did Sloane just text you?"

He turned his phone toward me: Ask your rock star girlfriend to move in with you already.

"I'm sorry," I said. "You know Sloane."

"You want to move in with me?" he repeated.

I studied his face, trying to read his expression. "Are you asking me or *asking* me?"

After a year, Oliver knew me well, because that question didn't confuse him. "I didn't need this text from Sloane. I was going to ask you as soon as we got home."

"Really?"

"Really," he said.

"Yes."

"Yes?"

We were almost to the front of the line when I saw Rob ahead ordering drinks, a very young blonde on his arm. Oliver had pretended Rob didn't bother him when Kari brought it up, but I knew better. The months of back-and-forth between Rob and me were hard for him to sit through without doing anything. And now, I knew Rob was one errant word away from getting laid out by Oliver's fist.

"I'm fine," Oliver said, reading my mind, like normal. "Are *you?*"

"You're really fine?"

"We won, Margot. I kind of feel sorry for him now. But if you want to avoid him, I understand. We can turn around."

I smiled up at him. "Yes, Oliver, I want to move in with you. I want you to be annoyed that I turn that nice chair in the corner of your room into my clothes chair and that I stack piles of books on the nightstand by the bed and that I only do dishes when the sink is full."

"And you can be annoyed that I don't hit the snooze button and I run every morning at the exact same time and I eat the exact same thing for breakfast regardless of my feelings."

"That is pretty annoying," I said. "But I'm already used to all that."

He kissed me softly. "You're good for me."

I laced our fingers together. "I get to use your toilet all the time now."

He let out a groan. "*Toilet* still doesn't mean what you're implying it to mean, Margot."

I laughed. "It will always mean that to me."

ACKNOWLEDGMENTS

My first adult book in the books! What a ride. I am so grateful that I had this opportunity to jump genres. And I'm so grateful for the readers who made the jump with me. Thank you! A lot of you have grown up reading my books and are now grown-ups reading my books. It means the world to me. I've had so much fun writing in this new-to-me market and I hope you had so much fun reading it.

Many thanks to my agent, Michelle Wolfson, who is always up for whatever I throw at her. Who is supportive and funny and amazing. I am so lucky to have her in my corner. And I've told her she's never allowed to retire. She's ageless, so I think this is a reasonable request.

Thank you to Sara Goodman, for giving me this opportunity and loving this book so much. And for helping me make it just right. I have enjoyed working with her so much. She is a dream editor. And also, thanks to the rest of the team at Saturday Books: Vanessa Aguirre, Cassie Gutman, Olga Grlic, Michelle

McMillian, and Merilee Croft. I know my book wouldn't be the same without all of you.

As always, thanks to my very supportive family. My husband, Jared, is always my first reader and always has a way of making me feel like the most talented writer in the world. Which is a good thing to feel when you're about to go into edits and find out everything wrong with your writing and story. I appreciate him so much. My kids, Skyler, Autumn, Abby, and Donavan (who are now adults), are my very favorite people. They're fun and creative and just lovely humans. I'm very happy to be a part of their lives and for the love they show me.

A special thanks to my dear friends, Bree Despain and Renee Collins, who have become my regular writing buddies. We have been writing together on the regular and it helps so much to have people you have to report to. It keeps me from wasting away on social media. Okay, I'm still wasting away on social media, but I'm wasting away LESS.

I have amazing friends who get me out from behind my writing screen as well. Jenn Johansson, Stephanie Ryan, Brittany Swift, Mandy Hillman, Emily Freeman, Megan Grant, and Misti Hamel. Thank you for always being ready to go on adventures or walks or dinner or lunch or whatever else we do to fight my reclusive nature. Love you all.

And finally, to my wonderful extended family who I adore with all my heart. I got lucky. I have the best family. Chris Thompson, Mark Thompson, Heather Garza, Jared DeWoody, Spencer DeWoody, Stephanie Ryan, Dave Garza, Rachel De-Woody, Zita Konik, Kevin Ryan, Vance West, Karen West, Eric West, Michelle West, Sharlynn West, Rachel Braithwaite, Brian

Braithwaite, Angie Stettler, Jim Stettler, Emily Hill, Rick Hill, and the twenty-five children and numerous children of children that exist between all these people. I love you all so much.

About the Author

credit Stephanie Ryan Photography

KASIE WEST is the author of many YA novels, including *Sunkissed, The Fill-in Boyfriend, P.S. I Like You, Better Than Revenge,* and *Pivot Point.* Her books have been named ALA-YALSA Quick Picks, Junior Library Guild Selections, and ALA-YALSA Top Ten Best Books for Young Adults. *We Met Like This* is her debut adult novel. When she's not writing, she's binge-watching television, devouring books, or on the Central Coast burying her toes in the sand. Kasie lives in Fresno, California, with her family.